Long Road to Cheyenne

Also by Charles G. West and available from Center Point Large Print:

Mark of the Hunter

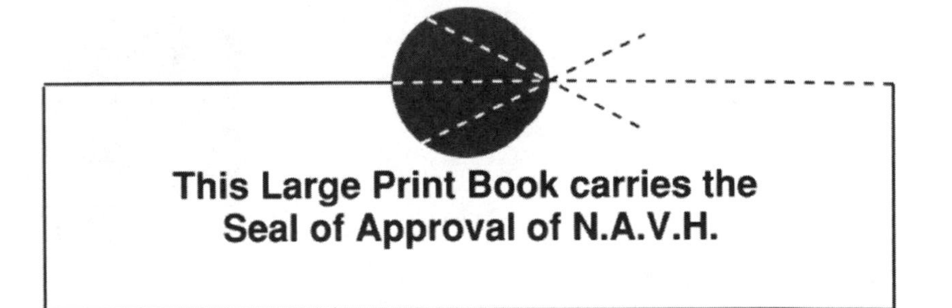

Long Road to Cheyenne

Charles G. West

Center Point Large Print
Thorndike, Maine

This Center Point Large Print edition is published in the year 2015 by arrangement with New American Library, an imprint of Penguin Publishing Group, a division of Penguin Random House LLC.

The text of this Large Print edition is unabridged.
In other aspects, this book may vary
from the original edition.
Printed in the United States of America
on permanent paper.
Set in 16-point Times New Roman type.

ISBN: 978-1-62899-699-9

Library of Congress Cataloging-in-Publication Data

West, Charles.
Long road to Cheyenne / Charles G. West. — Center Point Large Print edition.
pages cm
ISBN 978-1-62899-699-9 (library binding : alk. paper)
1. Widows—Fiction. 2. Stagecoaches—Fiction. 3. Robbery—Fiction.
4. Gold mines and mining—Fiction.
5. Black Hills (S.D. and Wyo.)—Fiction. 6. Large type books.
I. Title.
PS3623.E84L66 2015
813′.6—dc23

2015025200

For Ronda

Chapter 1

Cam Sutton wheeled his buckskin gelding around sharply to head off a reluctant steer and drive it back into the chute that led to a holding pen by the railroad siding. *That's the last one,* he thought, unknotting the bright red bandanna he had bought in Cheyenne and wiping the sweat from his face. He then turned the buckskin toward the lower end of the corral where his boss, Colonel Charles Coffee, stood with a tally sheet, watching the loading. The colonel turned to look at him when he rode up and dismounted.

"You ain't changed your mind?" Coffee asked hopefully. Young Sutton was a hardworking drover, and had been ever since he hired him three years before. Coffee hated to lose him, but he understood Cam's desire to leave. Coffee owned Rawhide Ranch in Wyoming's Rawhide Buttes, but lately the better part of each year was spent driving cattle from the Wyoming counties of Niobrara and Goshen, a short distance across the line to Nebraska where the colonel had established Coffee Siding. Cattle shipped from Nebraska were cheaper than cattle shipped from Wyoming because of the higher freight rates in Wyoming.

"I reckon not," Cam answered the colonel's question.

"Well, I guess I can't say as I blame you," Coffee said. "You're still young enough to have a hankering to see what the rest of the country looks like. I'd be glad to keep you on to work at Rawhide Ranch, but the days of free range are numbered. The settlers will be moving in before much longer."

"That's what I figured," Cam said, "and like you said, I've got a hankerin' to see some of the rest of the country before I decide to squat in one place." He had been thinking a lot lately about his future in the cattle business. It was his feeling that the colonel's range was going to be severely cut back in the near future. Coffee owned several ranches, but he didn't own the land they sat on. It was all free land, government owned, and open to homesteading. Already some sections of their range had been fenced off, and unlike some of the other large ranch owners, the colonel was averse to using violent tactics to scare homesteaders away.

When Cam looked his situation straight in the face, he couldn't say that he was unhappy riding for the Rawhide. If he had to define it, he would say it was more of a restless feeling, an urge to move on. Of course, he could always head back down to Texas and sign on with some outfit pushing a herd of cattle up north, but he was tired of playing nursemaid to a bunch of brainless critters. It didn't help his restless feeling when he witnessed the increased traffic on the Deadwood Stage Road taking adventurous souls to the mysterious Black Hills.

Soon after the Black Hills were opened to prospectors, the stagecoach line established a line of changeover stations from Cheyenne to Deadwood in Dakota Territory. Colonel Coffee's ranch in Rawhide Buttes was set up as one of the stops to change horses, so Cam had plenty of opportunity to see folks from all walks of life, all intent upon realizing the riches the Black Hills promised. Passengers were not the only cargo the coaches transported over the road. Every so often, a team of six horses pulling an ironclad Monitor coach, with a strongbox bolted to the floor, and a couple of extra *messengers* with rifles aboard, rolled into Rawhide on its way back to Cheyenne. He really didn't know much about prospecting for gold, but he confessed that he was one who was always tempted to *go see the elephant*. So he had decided to head up Dakota way to see for himself what all the fuss was about. He could then decide if he wanted to be a part of it, or to simply move on to someplace else. He had no family to concern himself with, so he was free to follow the wind if he chose. His thoughts were interrupted then by a comment from the colonel.

"I've got your wages here, up through the end of this month," Coffee said. "You thinking about heading out right away?"

"Well, if it's all right with you, I thought I would." Nodding toward the buckskin, he said, "Toby ain't worked too hard this mornin'. Might as well head on up toward Hat Creek. If it's all right," he repeated.

Coffee smiled. "Of course it's all right with me." It was typical of the young man to concern himself with the thought that he might not be entitled to a full day's wages if he had officially resigned. He handed Cam an envelope with his pay inside. "I added an extra month's pay in there. You're liable to need it. And listen, you come back any time you feel like it. I'll always have a job for you." He extended his hand in a parting gesture, joking as he and Cam shook hands. "And don't go telling the rest of the boys in the bunkhouse about the bonus. They'll all quit, probably wanting the same deal."

"I won't," Cam replied, grinning. "I 'preciate it, sir."

"You earned it. You take care of yourself, boy." He turned and walked toward the head of the siding.

Larry Bacon cracked his whip to encourage the six-horse matched team to maintain their speed up the incline. "Ha, boy, get up in there!" he called out to them. The team was not fresh but still had enough left to respond, and they would be changed at the Hat Creek Station, about five miles away. The horses answered Bacon's urging, hauling the big Concord coach through a notch in the breaks south of Sage Creek. Inside the colorful yellow coach were six passengers: Travis Grant, a businessman headed for Deadwood; a man named Smith, who claimed to be a cattle buyer; Wilbur Bean, an extra stagecoach guard; Mary Bishop, along with and her two daughters, Grace and Emma. Riding shotgun in the seat beside the driver was his grizzled partner, Bob Allen. Like Bacon, he was a veteran of the three-hundred-mile run between Cheyenne and Deadwood.

It was an unusually light load for the big eighteen-passenger coach, but there was additional freight that warranted the extra guard, or messenger, as the company called him. In the strongbox bolted to the floor was a neat bundle of currency totaling thirty thousand dollars. And the only nervous passenger in the coach was Travis Grant, who was planning to invest the money in the creation of a bank in the thriving town of Deadwood.

There had been frequent holdups of the Deadwood stage, four in one month's time by the notorious road agent Sam Bass and his gang. However, Bob and Larry were not expecting trouble on this run, in spite of the money they were carrying. Their reasoning was simple. The big gold shipments that the bandits were after were on the stages coming *from* Deadwood, and they were headed *toward* Deadwood. If any of

Bass's agents were watching the stage when it left Cheyenne or Fort Laramie, they would see that there was not a full load of eighteen passengers aboard, so not a worthwhile payday to go after. To be safe, however, the company sent Wilbur Bean along for extra protection. For these reasons, Bob Allen was taken completely by surprise when they topped the rise and he suddenly discovered three men standing in the narrow notch, their pistols out and aimed at him. He reached for the shotgun riding beside his leg as Larry hauled back on the reins to stop the coach.

"That'd be your first mistake," a voice warned from the side of the hill above him, and he turned to see the muzzle of a rifle aimed at him. "Suppose you just pick that scattergun up by the barrel real gentle-like and toss it on the ground."

Bob had no choice but to comply, so he did as he was ordered. "Damn," he swore as he dropped the shotgun over the side, exchanging a quick glance with Larry. Both men were thinking the same thing, hoping that Wilbur Bean wasn't asleep in the coach.

"Now you just drive them horses nice and slow down to the bottom of the hill," the gunman said after he jumped down to land on top of the coach. "Mind you, this here .44 has a hair trigger, so you'd best take it real easy."

"You fellers are goin' to a lotta trouble for

somethin' that ain't worth the effort," Bob said. "Hell, we ain't got but five passengers and three of 'em's a woman and two children. You ain't gonna make much offa this holdup. We ain't carryin' no gold shipment. Hell, word of this gets out and folks will be laughin' at Sam Bass and his gang."

"Who says it's Sam's gang?" the gunman asked.

"Well, if I ain't took leave of my senses, that feller with the black hat and the black mustache standin' in the middle of the road down yonder is sure as hell Sam Bass," Bob replied. "Ain't that right, Larry?" The two partners had had the unfortunate opportunity to meet Mr. Bass on another occasion while driving an ironclad coach between Custer City and the Cheyenne River crossing, so he was not likely to forget the man.

"I can't say for sure," Larry said, and shot a warning look in Bob's direction. "That was a while back. It's kinda hard to identify anybody after that length of time."

Seemingly amused by Bob's comment, the gunman prodded Larry in the back with the barrel of his rifle. "You just ease on down there, and we'll see if it's worth our time or not."

Realizing just then what Larry was trying to tell him, Bob said, "I reckon you're right. I don't recall ever seein' Sam Bass up close enough to know if it was him or not."

Inside the coach, the passengers were now

very much aware of what was taking place. Mary Bishop's two daughters moved in close to their mother's sides for protection, their faces tense with fear. "Ever'body just stay calm," Wilbur Bean whispered, and slid off the seat to crouch at the door, his rifle ready. A second later, he felt the impersonal barrel of a Colt .44 pressed hard against his back.

"I'll take that rifle, unless you're ready to meet your Maker right now," Mr. Smith informed him, and Wilbur released it immediately. Smith, whose real name was Cotton Roach, then addressed Travis Grant. "I'll take that peashooter you're carryin' in your inside coat pocket, too. And while you're at it, you can come up with the key to that strongbox—save us the trouble of havin' to break it open with a cold chisel."

His face drained of color, Grant hurried to do as he had been directed, knowing that the nightmare he had feared was even now unfolding before his eyes.

As the stage pulled slowly to a stop, the three men on the ground immediately surrounded it, brandishing their weapons and yelling orders for everyone to get out. Bob and Larry both locked their eyes on the door, anticipating some move by Wilbur Bean, expecting the possibility that he might come out firing. Neither of them had been relieved of his handgun, so they were poised to act when Wilbur surprised the bandits. They were almost stunned when he opened the door and calmly climbed down, Mr. Smith right behind him with a gun in Wilbur's back. A firm tap of the rifle barrel on the back of Bob's neck then reminded him that the gunman was still there. "Now, with your left hand, reach over and pull that pistol out of the holster and drop it on the ground," he ordered. "One at a time!" he scolded when Larry started to do the same. When Bob dropped his weapon, the gunman told Larry to do likewise. "Now both of you get on down." He remained standing on top of the stage while he watched Bob and Larry climb down to stand away from the coach with their hands raised. "Have any trouble in there?" he asked Cotton Roach.

"Nope, no trouble," Roach replied.

"Where's the man with the key?"

"He's comin'," Roach said. "He's peein' his pants right now, but he ain't gonna give us no trouble."

The outlaw still on top of the stage nodded to the man standing at the door of the coach now. Motioning toward Bob Allen, he remarked, "He said he recognized you."

Sam Bass nodded slowly, then turned to address Bob. "You think you know me?" he asked.

"I told you we shoulda wore them masks," one of his men said.

"Shut up, Joel," Bass responded while never taking his eyes off Bob.

Knowing he might have placed them all in jeopardy by his earlier remark, Bob tried to lessen the damage. "What I said was I thought you favored Sam Bass a little bit. Hell, I don't have no idea who you are." He glanced at Larry, who rolled his eyes heavenward in response. Both men shifted their gaze to the weapons lying in the dirt a dozen yards away.

Reading their thoughts, Bass said, "You wouldn't make it halfway there before we cut you down." Getting back to the business that prompted the holdup, he ordered, "Get yourself outta that coach!" Then when Travis Grant placed a trembling foot on the step, Bass grabbed him by the sleeve and yanked the terrified man out of the coach to land on his hands and knees. "Cotton," Bass called, "you got that box open yet?"

"Yeah, I got it, but we got some more folks in here."

"Well, tell 'em to get on out here," Bass said. He stood by the door then and politely helped Grace and her sister down from the coach. He then extended his hand to offer Mary Bishop his assistance, but she ignored it.

"I can manage myself," she said curtly, and climbed down to join her daughters.

"Yes, ma'am," Sam said with a wide grin, "you surely can."

At that moment, Cotton Roach sang out from

inside the coach, "It's all here, just like Ike said. I ain't counted it yet, but it sure looks like as much as we thought."

It was then that Wilbur Bean made his decision. Standing closer to the coach than Bob and Larry, he could see the barrel of his rifle on the floor where he had been forced to drop it. With the bandits distracted for the moment by Roach's announcement, he suddenly dived for the rifle. It was a brave but futile effort. The gunman still on top of the stage cut him down before he could reach the door. The reaction of the outlaws was immediate, with guns trained on Bob and Larry before they could even think about making a move. Thc two young girls screamed and pressed closer to their mother. The frightened Mr. Grant shrieked almost as loudly as the girls.

"I had a feelin' he was gonna try somethin' like that," the shooter said nonchalantly. He glanced up then to catch a scalding look from Sam Bass. "Hell, Sam, I didn't have no choice. I couldn't let him get to that rifle."

"Yeah, well, you've opened up a whole new can of beans now," Bass said. There was now the matter to decide whether or not they could afford to leave witnesses to the holdup. Jack Dawson had killed the guard, and that usually got the military stirred up. He had also called Sam by name, and he didn't particularly want the law to associate murder with his holdups. "Get down offa there and help Joel move these folks down the road a ways," Bass told him. "We can't stand around here all day." He turned to the remaining member of his gang. "Ben, go get the horses. Then unhitch them horses from the stage and scatter 'em. It'll be a helluva long time before they can catch 'em again and get to Hat Creek Station. We'll be long gone."

"Wait a minute," Jack Dawson said when he heard Sam's instructions. "What are you talkin' about, 'takin' them a long time to catch them horses'? You ain't thinkin' about leavin' them folks alive, are you? Why, hell, they can identify ever' last one of us!"

"Jack, you ain't rode with me long, or you'd know I don't hold to killin' women and children. Now, I admit I've had to shoot somebody now and again, but I draw the line at women and children. Besides, ain't no law gonna find us if we head back down to Texas. So you go on and help Joel herd them folks down the road a piece and start 'em to walkin'."

Dawson did not reply. He bit his lip in anger, but he held his tongue. He decided then that it was the last job he would pull with Sam Bass. He, Cotton Roach, and Ben Cheney had been doing all right on their own. It was Bass who asked them to come along on this job, and had they known he was squeamish about leaving no witnesses, they might have told him to go to hell, they'd do it without him. If it ever came down to telling the story to the law about what happened here, Dawson was the one who shot the guard, and he was willing to bet that Bass or Collins wouldn't hesitate to give him up. With that thought in mind, he turned abruptly and followed after Joel Collins, who was already herding the victims down the road.

"All right, folks," Joel said as Dawson caught up with him, "let's get them pockets emptied. It'll be a whole lot easier to walk if you ain't totin' a lot of money."

"What about our clothes and things?" Mary Bishop asked, making no effort to hide her disgust for the lot of them. "Are you going to take ladies' and children's clothes back to your hideout, or whatever pigsty you call home?"

Collins couldn't help chuckling at the woman's show of defiance. "When we're gone, I don't reckon there'll be anythin' stoppin' you from goin' back to the stagecoach to get 'em."

"Leave us something to buy food and shelter," Travis Grant pleaded. "You've got the money in the strongbox. Isn't that enough?"

"I wouldn't worry about it," Jack Dawson said. "You ain't gonna need no money." He casually aimed his .44 at the frightened man and pulled the trigger. The sudden report of the firearm startled bandits and victims alike. Mary Bishop couldn't suppress a cry of horror as the unfortunate victim's head jerked sickeningly to the side from the impact of the bullet in his brain. She grabbed her daughters and pulled them to her protectively.

Collins spun around in shock, thinking Dawson had gone crazy. He had ridden with Sam long enough to know he had not ordered execution for the victims, and now Dawson was turning to aim his pistol at Larry Bacon. Joel heard the solid thump against Dawson's chest at almost the same time a rifle discharged behind him somewhere. Dawson staggered backward a few steps, looking down at his chest in disbelief. A fraction of a second later, another shot ripped into his side and he cried out in pain. His rifle dropped to the ground beside him and he went to his knees.

Bob Allen did not waste time trying to figure out what was happening. He sprang on the dropped rifle and rolled with it until he was clear of the stricken bandit before coming up on one knee and cocking the weapon. Dawson was finished, however, so there was no call for swift action in his direction. Bob moved quickly back, jerked Dawson's Colt from his holster, and tossed it to Larry, who was already trying to shield Mary and her daughters from further gunfire. The slowest to react was Joel Collins, whose first thought was that Sam Bass had fired the shot after Dawson killed Grant. A general state of confusion set in with only one participant clearly focused on what he was doing—the unseen rifleman. Seeing Bob and Larry now armed, Collins threw one hasty shot in their direction and turned to run. It was a wild shot, hitting no one, but it caused the two stage employees to dive for cover, and resulted in allowing him to reach the idle stagecoach where Sam and Cotton Roach had already taken cover.

"What the hell!" Bass demanded. "Where'd them shots come from?"

"Damned if I know," a breathless Joel Collins answered. "Injuns, soldiers, I don't know. Did anybody see?"

"They mighta come from that hill on the other side of the draw," Roach said.

"One thing for sure," Bass said, "they ain't got around behind us, else we'd sure know it by now. I don't see no use in us hangin' around here to find out who the hell it is. We got what we came for. Where the hell is Ben with the horses?"

"We might better get them guns layin' in the dirt on the other side of this coach," Roach said.

"You go right ahead," Bass replied. "I ain't stickin' my nose out there to get shot."

"There's a good Winchester rifle layin' out there. I ain't ready to ride off and leave it," Cotton insisted. "I'm gonna see if I can slip around the back of this coach and pick it up real quick."

"It's your neck," Collins said.

Roach left the rear wheel of the coach, where

he had taken cover, and eased cautiously around the back of the coach to crouch behind the opposite wheel. He hesitated there long enough to satisfy himself that the stage driver and his shotgun rider had withdrawn from the road and taken refuge in a gully. There was no sound in the notch save that of the horses still hitched to the coach as they stomped nervously. He looked at the Winchester lying several feet from him for a second, then decided to see if he could fish for it with his own rifle. Almost successful, but just a few inches short of hooking the rifle, he strained to reach as far as he could. "Damn," he murmured under his breath, and crawled to the rim of the wheel, giving himself a few more inches of reach. He extended his arm as far as he could until he felt his fingertips rest on the butt of the Winchester. Two shots in rapid succession immediately sang out. The first threw dirt in his face. The second smashed the fingers on his hand. "That son of a bitch!" he cried out in pain, and quickly retreated under the stage, narrowly missing getting run over when the horses jumped at the sound of the shots.

"Let's get the hell outta here!" Sam yelled when the coach moved away from them, leaving them exposed. It was unnecessary to repeat it, for all three headed for the hill behind them as fast as they could manage, encouraged in their effort by the rifle slugs peppering the ground at their heels. They were met by Ben Cheney halfway to the gulch where they had left their horses. Taking no time for explanations, they jumped in the saddle and hightailed it—all except Cotton Roach. Seething with rage as he held his damaged hand up close to his chest, craving vengeance for the shooter crippling him, he pulled up short and turned to look back. "Come on, Cotton," Ben Cheney yelled back at him, but Roach ignored him.

Behind them, two astonished stage employees, a woman, and two young girls crawled warily out of a narrow gully, not sure what had just happened. Undecided if they were entirely out of danger or not, Bob Allen cocked the rifle he was holding and hurried to check on Wilbur Bean. "Nothin' we can do for Wilbur," he said when Larry knelt by his side. "He's gone under."

"Damn shame," Larry said, shaking his head. "He shouldn't never have tried it."

"He was a good man," Bob said. He turned to stare at the low ridge east of the road. "Somebody sure knows how to use a rifle," he commented, then added, "I hope to hell it ain't a party of Sioux Indians who happened to come along and is thinkin' about claimin' the spoils for themselves."

"Poor ol' Mr. Grant," Larry said, looking at the frail body lying near the dead bandit. He didn't really know the man, but he figured somebody back east would be grieving for him. The unfortunate little man was out of place in this rough country. That much he was sure of. He turned then to give Bob a serious look. "You know that son of a bitch—excuse me, ladies—that bandit was fixin' to shoot the lot of us." Thinking of how terrifying it must have been for the lady and her daughters, he asked, "Are you all right, ma'am? Things didn't look too good back there, did they?"

Mary didn't answer. She was distracted by the sight of a tall young man with a bright red bandanna around his neck leading a buckskin horse, just then emerging from a ring of pine trees along the base of the east ridge. "Look, Mama," Emma, her youngest, said, and pointed. Both Bob Allen and Larry Bacon spun around immediately, ready to face whatever threat might now be confronting them.

"Don't shoot," Mary exclaimed. "The man just saved our lives."

"Maybe he has, and maybe he ain't. Let's just wait and see what he's got on his mind," Larry said. He was not ready to trust anyone at this point. "Watch him, Bob." They were not alone in witnessing the appearance of the mysterious rifleman. Beyond the first grove of pines on the hillside, Cotton Roach stared hard at the broad-shouldered young man leading the horse. Not concerned that his fellow gang members were disappearing into the hills, he remained long enough to make sure he never forgot the man. Even though he could not see his face clearly at that distance, he could remember the way he strode easily across the stage road, and the bright red bandanna he wore. Roach tried to pull his rifle with his left hand, but it was clumsy and his right hand was throbbing in pain so intense that he couldn't use it at all. He finally gave up trying, knowing it would only waste a shot if he tried to shoot. Furious and frustrated, he finally wheeled his horse and went after his partners. "I'll run up on you sometime," he promised himself. "You ain't gettin' away with this."

"You folks all right?" Cam Sutton called out when still some yards away from the people standing in the middle of the road.

Seeing no need for the caution expressed by Bob and Larry, Mary answered, "Yes, we are, thanks to you. If you hadn't come along when you did, we'd all be lying in the dirt beside poor Mr. Grant."

"We're beholdin' to you, young feller," Bob said, still holding the rifle ready to use in case it was necessary. "The lady's right, they was fixin' to kill the lot of us, her and the young'uns, too, I s'pose. They got away with all the money we was carryin'. Ain't a dime left."

The insinuation was lost on Cam. "Well, I'm sorry I didn't get here soon enough to help that poor feller, but I was on the far side of that ridge when I heard the first shot." He paused a moment to look at the late Travis Grant, then walked over to stare down at Jack Dawson's body where it lay facedown after it had finally keeled over. It was the first man he had ever killed, and he was not sure how he felt about that. It was only for a moment, however, for he realized the consequences had he not acted. He reached down and turned the body over, so he could see the face. It was a cruel face, twisted grotesquely in the moment of death. *No different than killing a rattlesnake about to strike,* he told himself. Standing tall again, he said, "At least you still got your stagecoach." He turned to look a couple of hundred yards back up the road where the team of horses had stopped after being frightened by the shots. "I'll ride up and bring 'em back for you." He climbed into the saddle and rode off to retrieve the coach.

As they watched their rescuer ride away, five-year-old Emma spoke. "Mama, he sure is pretty, isn't he?" Her comment broke the tension of the moment, causing them all to chuckle.

"I reckon you're right, little missy," Bob said. "He sure looked pretty to me when he opened up with that rifle, didn't he, Larry?"

"That's a fact," Larry answered. Then his expression turned cold sober, as if the realization of their situation had just struck home. "We weren't a frog's hair from gettin' a ticket on the same train Mr. Grant and Wilbur took."

Her eyes still on the broad back of the rifleman, Emma wondered aloud, "Do you think he's an angel, Mama?"

Mary reached down and drew her daughter up close for a hug. "I don't know, honey. He might be, but not the kind of angel that came to take Grandmother up to heaven. Maybe he's just somebody an angel sent to help us when we needed help."

Grace gave her younger sister a long, patient gaze and informed her, "Angels don't shoot people, and they don't ride horses."

Mary smiled but said nothing. *This one might,* she thought.

Cam took hold of the lead horse's bridle and led the team back to the scene of the holdup, where Bob took over. "Mister," Bob said, "I'm mighty glad to make your acquaintance." He extended his hand. "I'm Bob Allen, and this is my partner, Larry Bacon. These folks here is Mrs. Bishop and Grace and Emma." He beamed at the two girls. "Did I get that right?"

"You did," Mary answered for her daughters, and extended her hand as well. "I'm Mary Bishop, and I thank you for your help."

"I'm Cam Sutton," he said after a brief handshake. "Glad I could help." He then turned to Bob. "You can't be much more than five miles or so from Hat Creek, if you were headin' north."

"We are," Bob said. "We're scheduled to stop there for the night."

"Maybe I'll ride along with you, just in case those fellows decide to come back, although I don't see any reason why they would."

"We'd appreciate it," Bob replied. "You never can tell. They was just about to clean all our pockets out when you showed up, even if they'd be damn fools to try it again." He nodded to Larry. "I reckon we'd best put Wilbur and Mr. Grant on the stage and take 'em in to Hat Creek."

"I don't reckon we oughta put them bodies in the coach with the lady and her girls," Larry commented.

Mary quickly replied, "We won't mind. I'm sure it won't be any worse than riding with that Mr. Smith. That man just looked evil, and he never said a word, just stared at us with those eyes that looked like glass."

Bob was in agreement with Larry, however. "Ain't no need for you to have to ride with a couple of corpses," he said. "Won't be no trouble to load 'em on top."

Contrary to what Bob said, it was a little more trouble to haul two dead bodies up on top of the Concord coach, but with Cam's help, they were soon loaded. "What about him?" Cam asked, indicating the one still on the ground.

"To hell with him," Bob said. "Let the buzzards have him." He hesitated, then decided. "We'll just drag him outta the road, though." He and Larry each grabbed an ankle and pulled the late Jack Dawson over to dump him in the gully they had taken refuge in before.

Chapter 2

By the time they rolled into Hat Creek Station, the sun was already poised on the horizon, preparing to settle down in the hills to the west. They were met by Fred Johnson, who was the acting manager in the absence of John Bowman or Joe Walters, the men who built the ranch. "You folks are running a little late, ain't you?" Johnson asked when greeting them. Taking note of the two bodies atop the Concord coach, he commented, "You've took to haulin' some unusual freight."

"I reckon you could sure 'nough say that," Bob replied as he climbed down from the seat. "One of them bodies up there is Wilbur Bean. He was ridin' messenger. The other'n is a passenger. I reckon we'll have to put 'em in the ground. I'll notify the office about the passenger, and they can contact his family. Then if they wanna come dig him up and have a funeral, that's up to them. Poor ol' Wilbur, he ain't got no family that I know of." He went on to tell Fred about the holdup. "The young feller on the buckskin is Cam Sutton. If he hadn't come along when he did, you and me wouldn't be talking about it right now."

Bob took it upon himself to get Mary and the girls settled in a room in the hotel while Cam helped Larry with the horses and the coach. There was the matter of the two bodies lying atop the coach that would have to be dealt with, but the first thing to do, after Mary was settled, was to notify the office in Cheyenne about the robbery and the deaths that resulted. Fred Johnson went with Bob to the telegraph office to send the message.

Cam had been to the stage station half a dozen times over the past couple of years, and he knew the hotel had a good cook. In addition to the hotel, there was a telegraph office, a post office, a bakery, a grocery, a blacksmith, and even a small brewery. It always seemed like a regular city to him with little else to be desired. Built below a ridge of pine-covered hills separating the high plain from the valley at the foot of those hills, it was not really located on Hat Creek. Back in 1875, some army troops were sent from Fort Laramie to establish a fort on Hat Creek in Nebraska to protect travelers from Indian attacks. The soldiers never got to Nebraska, but thought they had when they reached Sage Creek in Wyoming Territory. They called it Hat Creek anyway, and set up their camp. It never did develop into a fort, but it had turned into a fine stagecoach station now that the Indian threat was reduced and the Black Hills were open to prospectors.

"Let's go get ourselves some supper," Bob sang out when he returned from the telegraph office.

"Since we're so late, I thought we might skip it tonight," Larry said, and winked at Cam. He couldn't help japing his partner a little, knowing full well that Bob Allen would never swing through Hat Creek without visiting the hotel dining room. The little Japanese woman who ran the kitchen had caught his eye. Atsuko was the lady's name, and Bob got all tongue-tied whenever he tried to have a conversation with her. She seemed to know it and made a point of sidling up to his table and talking to him whenever he came in.

"Suit yourself," Bob advised him. "Damned if I'm gonna skip supper. I've had a busy day. I need some vittles." He then turned to Cam. "I know a young feller like you can always eat, so come on, I'll gladly buy your supper. I owe you a helluva lot more than that."

"You don't owe me anything," Cam insisted. "You'da helped me if it had been the other way around." He flashed a wide grin. "But I'll take you up on the supper."

"Good," Bob said, "let's go, then." He threw a hand up on Cam's shoulder as they started out toward the hotel. "I expect you'll want a room for the night, too."

"Ah, no." Cam hesitated. "I don't need a room. I expect I'll just find a place in the barn to bed down." He had to conserve what cash he had, so he didn't intend to squander any of it on a hotel bed.

Bob suspected as much but refrained from expressing it for fear of embarrassing him. "Sometimes the hotel rooms *can* get a little stuffy this time of year. You're welcome to bunk in the coach if you wanna."

"I'll take you up on that," Cam quickly accepted. As far as he was concerned, that was almost as plush.

"Might as well put your horse in the stable," Larry suggested, "feed him some grain. Fred can put it on the company's bill."

"Much obliged," Cam said.

"You watch ol' Bob when we get in there," Larry whispered to Cam.

All three men nodded respectfully toward Mary Bishop, who was already seated at a table with Grace and Emma. She acknowledged the greetings with a pleasant smile. Bob headed straight for a table opposite the kitchen door and seated himself so as to be able to see partway inside. He turned his plate, which had been lying facedown, over, tied the ends of his napkin around his neck, and waited anxiously. In a few minutes, a small, trim Oriental woman emerged from the kitchen carrying a large metal coffeepot. She smiled in their direction as she passed by on her way to fill Mary's cup. Bob's eyes followed her every step of the way. Larry nudged Cam and motioned toward his partner, grinning.

"Ah, Mr. Allen," Atsuko drew out in a voice almost lyrical when she came to their table. "You come to see us again." Larry nudged Cam again. He was thoroughly enjoying Bob's reaction. "Do you want coffee?" Atsuko asked.

"Yes, ma'am," Bob replied, almost choking on his tongue.

Larry chuckled openly. "We do, too, ma'am, me and Cam here." All three turned their cups over to be filled.

"You want steak?" Atsuko asked Bob. "You always want steak." He nodded, unable to organize his words to form a reasonable answer.

"I'll have the same," Larry announced loudly. "How 'bout you, Cam?" When Cam nodded, Larry went on. "With whatever else goes with it." She spread a smile around for the three of them, then headed for the kitchen.

Once the woman was out of his presence, Bob found his tongue again. "That's a mighty fine-lookin' woman there, from China or someplace."

"Japan," Larry corrected. "She's Japanese."

"Don't make no difference," Bob said. "She's a real looker, and her cookin's hard to beat. You can't ask for much more than that in a woman. Ain't that right, Cam?"

"Reckon not," Cam replied, "maybe if she was rich to boot."

Bob chuckled and said, "You got that right. I wonder why she ain't got no old man. I bet she ain't much younger than me. Some feller oughta be lookin' to throw a rope on her."

"That wouldn't be you," Larry teased. "She can't be that desperate."

"I don't know about that," Bob replied with a mischievous grin. He reached up with a finger to smooth his mustache, then removed his hat and hung it on the back of his chair. Running his fingers through his thick gray-streaked hair, he commented, "She just needs to meet a distinguished-lookin' gentleman like myself. Then she'd see what she's been missing all her life." He took a long sip from his coffee cup while Larry snorted a laugh. "Damn," he exclaimed, making a face, "that coffee's strong enough to float a horseshoe. Slide that sugar bowl over this way." He dropped two heaping teaspoons of the sugar into his coffee and proceeded to stir it vigorously. "Maybe that'll cut the bitter just a little." He glanced at Cam then and asked, "Want some sugar in yours?"

"No, thanks," Cam replied. He had never become accustomed to using sugar in his coffee, primarily because sugar had always seemed to be in short supply when driving cattle or riding the range. Further conversation on the quality of the coffee was interrupted when Grace Bishop got out of her chair and walked over to their table.

Tapping Cam on the shoulder, she said, “Mama would like to talk to you.”

“Right now?” Cam asked.

Grace shrugged. Her mother hadn’t specified when. She looked back at Mary as if hoping for an answer. “I don’t know,” she finally said.

Cam smiled. “All right, I’ll go over and talk to your mama.” He picked up his cup and followed Grace back to her table.

“Look out, Cam,” Larry whispered. “That woman mighta come out here lookin’ for a husband.”

“Watch your mouth,” Bob scolded. “Young’uns her age has got ears like a coyote. Besides, that lady might like a man a mite older than Cam, anyway.” He smoothed his mustache again and smiled. “If she was lookin’ for a husband, she’da most likely called me over to her table.”

“Did you need to talk to me?” Cam asked when he approached the table.

“Yes, I do,” Mary responded. “I didn’t mean to interrupt your supper, though. I should have told Grace that I just meant sometime before you decided to leave.”

“Yes, ma’am,” Cam said, “just whenever you say. It’s no interruption. She ain’t even brought my supper yet.”

Mary hesitated for a second, then suggested,

"Why don't you sit down here for a moment? What I have to say won't take long."

"Yes, ma'am." He pulled the empty chair back and sat down facing her.

"I haven't heard you say where you're going, or what you plan on doing," she began. "But I've been thinking about a business proposition that I'd like to hear your opinion of. I'm gambling here on a gut feeling about you, a feeling that you're an honest man. It's not a good idea for a woman and two young girls to travel alone in the country I'm bound for." She paused. "This terrible incident we just survived served to emphasize that fact. I'm determined to make my way to a little camp named Destiny. According to the map my husband sent me, it's about six miles from Custer City. That's why I want to talk to you. I have enough money to buy horses and supplies when we get to Custer City, and maybe enough left over to hire a guide to help me find Destiny. I've worried some over how I might find a man I could trust to guide me and help protect my family. I think you're such a man. Please tell me I'm right."

Her proposal certainly took him by surprise, and he had to stop and think about it for a few moments. "Well, yes, ma'am, you can trust me, all right, but if you don't mind me askin', how come you're travelin' up here by yourself? Where's your husband?"

"I don't know, Mr. Sutton. I received a telegram from him over three months ago, saying he was going to come home. He never did, and I haven't heard from him since. I'm hoping to find him, because he would have let me know if there was a reason he changed his plans. I fear something terrible has happened, and I need someone to help me. Will you?"

He hesitated while he tried to decide if he wanted to consider it or not. After a moment or two, he said, "To tell you the truth, I ain't sure where I was headed, or what I was gonna do when I got there. I just figured I'd decide when I did get there." He hesitated again, and turned to look back at Bob and Larry when Atsuko came from the kitchen with three plates of food. Unwilling to let his steak get cold, he quickly decided. "Well, like I said, I was just gonna do whatever landed in front of me, so I reckon goin' to Destiny with you and these young ladies is what came up. I'll do it."

"Excellent," Mary said, greatly relieved. "Now go back and eat your supper before it gets cold. We'll talk about your pay and anything else we need to after supper." She smiled warmly and extended her hand to shake on the deal.

Cam returned to his table and sat down to eat his supper, ignoring the pair of grinning faces beaming expectantly up at him, eager for a report. He took knife and fork in hand and sawed off a generous hunk of beef. “Pass me that shaker of salt,” he forced through the mouthful of tough steak.

“Pass me the salt, hell!” Bob responded impatiently. “What the hell was that little social all about?”

“Yeah,” Larry chimed in. “Me and Bob noticed that lady lookin’ you over a couple of times. She lookin’ for a daddy for them girls? She’d be a little too much for you, wouldn’t she? I mean, with a couple of young’uns already hatched.”

“Yeah,” Bob agreed. “She’d do better lookin’ at a man like me.” He cocked his head and winked. “You know, she ain’t a bad-lookin’ woman. I wouldn’t kick her outta the covers, and that’s a fact.”

Cam put his knife and fork down but continued chewing the tough bite of meat for a moment while his eyes shifted from one expectant face to the other, then back again. He rose halfway from his chair to reach across the table and grab the saltshaker. Seated again, he finally spoke. “I swear if you two don’t beat all I’ve ever seen. That lady ain’t lookin’ for nothin’ like that. She wants to hire me to guide her and her daughters to someplace outside Custer City, someplace she called Destiny. You ever hear of it?”

Larry shook his head, and Bob replied, “Can’t say as I have. It couldn’t be a very big place. What does she wanna go there for?”

"Lookin' for her husband, I reckon—said we'd talk more about it tomorrow."

"You gonna do it?" Bob asked, no longer joking.

"I reckon," Cam answered with a shrug. "I ain't really got nothin' else to do."

"Well, I think it's a damn good idea," Bob said, completely serious now. "That nice lady and them two little girls ain't got no business headin' off into the hills without no protection at all." He turned to look at Mary and her daughters when another thought entered his mind. When he turned back, he looked at Larry and asked, "Bishop, ain't that the name of that feller that got shot in that holdup near Cheyenne Crossin' a little while back?"

"Mighta been," Larry replied with a shrug while he gave it more thought. "Come to think of it, it was Bishop, same as hers. You reckon she's kin?"

Bob gave it another few moments' thought, then decided. "Nah, I doubt it. There's a heap of folks name of Bishop."

Mildly curious, Cam asked, "What happened at Cheyenne Crossin'?"

"Like I said," Bob replied, "a couple of fellers held up the stage a few miles north of the Crossin'. Johnny Peaks was drivin' it. He said they wasn't carryin' anythin' but passengers—wasn't even drivin' one of the big coaches. Johnny said one of 'em was carryin' one of them big ol' Sharps buffalo rifles. Anyway, they made ever'body get outta the coach, and they took whatever the passengers had on 'em. They didn't get much and I reckon it riled the two bandits, because the one totin' the Sharps turned it on one of the passengers, this feller named Bishop, and blew a hole through his chest big as your fist. Then they jumped on their horses and lit out. Johnny said there wasn't no particular reason to shoot the feller. He didn't say anythin', just turned his pockets inside out like everybody else. I reckon they just didn't like his looks."

"They never caught them two," Larry commented.

"That ain't surprisin'," Bob remarked. "They most times don't."

Cam took another glance at Mary, wondering if there could possibly be any connection with the Cheyenne Crossing victim. *Maybe I'll find out after supper,* he thought. Back to Bob then, he asked, "How long will it take you to get to Custer City?"

"I ain't sure," he answered. "I aim to get outta here early in the mornin'. And if there ain't no trouble at any of the changeovers, we might be able to make it to Custer City late tomorrow night."

Cam nodded thoughtfully. As best he could estimate, Custer City was probably around ninety miles, give or take, and it would take him two days, maybe more, to cover that distance on Toby.

That would have to be discussed at his meeting with Mary Bishop.

"Well, Mr. Sutton," Mary said as she led him into the hotel parlor, "are you still planning on guiding me to Destiny?"

"Why, yes, ma'am," Cam replied. "We shook on it." He was a little uncomfortable for having been addressed as *Mister*. "Please, ma'am, just call me Cam."

"All right, Cam," she said, her tone businesslike but friendly. She then proceeded to tell him that her husband and his brother had gone into the Black Hills in search of gold. "He was going to stay for one year only, and then return whether or not they had been successful. As I've already told you, three months ago, he sent a telegram from Custer City, telling me that they had had some luck, and he was coming home the following week." Her eyelids blinked nervously at this point, but she maintained her demeanor. "That telegram was the last contact I've had with my husband. He never came home. I've sent several telegrams to him at Custer City, but they were never answered. And looking at the map he sent me, I would have to assume the telegraph office had no way to know him or where to find him."

Cam swallowed hard, knowing that the man killed in the holdup at Cheyenne Crossing had to have been her husband. It was too close to be a coincidence involving similar names. He hesitated a few moments, trying to decide how best to tell her what Bob had told him. In the end, he felt it would be wrong not to tell her. "Mrs. Bishop—" he started.

"Mary," she interrupted.

"Mary," he corrected. "I don't like bein' the one to tell you this, but I think it's somethin' you oughta know." He proceeded to tell her about the fatal holdup. Her expression was one of profound shock, but she managed to hold on to her emotions. He could guess the total despair his news had wrought, and he tried to give her some hope. "That mighta been some other man named Bishop. The stage company oughta be able to tell you the man's name. If you want, I'll go with you to the telegraph office here and see if they can wire Custer City and find out." He paused, seeing she was trying to collect her nerves. "Or I can go find out for you," he suggested.

"No," she said softly, "I can do that myself." Feeling suddenly faint, she fought to maintain her composure. She had tried to steel herself to the possibility of finding out such news, for deep down she had known that something this tragic had to have happened. But to actually hear it was devastating. In a moment, she felt she was in control again. She pulled herself upright and announced, "I'll go do that now. I'll let you know what I find out when I get back." She got up to go. "Where can I find you? Do you have a room in the hotel?"

"No, ma'am. I'll be sleepin' in the stagecoach tonight, so I'll be there." He walked out the door behind her and stood watching her from the porch as she made her way across the clearing toward the telegraph office. *Well, I didn't hold that job for very long,* he thought, certain that the murdered man had to have been her husband.

It was a couple of hours before she returned. Walking out to the corral where the stage was parked, she found him already in his blanket, asleep in the coach. She called out his name softly and he immediately responded. "Were you asleep?" she asked.

"Yes, ma'am. I just naturally wake up easy." He stepped out of the coach and stood up. "I had a little fire goin', but it went out." Actually, he was surprised to see her again. He assumed that if she verified her husband's death, she'd cancel her trip to Destiny and go back home, wherever that might be. Had he not thought so, he would not have turned in for the night. "Did you find out about your husband?" he asked.

"Yes, I did," she replied. "The man murdered by that outlaw was my husband, William Warren Bishop. He still had the watch I gave him on our fifth anniversary. The bandits didn't even take it."

"Well, I am right sorry, ma'am. I hated to be the

one to tell you about it, but I figured you'd surely want to know, instead of goin' all the way to Custer City to find out. I expect you'll be stayin' over here and wait for a coach headin' back to Cheyenne."

"No," she said. "I'm still going to find Destiny. My poor husband's brother should know that Warren never got back. If I don't find him, he may never know that his brother was killed."

He was surprised, but when he thought about it, he could see that it was the right thing to do. "So you still want me to go up there with you?"

"Yes, I do. I've never had to hire a guide before, so maybe you have a figure in mind. How much do you think it's worth for your help?"

"I've never done it before, either," he replied, and gave it a few moments' thought. "I don't know. Is ten dollars too much?"

She couldn't help chuckling. "No, that's not too much. It's worth more than that. I was thinking more along the lines of fifty dollars." When he hesitated, she said, "You know you're going to have to travel with two precocious little girls. Fifty might not be a fair amount."

He shook his head and grinned. "Why don't we settle on forty?" he said.

"Agreed," she said at once; then she remarked, "You'd make a mighty poor businessman." They shook on it again. "Now, we'll take the stage to Custer City in the morning, and when we get there, I'd like your help in buying horses and supplies."

"I won't be goin' with you in the mornin'," he replied. When her eyebrows went up in surprise, he explained. "I can't just tie my horse onto the back of the stage and go with you. That would wear my horse plumb out. It's gonna take me at least two days to get up there and maybe a shade more. I can make pretty good time on that buckskin of mine, but I expect you'll get to Custer City at least a day ahead of me and Toby, even if you stop over for one night."

"I'm sorry. I forgot that they change to fresh horses every ten or twelve miles." She made an impatient face, then thought about it a moment. "Of course you can't leave your horse behind. Well, I guess there's no longer a need to hurry. I plan to take a room in a hotel, if they have one."

"Yes, ma'am, they have two is what I heard."

"All right, when you get there, come find me, and we'll get on with our business then. All right, partner?" She gave him an encouraging smile.

"All right," he said, "I'll get up there as soon as I can."

Chapter 3

He rode into the town of Custer City late in the morning of the third day after leaving Hat Creek Station. Seeing a sign that declared a new two-story building at the end of the street to be the Custer House, he figured that was where he might find Mary. So he guided Toby in that direction. Inside, he told the clerk he was looking for Mrs. Mary Bishop. "Yes," the clerk responded. "Mrs. Bishop is staying here, but she's not in her room at the present time. She said that you might be looking for her, and to tell you that she and the girls are down at the other end of the street at the stable. I think she said she was looking to buy some horses."

"Much obliged," Cam said.

"Well, I see you made it," Mary called to him when she saw him approaching, leading his horse. Standing beside the corral, with a daughter on either side of her, she had been talking to the owner of the stable, who was inside the corral with the horses. "Mr. Bledsoe has been showing me some horses he has for sale. You got here just in time to give me your opinion." A genuine look of disappointment captured Bledsoe's face as Mary continued. "See those two tied at the corner, the red one and the black one? He's offering what he says is a good price for them, and now we're looking for two more."

"Is that a fact?" Cam replied as he dropped Toby's reins to the ground. "You think you need four horses?"

"Why, I suppose so," she answered, "one for each of us, and one packhorse."

"Well, it's your money, but I figure you don't need but three. Grace and Emma can ride on one, you on the other, and the other'n for a packhorse. The girls won't be much of a load for a horse."

"Maybe you're right," she reconsidered. "I guess I wasn't thinking."

"Cam's right," Emma interrupted. "I don't wanna ride a horse by myself."

"Then I guess you can ride behind your sister," Mary said. She smiled at Cam and suggested, "Why don't you take a look at the two we've already picked out?"

Bledsoe stepped in at that point. "Howdy, young feller. I'm Ned Bledsoe. I've been tryin' to get the lady as much horse for the money as I can—you know—and put 'em on somethin' that's gentle enough for a lady and the little girls." He followed Cam along the side of the corral. "You're welcome to look 'em over," he said when Cam climbed over the rails to inspect the horses. "Both of 'em's been gelded."

Cam's inspection didn't take long. "I wanna throw a saddle on the black one. He'll do if his wind ain't been broke." He also wanted to test the horse's disposition, since he might be ridden by Mary or the girls. "We won't be wantin' the chestnut," he then told Bledsoe. "He's a little slack in the girth and has weak-lookin' quarters. Those long legs tell me he ain't likely to hold up under a load."

"Well," Bledsoe offered weakly, with thoughts of high profit combined with getting rid of some weak horseflesh fading away, "like I said, I was tryin' to give her somethin' gentle, but I got others."

"He oughta be gentle, all right," Cam remarked, "but where we're headin', we ain't lookin' for a pet."

The purchase of Mary Bishop's horses went on a good bit longer than Ned Bledsoe had estimated in the beginning. Cam saddled the black and rode it full gallop out the end of the main street to judge the horse's heart and wind. "He'll do," he told Mary when he returned. He settled on a sorrel and a bay to round out Mary's string, including two saddles and a packsaddle.

"Mister," Bledsoe told him, "you're a helluva man to bargain with. I can't make any money dealin' with you. You looked at them horses every way in the world. I was expectin' you to crawl up their hind ends to take a look inside 'em."

"You got a fair price for the three of 'em," Cam said. "I knew you didn't look like the kinda man who would take advantage of a lady. I saw an old pack rig hangin' up in the tack room back there. Since the lady bought two saddles from you, too, I expect you'll throw that in to boot."

Bledsoe snorted and shook his head. "I reckon," he said, knowing when he was beat. "I expect you'll be boardin' 'em here," he remarked hopefully.

"Don't know," Cam answered. "It's up to the lady." He walked back out to the corral, where Mary waited. "How soon do you wanna get started for this camp where your brother-in-law is? There's still plenty of daylight left today if you don't wanna wait till the mornin'."

"I don't see any reason to wait," she replied. "Let's get started today."

He smiled. "Have you got any money left for the supplies we're gonna need?"

"I think so," she said. "At least we'll find out."

"Let's go, then," he said, and led the horses out of the corral. "Come on, Grace." She came to him and he picked her up and sat her in the saddle. Next, he placed Emma up behind Grace and told her, "Hang on to your sister." He then helped Mary up on the black gelding, and they waited while he put the packsaddle on the sorrel. Stepping up on Toby, he said to Bledsoe, "Pleasure doin' business with you."

"Come back when you need another horse," Bledsoe called after them. "Remember you got a good deal here." *Sharp-eyed son of a bitch,* he thought. *He cost me a helluva lot of money.*

Cam waited downstairs while Mary changed into a pair of denim trousers she had purchased the day before at the dry goods store. When she came down, carrying her suitcases, he was pleased to see that she had gotten some sensible clothing, something more suitable for the trip she was determined to take. Grace and Emma were similarly attired. Grace carried a small suitcase and Emma dragged a carpetbag behind her. He wasted no more than a few seconds to scrutinize the luggage before suggesting she should get rid of the suitcases and carry her things in sacks. "These are a matched set of suitcases," she complained. "Why would I want to discard them? And where on earth am I going to find cloth sacks?"

"Maybe the grocery," Cam suggested. "If they ain't got any, we oughta be able to find some at the feed store."

She frowned as she considered his suggestion. "No," she decided, "this is perfectly good luggage and I don't wish to part with it. We'll just have to tie it on our packhorse." Leaving no room for further discussion, she continued. "Now, I expect we should go to the store across the street and get what supplies we need. I'm going to need a frying pan and a coffeepot, too, if I have to come up with something for you and the girls to eat."

"Yes, ma'am, you're the boss. I'm gonna need

some extra rope. I've got a fryin' pan and a coffeepot, but they ain't very big ones. I never did much entertainin'."

"I'll need to buy some new ones," she said decidedly. "I've seen yours."

He grinned sheepishly. There was no need to comment.

"You ever hear of a camp called Destiny?" Cam asked the owner of the general store when he carried the last of Mary's purchases out to tie onto the sorrel.

"Destiny?" Grady Simpson responded. "Can't say as I have, but there's a lot of little pockets of folks up in those hills. Somebody will strike a little color, and pretty quick other folks move in, and before you know it, there's a sizable little settlement sprung up. But Destiny, I don't recollect hearin' that name." He hesitated for a moment when another thought struck him. "Martha," he called to his wife, who was standing on the front step talking to Mary. "What was that name those two brothers called their minin' camp?"

"Destiny," Martha said without having to think twice about it.

Her reply caught both Cam's and Mary's attention. "That's my husband's camp," she quickly stated. "He and his brother staked a claim and called it Destiny."

"I declare," Grady remarked, "that's right. I had

plumb forgot. Tell you the truth, I thought it was a peculiar name to call a placer mine. But Martha's right." He handed Cam the sack of flour he had been holding and stood back to judge his proficiency in tying a secure packsaddle. "They musta struck good color, because they quit comin' into town together. First one of 'em would come to the store. Then next time the other'n would come. I figured they musta been settin' on a sizable strike, and they figured somebody needed to guard their claim." He turned to Mary then. "Which brother are you married to?" She told him that Warren was her husband. "So now you've come to join your husband?"

"Her husband was killed, Grady," Cam quickly told him before he went further with his questions. "She's looking for his brother, so she can tell him the sorrowful news."

"I'm right sorry to hear that, ma'am," Grady stated awkwardly. "We never got to know either one of 'em very well, but they struck me as fine gentlemen, both of 'em."

"You have any idea where that camp might be?" Cam asked.

"Why, no," Grady replied. "They were mighty tight-lipped when it came to talkin' about their claim. It's just somewhere up in those mountains northeast of here. They always rode out the north end of town when they left, but I'm afraid that's all I can tell you."

"Much obliged," Cam told him while Mary said good-bye to Grady's wife. When Mary was aboard her new black gelding, Cam perched the girls on the back of the bay. Each girl had a piece of peppermint in her mouth, a gift from Mrs. Simpson. With everybody set to start out on their wilderness adventure, Cam led his little party out the north road. Beyond the last building in town, and away from curious eyes, he pulled Toby to a stop and Mary handed him the map her late husband had sent her in one of his letters.

Cam studied the roughly sketched map carefully. "Accordin' to this, we oughta see a smooth round rock about the size of a haystack, close to four miles north of town. It's settin' right beside a wide stream comin' down outta the mountains. We're supposed to follow that stream up through the hills till we get to a smaller stream that feeds into it." He handed the map back to Mary. "Sounds simple enough so far."

They found the round rock beside the stream after traveling a distance that seemed far more than four miles, but they decided it had to be the right stream, so they followed it up into foothills that were thick with dark pitch pines, broken here and there with maples and quaking aspens. Higher they rode, past traces of abandoned claims along the stream, evidence of played-out strikes, their former owners no doubt having left to join the horde that rushed to Deadwood. By the time they reached the fork where the smaller stream flowed in from the eastern mountains, the sun was threatening to drop out of sight. So they decided it best to make camp while there was light enough to do so. "If your map is right," Cam said, "that camp shouldn't be too far from here. We oughta strike it pretty early in the mornin'."

He pulled the saddles off the horses and hobbled the three Mary had just bought. He didn't hobble Toby. When Emma asked why, he told her that Toby was more like a dog than a horse, and the buckskin would never stray far from where he was. This delighted the little girl, and she told her mother that she wanted to name the new horses. "All right," Mary told her, "you and Grace can have that job, but think of some good names, because they'll be stuck with them. While you're thinking about that, you two can help me build a fire and we'll try out our new pan. Grace, you know how to make coffee, so you can do that as soon as we get a fire started. Now, Grace, don't skimp with the coffee grounds. Put enough beans in the mill to fill that little drawer. We don't want Cam to faint because of weak coffee."

"It might be a good idea to build your fire in that little hollow over there," Cam suggested, and pointed to a spot just below a steep outcropping of rock. "It ain't a bad idea not to make your fire too easy to see when you're in country you ain't familiar with." Seeing his point, Mary directed the girls to gather wood and pile it where he suggested.

Supper that night was simple, since Mary had little time to prepare. It consisted of fried pork and pan bread, washed down with plenty of coffee. It satisfied Cam's plain taste, but Mary said she would make up for it when they reached Destiny. In return, he said he would furnish some meat other than bacon, since he had seen abundant deer sign ever since they started up into the hills.

When it came time to turn in, an awkward sense of modesty descended upon the camp since it would be the first time she would close her eyes in the presence of the strapping young man, and there were no doors to lock. In spite of riding a horse all afternoon, she decided she would forgo an urge to bathe before retiring. "Grace, you and Emma can spread your blankets up next to me," she told them. "It might get a little chilly during the night." They gladly followed her suggestion, not so much out of fear of a chill. It was black as soot outside the ring of their firelight, and a little girl's imagination was capable of conjuring all manner of night creatures roaming the woods. She found a low mound of dirt at the edge of the circle of firelight that appeared to be just the thing for a pillow for her and the girls, so she spread a blanket over it. Cam watched her preparations for sleeping with interest, but without comment. In spite of her feelings of uncertainty about their first night alone with Cam in these mysterious hills, long sacred to the Sioux and Cheyenne, she felt a bit sheepish when he announced that he was going to sleep close to the horses. *I owe him an apology,* she thought, *but damned if I'll ever tell him why*. She then reminded herself that she owed so much to this stranger, her life and her children's lives, in fact. Thoughts of the stage holdup returned to her, and the terrifying road agents that were prepared to kill them all, had it not been for the fortunate hand of fate that sent Cam Sutton to help them.

Perhaps not entirely by coincidence, the outlaws Mary brought to mind were also thinking about the holdup, although some sixty miles away from Destiny. "That son of a bitch," Cotton Roach cursed, thinking about the rifleman who had torn a hole through his hand. "By God, I'll find out who he was one of these days, and when I do, he's a dead man."

"How the hell are you gonna find a man you ain't even got a good look at, and you don't even know his name?" Ben Cheney asked.

"I got a good enough look at the bastard. That stage was headed to Deadwood, so I reckon that's where he was headin', too. There's bound to be talk about the holdup. I'll find him."

"He might notta gone to Deadwood, mighta stopped at Custer City or somewhere," Cheney said. “We might better wait till your hand heals up. There’s folks that could identify you.” Cotton was easy to identify, with shoulder-length, almost white, blond hair and piercing blue eyes set deep under dark eyebrows. He had the look of a predator. Cheney watched while Roach fumbled with his spoon in his left hand in an effort to eat his supper, and couldn’t help chuckling. “Next time you have to reach for a rifle, you’d best use your left hand, partner. It makes it kinda hard without your right hand, don’t it?” He laughed again. “Hell, that’s your wipin’ hand, too.”

“I’m glad my miseries bring you so much enjoyment,” Roach snarled. He held his wounded hand up before his face to examine it. The bullet had gone straight through, but it must have done major damage. At this stage in the healing, he wasn’t sure if it would remain permanently stiff, or if the flexibility would gradually return. In the meantime, he had been forced to reverse his hand gun and wear it on his right side with the handle facing forward. Worse than that, firing a rifle with any accuracy was almost impossible. He was glad Cheney felt the same way about splitting up the gang after the holdup when Sam Bass and Joel Collins wanted them to run to Texas with them. The thought of their former partners caused further comment. “At least we got our share of the money. Pickin’s are a helluva lot better in the Black Hills right now, and there ain't a damn thing I want in Texas." He released a painful sigh. "Yeah, I'll find that son of a bitch."

"Maybe," Cheney remarked. In his opinion, the odds of Roach catching up with the man who shot him were pretty slim. But he had ridden with Roach long enough to know he was a dangerous man to have on your trail, and Lord help the rifleman if Roach ever did find him. Roach never said a word about losing Jack Dawson, a man who had ridden with them for a year. As far as Cheney knew, he was the only man who had been able to stick with Roach for any length of time. "We got a little money to lay back for a while, and you're gonna need some time to let that hand heal. Why don't we ride on down to Bill Foley's place and drink up all his whiskey?"

The morning broke bright and clear in the camp by the confluence of the two streams. It would be almost impossible not to enjoy the serenity of the dark pine-covered hills, and the lack of the dry parching winds that typified most of South Dakota. The stream that they were to follow that morning would lead them higher up toward the mountaintop. Cam stood near the horses and peered up at a waterfall high above them. According to Mary's map, the camp named Destiny was at the foot of that waterfall. His attention was distracted then by the sounds of the girls waking up, so he walked down to rekindle the fire. "Mornin'," he said when Mary turned back her blanket. "You ladies sleep all right?"

"Yes," Mary replied cheerfully, "I think we did. At least I slept like a rock, and I think the girls did, too. Is that right, Grace?"

"Yes, ma'am," Grace replied, and pulled her blanket up around her shoulders to protect against the morning chill.

"We'll have this fire goin' in a minute," Cam told her. When Emma came to stand close by the fire, he handed her a broken ax handle he had found near the stream. "You can put that on the fire when it gets goin' a little better." When he saw the look of curiosity in Mary's eye, he explained. "Found it by the stream. Like I figured last night, it looks like somebody musta been pannin' for gold right here at the fork. Looks like they mighta had a little bad luck." He pointed to the mound of dirt Mary and the girls had used for a pillow. "Looks like that's where one of 'em's buried."

His casual comment caused Mary to jump quickly away from the mound. "What!" she demanded. "That's a grave?" She quickly reached down and jerked the blanket off it. "You knew it was a grave? Did you know it was a grave last night?"

"Well, I suspected that's what it was. I didn't know for sure. I couldn't think of no other reason for a pile of dirt that size to be there." He glanced down to see two scrunched-up faces on the girls. "Figured you didn't care."

"Ooh." Mary shivered in disgust. "We were sleeping on top of some old dead miner?"

"You said you slept good," he reminded her.

"Well, I shouldn't have," she replied, still trying to decide how perturbed she was going to be with him for letting her lay her head on a grave. After a minute, she grudgingly admitted there had been no harm done. "Don't you ever let me do something like that again," she ordered with one last shiver.

Breakfast was another hurried affair, since they were so close to their destination, and the girls were eager to see their uncle Raymond. Mary explained to Cam that Grace and Emma had never been around their father's older brother to know him really well, but they had heard tales of his adventures in Virginia City and Bannack, so he was somewhat of a hero in their minds. When the horses were saddled and all were packed up, they started up a path no wider than a game trail that held close to the stream.

All along the way, where the stream had furrowed out a deeper and deeper gulch, they saw the evidence of a once busy mining strike, strewn with trash and piles of earth left by the bank, but the miners were gone. Halfway to the waterfall, they came upon a camp that was still inhabited, however. Two men were working a sluice box, unaware of the travelers on the path until they were almost upon them. “Mornin’,” Cam called out.

Both men stopped to gape at the strangers for a long moment before one of them returned the greeting. “Mornin’,” he said, eyeing Mary and the girls openly. “You folks lost?” he then asked. “If you’re thinkin’ ’bout lookin’ for gold in this stream, you’re too late. What was here ain’t here no more.”

“We’re looking for a camp called Destiny,” Mary told him.

Her comment brought a laugh from both men. “You found it. This is Destiny, at least that’s what some folks called it. A year ago, there were close to twenty claims between here and the waterfall. Now you’re lookin’ at what’s left of Destiny, the two of us, and one other feller up at the falls. There was color here for a while, good color, but it didn’t last long. That other feller got most of it. We stayed on ’cause we were still gettin’ a little color, but we’re about ready to admit we’re whipped.”

“We’ve come to find Raymond Bishop,” Mary said. “Do you know if he’s still here?”

“Bishop? Yeah, we know him, all right. He’s the other feller I was talkin’ about. Yes, ma’am, he’s still up there, squeezin’ every last ounce outta this mountain.”

“You kin of Bishop?” the other man asked.

"I'm his brother's widow," Mary answered.

"His brother's widow?" It was a surprise to both men, and the one who had been shoveling dirt into the back of the sluice box walked over to stand beside his partner. "You mean the one named Warren Bishop? He's dead?"

"That's right," Mary said.

"I swear, that's sure 'nough bad news, ma'am. I'm right sorry to hear it. He seemed like a good man, what little bit we talked to him. The older one, the one still up there, he didn't ever have much to say to us." He paused then. "Excuse my manners, ma'am. My name is Cecil Painter. This here's my partner, Everett Jones. I'm right sorry to hear about Warren's death. He just left here a few weeks ago, said he was headin' home. He looked as healthy as a horse then. What happened?"

"He was murdered by road agents," Mary stated without emotion.

"Oh my goodness," Everett sighed, though not entirely convincingly. "I sure am sorry, ma'am."

"We're on our way to tell Raymond about his brother's death," Mary said, and signaled Cam that she was ready to get on with it.

"You folks be careful when you start up to Bishop's camp." Cecil spoke directly to Cam. "Sing out loud and clear before you go ridin' into his place. He's a mite touchy about anybody he thinks is sneakin' up on him."

"He's the only one's got anythin' to protect," Everett added. "I'd be touchy myself."

"We'll let him know we're comin'," Cam assured them. "I expect he'll be glad to see his sister-in-law and his nieces."

"Good day to you, ma'am," Cecil said as Mary nudged her horse to follow Cam. "Ladies," Cecil acknowledged as the girls on the bay passed by him, following along behind Mary's horse.

The two miners stood and watched them depart. When they were well out of earshot, Cecil said, "I hope that ol' badger don't shoot at 'em before they get a chance to tell him about his brother."

"That's a shame about Warren," Everett said. "He had a fine-lookin' family, didn't he? And he was on his way home to see 'em."

"He did," Cecil replied, "and enough gold to live high on the hog for the rest of his life. Well, I reckon he left a wealthy widow. She won't have no trouble catchin' another husband."

"I'll volunteer, if she has any trouble."

Cecil chuckled at Everett's remark. "I said she was fine-lookin', not desperate-lookin'. They never said who the feller with her was. He might have his eye on the widow's share of that gold."

"Well, she says she's come all the way up here just to tell poor ol' Bishop his brother's dead, but I'd bet she's more likely comin' to make sure she gets her husband's share of all that dust they been washin' outta that hill."

"I expect so," Everett said, "and that young feller totin' the rifle don't look like he's just a friend of the family. Maybe ol' Bishop better watch he don't turn his back on 'em."

"I expect," Cecil agreed. "Hell, they better watch out they don't turn their backs on Bishop. That ol' son of a bitch ain't likely to share anythin' with that woman. If anybody oughta have a share in whatever he's got hid up there, it'd be us. We're the ones been siftin' through his leavin's."

"Wouldn't it be a damn shame if ol' Bishop and that young feller got into a tussle and shot each other?" Everett said facetiously. "Then we'd have to go up there and take care of the lady and her gold."

Chapter 4

Not much escaped the watchful eye of Raymond Bishop. It was a vital trait to possess for a man sitting on a fortune in gold, and this was the fact in Raymond's case. He was the one who first realized the potential the little stream below the waterfall concealed, but in all fairness, the initial discovery was made by Warren. While watering their horses in the little pool at the bottom of the fall, his brother decided to get out his gold pan and work some of the gravel at the edge of the stream. Much to their surprise, he sifted out about fifty cents' worth of gold in his first pan. They immediately made camp right there and went to work to see if the potential they hoped for was really there. It had proven to be a genuine strike, one that Raymond could appreciate much more than Warren, because Raymond had already invested years of fruitless search for the strike that would justify his frustrations. For Warren, this expedition with his brother was his first endeavor to gain instant wealth.

They staked off their claim and began to work it day and night in an attempt to amass a fortune before anyone else happened along. The pace soon became too much for Warren, but he was spurred on by his older brother, who was consumed by his lust for every ounce of gold the mountain had hidden. He sent Warren back to the sawmill in Custer City to buy boards to build a sluice box. It was a welcome break away from the constant toil for the younger brother, but the trip created almost instant competition for them. A pair of curious prospectors found it interesting when they saw Warren leading a packhorse loaded with pine boards on the road out of town. Having no real prospects of their own at that time, they decided to tail him just in case he was onto something they might be able to take advantage of. So Cecil Painter and Everett Jones staked claims next to the Bishop brothers'. The incident caused an argument between the two brothers, creating a rift between them that lasted for several days, with Raymond faulting Warren for carelessly leading the two interlopers to their strike.

Painter and Jones were soon followed by others who somehow got wind of the strike, and the little stream became the site of frantic clambering to strip the mountain of its gold. Their activity only served to encourage Raymond to work longer and harder, and he was quick to tell any who approached him that this stream was his destiny, and his alone. Before long, the other miners began to refer to the area as Destiny, a fact that Warren found amusing. The second argument between the brothers came about when Raymond found out that Warren had drawn a map of their claim and sent it to his wife, thinking she would find it interesting to know exactly where her husband toiled. That disagreement was still unresolved when Warren announced that he had been away from his family for too long, and he had decided to go home to see them. Raymond ranted in protest, but Warren was determined to go, promising to be back in a month. And that was how they left it.

Now, on this morning, Raymond's ever-watchful eye caught sight of the party of strangers heading up the trail toward his camp. Instantly aggravated, he dropped his shovel and picked up his rifle. "Now, what the hell . . . ?" he muttered, and walked forward to meet them.

"Hello the camp!" Cam called.

"Hello yourself," Raymond roared. "What the hell do you want?"

"Raymond!" Mary called out then. "It's Mary!"

"What?" Raymond returned, shocked. "Mary, is that you?"

"It's me and the girls," she replied, and pushed past Cam.

Still clutching his rifle, Raymond stood there, a man fully astonished, as if seeing ghosts approaching his camp. "Warren ain't here," he finally muttered.

Watching off to the side, Cam found it to be an odd reaction to the sudden appearance of his sister-in-law. The bay carrying Grace and Emma edged up to stand beside him, and the two little girls stared at the gruff-looking, silver-haired man, glaring at them in return, with such inhospitable eyes. Cam glanced toward them and said, "I reckon that's your uncle Raymond."

"He looks so old," Grace remarked.

"He looks mad," Emma commented.

"He most likely ain't as old as he looks," Cam told her. "Hard work will make you look a lot older than your years sometimes." He dismounted and said, "Here, I'll help you down." When he had lifted both girls off the horse, he waited while they ran forward to join their mother, who had already dismounted.

Raymond Bishop stood like a man turned to stone until Mary extended her hand to him.

"Raymond," she said, and gave him a polite peck on his cheek, "I'm afraid I have come to bring you some very sad news."

"Mary," was all he seemed able to say, as if still finding it hard to believe, all the while looking beyond her at the strapping young man by the horses.

Noticing his obvious curiosity about her guide, she said, "That's Cam Sutton. He's a friend and our guide." Raymond nodded slowly when Cam touched a finger to his hat to acknowledge. "And this is Grace and Emma," Mary went on, trying to dispel the icy atmosphere between them. "Emma was just a baby the last time you saw them. Girls, say hello to your uncle Raymond." Their response was less than enthusiastic, bordering on fearful, since their uncle seemed a baleful sort. Grace managed a cautious hello, while Emma chose to cling to her mother's leg. Raymond lowered his gaze only briefly to look at his nieces, equally disinterested in a reunion. Mary delayed no longer in giving him the news about his brother's passing.

When she had finished giving him all the details she knew about Warren's murder at the hands of a road agent, Raymond at last responded in a more normal nature. "Warren dead?" he gasped, and shook his head in disbelief. "Murdered, you say?" She nodded mournfully. He shook his head slowly back and forth. "That is truly sorrowful news. I tried to tell him to wait till I could go with him. I wish he had listened." He glanced again at Cam before asking, "What are you gonna do now? I ain't got much of a place here." He turned to gesture toward the tent he had been living in.

"I guess I'll be going back to Fort Collins after we've rested," Mary said. "I just felt that we should make our way up here to tell you of your brother's passing. It was the least I could do."

Her last statement seemed to give him visible relief, and he warmed a bit. "I sure appreciate it, Mary." He looked around at the tent again. "I wish I had some more comfortable accommodations for you." He then smiled, for the first time since their arrival. "Warren and I didn't build a camp with comfort for ladies in mind." Quickly reverting to his expression of sorrow, he said, "That sure is bad news about Warren. He and I worked hard on this camp. We got a little bit of dust outta this stream, so I reckon half of it belongs to you now, might be enough to help you get back to Colorado. I'm afraid I'm running awful short of supplies right now, though. I ain't been able to get down to Custer City since Warren has been gone."

"That will certainly help," Mary said. "It cost me almost everything I had just to get out here, but we've got some food with us."

An interested witness to the conversation, Cam wondered what the man planned to do when he ran out of food. Remembering what Cecil had said about Raymond being the only one who had anything to guard, he could pretty well guess that he was virtually a prisoner of his success. He couldn't leave his camp unguarded long enough to go after supplies. Curious, he took a longer glance at Raymond's tent; the little trench dug around it to drain water away, the large pile of dirt behind it. The pile looked to be enough dirt to fill a hole three or four feet deep, the size of the tent. *He's dug himself a fort under that tent,* he thought, *and I wouldn't be surprised to find it's lined with little sacks of gold dust. I'll bet the cheating bastard's planning on keeping Mary's share of her husband's gold.* He decided then that he wasn't going to let him get away with it if he could help it. Since it was obvious that food was in short supply, he volunteered to provide some. "I reckon we're gonna be here long enough for you folks to visit a little, so I think I'll go on around the other side of this mountain and see if I can find one of those deer I've been seein' sign of. A little fresh meat would help out."

Raymond addressed him for the first time. "That would sure help out," he said. "I've been thinking about going hunting myself, but I ain't been able to find the time."

"I was gettin' a little tired of Mary's salt pork," Cam said, with a grin for the lady. "We'll see what kinda luck I got." He climbed back into the saddle and turned Toby around. "If I get some luck, I oughta be back by suppertime with fresh meat."

Raymond watched him closely as he rode away, and as soon as he rode out of earshot, he turned to Mary and asked, "Where'd you hook up with him? What do you know about him?"

Surprised, Mary replied, "Truthfully, I haven't known Cam for very long, but I trust him completely." She went on to tell him about her initial meeting with Cam when he appeared out of nowhere to stop what could have been a fatal stage holdup. Raymond made no further comment, but he was not ready to disregard his suspicions about the man's true intentions.

Cam figured it was too early in the day for deer or elk to be feeding, so he rode along the ridges, looking for likely spots where they might be resting in the dense pine belts. While he looked, he thought again of Raymond Bishop. The man didn't appear too happy to see Mary and the girls. *And he eyed me with a definite look of suspicion.* He remembered Painter and Jones joking about Raymond's inhospitable ways, and his claims on the mountain as his destiny alone. After meeting the man, Cam could readily understand why he wasn't thought of as neighborly by the other miners in the small gulch. Then his thoughts went to Mary and her daughters. He supposed that his agreement with her was completed. She had asked him to take them to Destiny, and in Destiny they were. But he felt that to do his part, he should see them safely back to Custer City, where they could catch the stage back to Cheyenne. Then there was the question about Mary's rightful share of the gold Raymond and her husband had found. *The man was his brother, for God's sake,* he thought. Further speculation was interrupted by a slight movement in a pine thicket below him.

I can't be that lucky, he thought, but grabbed his rifle and dismounted anyway. Dropping Toby's reins to the ground, he made his way down through the trees on foot, moving slowly and cautiously, stopping frequently to look and listen. They were lying near a tiny trickle of water that wound its way between the trees that sheltered them. It was so dark beneath the branches that he could not tell how many there were, and he had only shadows for targets, so he had to get closer. As he strained to keep his eye on the shadows, his foot caught on a root and he stumbled and caught himself on one knee. It was enough to cause alarm in the resting group of deer, resulting in a flurry of motion among the shadows. With only seconds to pick a target, he raised his rifle and fired at the silhouette of a deer's neck. It disappeared, but so did all the others, so he wasn't sure if he had hit anything or not.

By the time he made his way down through the thicket, all the deer had fled, all except the one doe that lay dying on the ground. He quickly put the deer out of its misery. *Lucky shot,* he thought. *I won't be bragging about that one. I almost fell on my ass and let them all get away*. The result, however, was fresh meat, so he dragged the carcass out of the thicket, then went to get his horse. *Anyway,* he thought, *I won't have to go back to that camp with a rabbit or squirrel after I said I'd get them a deer*. It was a fair-sized doe, causing him to grunt a little when he hefted it up on Toby. "Damn," he said to the horse, "maybe I shoulda butchered it here."

When he returned to the camp, he found that Mary had built a fire and had coffee on to boil. It was still a strange picture, with Raymond sitting apart from his guests on a bench-high boulder. When she heard his horse approaching, Mary turned to greet him. Apparently it had been a difficult task trying to make conversation with her brother-in-law, so she was doubly glad to see Cam again. She got up from her seat on a blanket to help him with the deer. Emma's eyes got bigger and bigger when she saw the carcass draped across Toby's withers. The girls had never seen a dead deer before. She and Grace ran after their mother to get a closer look.

Raymond got up from the rock he had been seated on, his interest definitely aroused. "You work fast," he commented to Cam. "I heard the shot."

"Didn't take long to find 'em," Cam replied with

no elaboration of the details. He was thinking that it took the prospect of fresh meat to foster any animation on the part of their stoic host. It was a sign of the desperation the man must certainly be in. *He must have been eating grass,* Cam thought. It caused him to make an offer to help. "Say, if you need to get into town to get supplies, I could stay here and watch your claim for you." He figured Mary and the girls could go back to Custer City with him. But as soon as he said it, he saw the narrowing of Raymond's eyes and his look of concern.

"I don't need anybody to sit on my claim for me. I don't need supplies that bad, and I'll be leaving here for good pretty soon."

"Well, I was just offerin'," Cam said, shrugged, and went to work skinning his deer. Mary volunteered her help, but he told her he had butchered enough game to have his own methods of doing it. "You just take care of the cookin'," he said. "Besides, it looks like I've got all the help I need," he added, nodding toward the girls, who were crowding in to get a closer look at the procedure.

Before long, there were strips of fresh venison roasting over the fire on a spit that the brothers had fashioned, but that looked to have not been in use for some time. Mary served the hot meat as soon as it was done, and no one was more eager than Raymond. *Like he ain't had anything solid in days,* Cam thought. He began to suspect that

Raymond might have been searching for gold for too many years. He had heard of men who had spent so many lonely years of hard labor, brutal weather, and danger from Indians and outlaws that they had gone crazy in the head. The image of Raymond, choking down strip after strip of meat like a hungry wolf, easily verified his suspicions. When all had had their fill, Cam finished the butchering, portioned out some to cook later, and prepared the fire to dry out the rest, smoking it over the flames.

The only occasions when Mary could talk to Cam without being overheard were when Raymond would have to walk back in the woods to answer nature's calls. To satisfy his curiosity on one such occasion, Cam opened the flap on the tent and stuck his head inside for a quick look. It was as he had suspected. The tent was over a hole more than three feet deep. It had been carved out in the shape of a square, just inside the area covered by the canvas, in effect, a short room. There were two beds, one on each side, and a small stove in the center with a stovepipe that extended up to a smoke hole in the top of the tent. In one corner of the hole, he saw a small pile of three cloth bags, containing gold dust, he assumed. *Not much to show for the time the two brothers had spent here,* he thought. He had no need to linger, for he had seen all there was to see, and the heavy stale air inside the hole made him crave a lungful of fresh air. He backed away and closed the flap, then turned to meet Mary's questioning gaze. Shaking his head vigorously and snorting like a buffalo, he said, "You don't wanna go in there."

She started to question him, but Raymond returned at that moment. "When are you folks planning to start back?" he asked.

"I guess we'll leave tomorrow," Mary answered. She then turned to Cam. "Is that all right with you, or do you need more time to tend the venison?"

"That's fine with me," Cam replied. "I'm leavin' most of that meat here for Raymond to finish up. We oughta be able to head out before noon."

His answer was well received by Mary. This whole reunion with Raymond had been a depressing encounter, one she almost wished she had not undertaken. Raymond had changed, and for the worse, she guessed, and she was eager now to leave him here in his *Destiny*. Had it not been for the need to rest the horses, and for the smoking of the meat, she would have been ready to ride back down the mountain immediately. *Just as well,* she told herself. *The girls can have an afternoon to rest.*

She had just begun to prepare supper when Raymond went into his tent and came out with two of the sacks Cam had seen in the corner of his fortifications. He carried them over and dropped them at Mary's feet. "Like I said, Warren and I managed to dig up a little pay dirt. I weighed these sacks out at five pounds apiece. I've got three of 'em, so I'm giving you two, and I'll keep one. I think that's fair, since you've got children to feed, and those two sacks are worth about thirty-three hundred dollars."

Almost stunned, she didn't know what to say at first. "Oh, that much?" she gasped. "But that's not fair to you, Raymond. I think we should at least split the gold fifty-fifty. That's much too generous. I want to be fair."

"I insist," he said. "I'll get by with my share. I don't want it said that I didn't take care of Warren's widow."

Gleeful over the prospect of having enough money to decide where she and the girls could find a place to settle down, Mary gushed, "Thank you so much, Raymond. This will make our lives so much easier. I know Warren is thanking you right now for your kindness."

More than a little interested in the conversation he could overhear, Cam turned his attention away from the stream, where he had been watching Grace and Emma playing a game of stepping stones. The winner was the one who could walk across the water without slipping in, by stepping from stone to stone. "That's the least I can do," he heard Raymond say in response to Mary's thanks.

That's the least you can do, Cam thought. *You got that right*. Judging by Raymond's attitude from the first moment since they had shown up, he couldn't figure him to be generous worth a damn. While he had whiled away the afternoon, watching the meat he was preparing, he couldn't help visually searching the campsite for possible places to hide the bulk of Raymond's fortune, and there were many. One thing he felt certain about was the probability that those three sacks of dust were a minor portion of that taken out of the gulch, and were kept inside his tent to mislead anyone intent upon robbing him. He paused then to ask himself if it was any of his business. *It's a family affair,* he thought, and considered that for a moment. He picked up a small stone and tossed it into the pool at the bottom of the falls, close enough to Grace to make her squeal when a little water splashed on her leg. *I don't care if it ain't my business. She deserves half of what's been found so far*.

Unnoticed by the idle young man, or anyone else on this lazy summer afternoon, a dark rider sat on a gray horse, surveying the camp from the ridge above. Dressed in black, from the flat-crowned, wide-brim hat, down to his black Spanish boots, he watched with interest what appeared to be an idyllic family scene: meat smoking over a fire, children playing in the water, a comely mother smiling sweetly as Raymond Bishop handed her two sacks of gold dust. He took an extra minute to study the younger man tending the smoked meat. *Hard to say,* he thought, and reached down to make sure the .44 was riding easy in its holster. "Look's like a family picnic," he told the dappled-gray gelding. "Let's go down and join the folks." He gave the horse a nudge with his heels and descended the ridge.

With his back turned to the ridge, Cam didn't realize they had a visitor until he saw the angry surprise in Raymond's face. He turned then to see the dark rider emerge from the pines. His natural reaction was to reach for his Colt, only to recall that it was on his saddle with his rifle. There had been no thought that he would have need of it. Maybe he wouldn't. He had no choice now but to wait and see. Taking a quick glance at Raymond, he guessed that Mary's brother-in-law knew the rider, and from the expression on his face, he was not especially glad to see him.

Sensing something was wrong, Mary stepped away from Raymond and hurried to gather her daughters up close to her. The stranger smiled menacingly at her as she called to Emma, who had paused to gawk at the visitor. Aware that Cam had gotten to his feet, the rider pulled his horse to a stop between him and the saddle on the ground where his weapons lay. He then glanced at him, still with the confident smile in place.

"What are you doing here, Rafer?" Raymond asked, clearly angered.

"Hello, Mr. Bishop," Rafer replied, making no

effort to disguise a sneer. “You don’t look happy to see me again.”

“What do you want?” Raymond demanded.

“I came to collect for that little piece of business I done for you.”

“Our business is finished,” Raymond shot back. “You got every bit we agreed on, and our deal was that you would never come back here again.”

Rafer glanced at Cam again to make sure he wasn’t about to make any sudden moves toward his weapons. “Yeah? Well, I’m changin’ our deal. I think you bought me off too cheap, Bishop. I got to thinkin’ about it and I think that job I did for you was worth twice as much as you paid me. So why don’t you just come up with the other half of my payment, and maybe I’ll ride away and not bother this little family picnic?” He smirked, enjoying his advantage over the two men. “You know, money’s the only thing that keeps my tongue from waggin’ too much.”

“You son of a bitch,” Raymond blurted. “We had a deal, and I kept my end of it.”

“And I kept mine,” Rafer roared back. “The son of a bitch is dead.”

“Shut your mouth!” Raymond demanded, looking anxiously back and forth between Mary and Cam.

“Like I said, nothin’ shuts me up like a few bags of gold dust, and it looks to me like you’re handin’ ’em out right now.” He nodded toward Mary.

"There isn't any more," Raymond insisted. The situation was becoming more desperate with each statement that came out of Rafer's mouth. Not anxious to explain any more than had already been said, he decided it better to try to buy Rafer off. "All I've got left is one more five-pound sack. I'll give you that if you'll go away and leave me alone."

"You think you're dealin' with a damn fool?" Rafer shot back, irritated by what he considered a cheap attempt. "Yeah, I'll take the other sack, and them two the woman's holdin'. Then we'll dig up some of the rest of that dust you've hid, and the sooner you get to it, the sooner we'll be done."

Feeling helpless to do anything about the confrontation between the stranger and Raymond, Cam could only hope for some opportunity to make a move to protect Mary and the girls. He was afraid of what he felt certain was slated to happen. This man Raymond called Rafer was a gun hand, a killer, and Raymond had evidently paid for his services. It was not difficult to imagine who the victim might have been. Rafer, like Cam, knew without doubt that there was a helluva lot more gold dust hidden somewhere around this camp. And Cam also knew that it was highly unlikely that Rafer planned to ride away, leaving live witnesses behind. He glanced furtively under the belly of the gray horse at the rifle and pistol he could see lying on his saddle, so close, yet they might as well be fifty yards away.

Mary, frozen in fear moments before, began to think rationally again, and she gradually realized the same thing that Cam had figured out. The more she thought about it, the more angry she became, to the point where she ignored the risk and demanded, "What did you pay this man to do? Kill someone? Who did you have him kill?"

Raymond recoiled as if having been struck with a club, his face contorted into a mask of anger. "Stay out of this, Mary. It ain't got nothing to do with you."

Mary's outburst seemed to amuse Rafer. "Yeah, Bishop, why don't you tell her who you hired me to kill?"

"All right, dammit!" Raymond blurted. "I'll pay you what you want! Just take it and get the hell away from here."

"Now you're startin' to make sense," Rafer said with a chuckle.

"I'll get the other sack out of the tent," Raymond said.

"You do that," Rafer said, and as soon as Raymond disappeared into the tent, he drew the .44 from his holster, leveled it at the tent flap, and waited.

Cam, aware of what was about to happen, knew there was only going to be one chance for him to act, and it was going to be desperate at best. While Rafer's gaze was fixed upon the tent flap, Cam slowly lowered himself to one knee. With his eyes on Rafer, he felt around for a stone bigger than the ones he threw in the water to splash the girls. When his hand settled on one the size of a biscuit, he closed his fingers around it and waited. It was no more than a few seconds before he saw the tent flap move and the barrel of a shotgun emerge. Expecting such a move, Rafer did not hesitate. He pumped three shots into Raymond before the unfortunate man completely cleared the tent. He was about to cock his pistol for a fourth shot when he was startled by the solid thud of the stone on his back. Thinking he had been shot, he turned to find Cam charging him, his body already about to be launched. Rafer tried to bring his .44 to bear on the human missile, but he was knocked off his horse before he could get off another shot.

Landing hard on the rocky stream bank, the two men fought desperately, each trying to gain the advantage. Rafer tried to force his gun hand down to aim at Cam's chest, but he had not reckoned on the strength of the rugged young man. Gradually, Cam forced Rafer's wrist back until he could no longer keep his grip on the pistol and it fell from his hand to land in the edge of the water. Straining mightily, the two men rolled into the stream, turning over and over in the water, each man struggling to land on top. The contest finally ended when Cam managed to get both hands on Rafer's throat and forced his head under the icy water, and held him there until his hands ceased their frantic clawing and flailing, and his body went limp.

Still holding the gunman under the water long after he knew he was dead, Cam looked up to see the shocked faces staring at him, the one most horrified that of little Emma. Exhausted, he released his death grip on Rafer's body and crawled out of the water to drop onto the ground. At last able to gather her wits about her, Mary hurried over to him. "Are you all right?" she asked.

He nodded, then gasped, "Just give me a minute and I will be." In a few seconds, his breath began to come a little easier and he said, "I'm sorry the girls had to see that."

When she saw that he really was all right, she said, "I guess they'll get over it. You'd better get out of those wet clothes and put them by the fire to dry. I'll go see about Raymond." When he appeared reluctant to do it, she told him, "You can wrap your blanket around you till your clothes are dry."

He was amazed that she was already calm so soon after what had to have been a frightening experience for her. "I'll drag him outta the water first," he told her, "so Grace and Emma won't have to look at him no more." He got to his feet and walked down the stream a dozen yards where Rafer's corpse had lodged itself against a rock.

It was the first time she had seen the inside of Raymond's tent, and even though Cam had told her of the excavation, she was surprised to find the pit Raymond had dug for his protection. It had all been for naught when the crucial time came, however, for she found him lying on the floor of the pit with three bullet holes, all high on his chest. She glanced around the earthen enclosure, lingering for a few moments on the one bunk with no blankets. It struck her that this was where Warren had slept, so many miles away from her, and she felt the tears begin to well up in her eyes. She had reached up to brush a tear from her cheek when she was distracted by a low moan from the body she had thought to be dead.

"Cam!" she cried out. "He's alive!" She looked back to see if he was coming; then when he started walking toward her, she dropped down inside the tent. Raymond was alive, but just barely. "Pull that flap away, so we can see in this dark hole," she told Cam. Raymond's eyelids fluttered weakly as he tried to tell her something, but he could scarcely make a noise. Knowing that he was rapidly dying, he forced himself to make a sound. "What is it you're trying to say?" Mary asked.

"Sorry," he whispered, his voice rasping from the effort it took for him to speak. "I'm sorry." Cam pulled back the flap and part of the front of the tent, and stood looking down into the hole. Raymond's eyes opened wide for a moment and he moaned. "Warren! I'm sorry, Warren. Forgive me." His voice trailed off then and he made no further sound, although he still stared up at Cam.

After a long moment, Cam stepped down beside Mary, placed his fingers on Raymond's eyelids, and closed them. "He's gone," he told Mary. "He was tryin' to make his peace."

"He thought you were Warren," she said, then looked up at him, a question in her eyes.

Understanding, he answered the unspoken question. "I reckon that's the truth of it, what you're thinkin'. It all adds up to it."

She slowly nodded. He didn't have to spell it out. Raymond had paid Rafer to kill her husband, his own brother. That explained why Warren's killer was not interested in his watch or his money. It was a planned assassination. She got to her feet and stood over him, staring down at the lifeless body of her brother-in-law, the brother that Warren had so looked up to. Finally she spoke softly. "I hope you go to hell." She turned away and started to climb up the front of the pit. "Help me out of this damn hole," she said to Cam, completely dry-eyed now. When he took her arm and gave her a boost, she said, "Take that other sack of gold. I promised I'd pay you for coming with me."

"Yes, ma'am," he replied politely, "but I don't believe we agreed on as much as there is in that sack." Being of a more practical nature, he looked around the hole under the tent for anything else that might be of use to them. There wasn't much of anything that they didn't already have, so he picked up the sack of dust and climbed out behind her.

While Mary tried to comfort her two daughters, Cam pulled up the tent pegs and moved the canvas away, leaving only a square hole in the ground with Raymond's body lying at the bottom. Mary glanced at him, refrained from questioning his actions, but asked, "When are you going to get out of those wet clothes?"

"When I'm done with buryin' 'em," he answered.

"I guess we should dig a grave for his brother," she said.

"Grave's already dug," he replied. "All I've gotta do is fill it in." He walked over then and grabbed Rafer's body by the heels of his Spanish boots and dragged it over to the pit. He parked it at the edge of the hole, then rolled it over to drop in beside Raymond. "I think it'll be easier on the girls when these bodies are in the ground," he remarked as he picked up a spade and started shoveling dirt into the hole from the large mound behind it. "I think what we'll need is a big pot of coffee after I get this done, and maybe some of that venison." He was trying to think of things for her to do in case she was going to let her mind dwell on the tragic incident just witnessed.

It took him over an hour to get to the bottom of the dirt pile, but he wanted to finish the job as quickly as possible. When it was almost level with the ground, there was still a small mound of dirt remaining. He hesitated, thinking it was good enough, but decided to go ahead and finish it off. So he thrust the shovel back into the mound, and when he did, it snagged on what he assumed was a pine root below the ground. When he raked the dirt from around it, however, it turned out to be a canvas sack. *Well, I'll be damned,* he thought, *they hid some of their dust under the dirt.* "Mary," he called, "come look at this."

By the time he shoveled away the last of the mound, he had unearthed four additional sacks, all appearing to be the same size as the three Raymond had left in the tent. The discovery of such a quantity of gold at once triggered contrasting emotions in Mary's mind, causing her to trouble over the source of the wealth. "I don't know," she said, and backed away from the sacks as if they held an evil power. "I don't know if I want that blood money. It comes from greed and murder."

Cam stood gazing at her for a moment while he thought about what she had just said. Then he calmly spoke his mind. "Well . . ." he drew out, "I reckon we could just empty all the sacks in the stream, and give the gold back to the mountain. On the other hand, you've got the rest of your life and the lives of your daughters to think about. Seems to me your husband woulda wanted you to have the gold he worked so hard for." He picked up one of the sacks as if to examine it. "You know, there ain't no evil in gold. It can't help what kinda person gets a hold of it. So I'm sayin' you need to thank Warren for takin' care of you for the rest of your life. The gold didn't come from evil-doin'. It came from your husband's hard work."

"You're right, of course," Mary admitted. "I think I just had a little holy moment there." She picked up one of the sacks. "Thank you, Warren," she said softly. "Your girls love you and appreciate what you have sacrificed your life for." She cocked an eyebrow at Cam and said, "It's a lot, but I don't think it's enough to take care of us all our lives."

"This ain't all of it," Cam replied confidently. "I'm bettin' there's more hid around here somewhere." He slowly turned in a complete circle, looking at possible places. "The way I figure it, your husband and his brother musta hit right in the middle of a strong vein of gold. I think that's the reason they decided they needed a fort to protect against claim jumpers. Figured they could just hunker down in that hole and hold anybody off. And if they had struck it that big, they most likely were hidin' their gold somewhere before they decided to dig that hole."

"You may be right," Mary said, trying now to hide the excitement that the prospects promised. "Where do you think we should look?"

"Everywhere," he replied. "First place is that

boulder he was always settin' on." He went immediately to the boulder in the middle of the clearing and put his shoulder against it. It wouldn't budge, but that did not discourage him. He brought his horse into the clearing, looped a rope around its neck, then took a couple of turns around the rock. Taking hold of the bridle, he led the buckskin until the slack was out of the rope. "Come on, boy," he encouraged. The horse hesitated when it felt the resistance, but with Cam's encouragement, he pulled against the rope until the boulder rolled over half a turn, enough for Cam to see where it had sat. He immediately looked to see evidence of a hole, but there was nothing but hard ground. "Damn," he muttered. "I reckon that rock's been there longer than I thought. It's a wonder Toby could move it." He patted the buckskin's broad chest and removed the rope. He looked at Mary apologetically. "That's where I woulda buried it. I reckon I'm gonna have to do a little more lookin'."

"You're not going to do much of anything if you catch pneumonia," Mary scolded. "Get out of those wet clothes."

"They are a little chilly," he admitted. "But they dried a little bit since I filled in that grave."

She walked over, picked up his blanket, and handed it to him. "Here, go over behind those bushes and get out of your clothes—*everything,*" she emphasized. "I'll put them by the fire to dry.

We can look for more gold dust tomorrow. I need you well, not lying around dying of pneumonia." He did as she instructed and returned to surrender his clothes. "I'll get you a bar of soap and a towel," she said. "You might as well take a bath while you're at it." When he started to protest, she said, "It's not gonna hurt you."

He had to confess that it had been a while since he had stripped down and had a good bath. He wondered if he was starting to smell a little rank. He hadn't noticed it himself. Maybe women have a sharper sense of smell. *What the hell?* he thought. *I'm already freezing. A little more won't kill me.* He took the soap and towel and walked around the bend in the stream where it split to flow on either side of a large rock, tall enough to hide him from the camp. *Made to order,* he thought as he placed his blanket and towel on top of the rock and went to work with the bar of lye soap.

It occurred to him that naked and unarmed, he was now more vulnerable than he had been when Rafer rode into their camp. The thought encouraged him to hurry. He would have, anyway, because of the cold water he bathed in. Finished, he shivered as he stepped up on a small rock to reach for the towel and almost fell backward when the rock moved under his foot. "Damn," he cursed, thinking that he could have been on his behind in the stream and his towel soaked with him. Hurrying to dry enough to put the blanket around him, he was suddenly struck by a thought from out of nowhere. He stepped back in the water and reached down to test the small rock he had stepped on before. It moved, but not easily. "What the hell?" he muttered, put his towel and blanket back on the large rock, and bent down to get a good grip on the smaller one. It resisted, but moved a little, so he put some muscle behind it and pulled it away to reveal a hollowed-out pocket in the large boulder. Inside the pocket lay Mary Bishop's fortune, in a double row of canvas sacks. Anxious to give Mary the news, he splashed ashore and started to yell for her to come, before realizing he was completely nude. He stormed back into the chilly water and snatched his towel from the rock, then ran around the bend barefooted to tell her of his find.

Chapter 5

Mary was in shock and close to fainting when informed that she was now a very rich woman. She stood on the bank of the stream, her eyes wide open and her mouth agape, as Cam waded back and forth from the rock to the bank, carrying two sacks at a time while clutching the towel around him and trying to walk carefully on the rocky streambed. Grace counted each pair of sacks as they came out of the water, while Emma seemed fascinated more by Cam's struggles with the towel. “Well, that’s the last of ’em,” he finally confirmed, after squatting down in the cold water again to feel up under the rock. “How many is it, Grace?”

“Twenty-two,” Grace replied confidently.

“Well, I ain’t much good with figurin’ numbers,” Cam said to Mary. “But last I heard, gold was tradin’ at around twenty, twenty-one dollars an ounce, so that’s gotta add up to a good sum of money.”

She stared at him as if he had spoken a foreign language for a long moment before she brought her emotions under control. “Oh my God, my God,” she finally uttered, and pinched herself to make sure she was not dreaming. In command of her senses again, she knelt on the ground and started scratching out numbers in the dirt, using a stick for a pencil. Her mind went blank for a moment, and she had to ask, “How many ounces in a pound?”

Cam hesitated. “Sixteen, I think.”

“Sixteen!” she exclaimed, remembering then. “Sixteen, that’s right.” She resumed her scratching in the dirt until she dropped the stick and sat back on her heel, hardly able to believe her figures. “I don’t know if that’s right, but even if it isn’t, there’s a lot more money there than I ever believed existed.”

“I’d say your husband took pretty good care of you,” Cam said, enjoying her good fortune almost as much as she. He could not resist the temptation to scan the trees on both sides of them to make sure no one else had observed the discovery. Then he got to his feet and wrapped his blanket around him, and tied two corners of it in a loose knot. With both hands free, he loaded his arms up with as many of the five-pound bags as he could manage and began moving the gold to the campsite. She came behind him with as many as she could carry, followed by Grace and Emma with one bag each.

When the gold sacks had all been moved to a spot where they could keep an eye on them, Mary helped Cam place some tree branches over the pile. There was no pretense that the gold was sufficiently hidden, but at least it didn't stand out so obviously. When that was done, Cam at last had the chance to put his clothes on. They were still a little damp, but he had a change of dry underwear and socks, so he was not uncomfortable. With the excitement of finding the large cache of gold, damp britches claimed very little of his concern.

Settled down enough by then to make fresh coffee, Mary sat by the fire and tried to think about what her new financial status would mean for her and her daughters. It was hard not to feel some guilt for the means by which she had gained her wealth, but the enormousness of the treasure pushed thoughts of grief to the back of her mind. Besides, enough time had passed since

Warren's death that she felt he would understand.

Watching her intently as he sipped the hot coffee, Cam could see the deep expression of concentration in her eyes, and knew she was far away from there in her mind. "You figured out what you're gonna do now?" he asked.

"Not exactly," she answered, "but I'm thinking about it."

"You still goin' back to Fort Collins?"

"I don't know." She hesitated, still thinking hard. "I guess I will. I don't know of any place else I wanna go. There isn't any other place that I know much about," she added. "I'm thinking that I might want to build a rooming house. I could run a rooming house, and it would be something that should support me for the rest of my life."

"That sounds like a fine idea," Cam said. He looked down at Emma, who had seated herself beside him. "Don't you think so, Skeeter? You could help, couldn't you?" He received a shy giggle in return. Back to her mother then, he remarked, "You might not have to worry about runnin' a roomin' house. A fine-lookin' woman like yourself, a rich widow, why, you'll have every man in town knockin' on your door."

"Is that a fact?" Mary said with a chuckle. "Well, a fat lot of good it will do them, because the last thing I'm looking for is a husband."

More serious concerns came to mind then, when he glanced at the stack of gold dust sacks under the branches. "If you're sure about Fort Collins, I reckon we'd best get started pretty soon before somebody else shows up here who mighta known they were pullin' pay dirt outta this claim."

"Maybe you're right," she agreed. Another thought then came to her. "You know, of course, that you'll have a share in the gold. Without you, we probably wouldn't be sitting here drinking coffee."

He smiled. "No, ma'am, I don't figure I've got a share in your husband's gold. That dust belongs to you. Besides, we already had a deal on what my pay was gonna be. I just wanna make sure you get where you're goin' safely."

She smiled back at him, the appreciation clearly showing in her eyes. "I should have known you'd say that. I'm going to pay you for what you've done, and it's going to be a lot more than forty dollars." She paused when he shook his head, objecting. "You only agreed to bring me here, so you can just put me on the stage in Custer City, and the girls and I can manage from there."

"No, ma'am," he insisted. "I can't rest my mind till I know you're back home in Fort Collins. If anybody got wind of a woman carryin' that much gold on the stage, there'd be a holdup for sure. I don't think you oughta take the stage. There're too many outlaws watching the road for stagecoaches coming out of the Black Hills as it is. I think you'd be better off goin' horseback. It'd take longer, but

I'd have a better chance of gettin' you home safe."

"You'd take us all the way back to Fort Collins?" she asked.

"I would," he replied.

"I knew you would," she said, nodding confidently. "At least, I hoped you would."

"I reckon I'd better rig up a packsaddle for that gold," he said, and got up to take a closer look at the gray gelding that Rafer had ridden. It was a sturdy-looking horse, dappled all over its body, with black stockings. The oddest thing about it was the dark half circle under one eye that gave the appearance that the horse was glaring at you. He took some extra time to consider the three-quarter, double-rigged saddle with silver inlaid on the oversized horn and along the back of the cantle. It was not a Mexican saddle, but it had been made to resemble one, and maybe to match Rafer's Mexican boots. There was a special-made rifle scabbard attached to it, and when Cam drew the weapon, he realized it was a Sharps, the model commonly used to hunt buffalo. The comment that Bob Allen had made came back to him, the man that killed Mary's husband had killed him with a Sharps rifle.

He had no desire to swap his saddle for Rafer's, even though it probably cost the previous owner a pretty penny, but he was reluctant to discard it. He could most likely sell it, maybe at Fort Laramie, or Cheyenne. He could use the money, for he honestly felt no claim on Mary's fortune. He decided to see if he could rig a pack for the gold dust, fashioning it around the saddle. It would have to be secure, for it would carry a little over a hundred pounds.

While he worked with the packs, Mary, with the girls' help, wrapped the smoked venison in preparation to take it with them. Everyone worked with a sense of urgency, for no particular reason other than a feeling that it was important not to remain at the camp with that quantity of gold out of the ground. Already there were too many people who knew that Raymond and Warren Bishop had been sitting on a rich claim. Cam wanted Mary and the girls to be ready to ride out of there early the next morning.

"I'm tellin' you, they're fixin' on movin' outta there," Everett Jones whispered to Cecil Painter.

"Most likely first thing in the mornin'," Cecil replied. Both men pulled back from the bank of berry bushes from which they had watched the activities going on in the camp after hearing gunshots. It was the same spot from which they had kept an eye on Raymond Bishop before. "That's one helluva big pile of gold dust they stacked up under that brush. I knew that son of a bitch was settin' on a pile of gold. How much you reckon it's worth?"

"I don't know," Everett answered, "but it's a

helluva lot, and we oughta have a share of it. Hell, them folks fixin' to tote it off ain't done a lick of work to earn it."

"Whaddaya think we oughta do about it?" Cecil asked. "We could walk up and ask 'em to give us a share, and say 'pretty please,' but I don't think that would do the trick. Me and you has been workin' this claim for a year, and gettin' nothin' for our efforts, while they've been gettin' rich. We're gonna have to decide how bad we want that gold, and if we're ready to do somethin' about it."

Everett knew full well what Cecil was thinking, and it was a tough decision to make. "I don't know," he said, after a few seconds' hesitation. "I don't like the idea of shootin' those two little girls—or their mama, either."

Cecil didn't like the idea any better than his partner, but they had been following gold strikes all over the Rockies with no luck other than grub money. Sitting downstream from the Bishop brothers had been as close as they had ever come to a big strike. And now it appeared that it had played out and they had come up empty again. Otherwise, why would those folks leave it? "Dammit!" he blurted. "We got as much right to that gold as they do—more right, in fact." He was reluctant to put it into words, but he finally spat it out. "If we do it, we got to kill 'em all. We can't leave nobody to tell about it."

"I ain't never shot nobody," Everett confessed.

"Well, I've got to know if you're gonna do your part or not. I ain't havin' this whole thing on my shoulders. If we're partners, then we gotta be partners all the way." When Everett still hesitated, Cecil went on. "I ain't never shot nobody, neither. But damn it, the years are runnin' out for me and you. And it looks like we've been handed the only chance we're ever gonna get to pay us for all the nameless gulches we've groveled in, sweatin' out the summers and freezin' our behinds off in the winter." Still Everett hesitated. "Damn it! It ain't right! Those people don't have no right to any of that gold, especially that hired gun she brought with her. It's the same as if they stole it from us. I don't know why we oughta feel bad about killin' them. Damn it, they killed ol' Raymond, didn't they?" He naturally assumed that the gunshots they had heard had come from the man riding with the woman and her children.

"I don't know," Everett muttered with a shake of his head. "I reckon you're right. I just don't like the idea of shootin' women and children."

"Ain't nobody gonna know about it but us," Cecil said. "We'd be doin' the world a favor by gettin' rid of that gunman, and that woman don't deserve to live after what she done to her own brother-in-law. It's a shame about the young'uns, but they'll be better off dead, instead of bein' left alone in these mountains." He waited for Everett's response. "There's enough gold there for me and you to live out the rest of our lives as rich men."

"Ah, damn," Everett finally muttered, "I'm already goin' to hell, anyway."

Cam awoke to a light drizzle sometime before daylight. It was not totally unexpected, for a heavy shroud of dark clouds had settled upon the mountaintops the night before. As a precaution, he had fashioned a makeshift cover over Mary and the girls, using most of the canvas that had been Raymond's tent. For his own protection, he had spread his rain slicker over him. It had given him adequate protection until rain began to form pockets in the folds so that they began to find avenues into the blanket underneath. When it became too bothersome, he got up and put the slicker on, figuring he might as well get the horses ready to travel. When he walked by the shelter he had built for the girls, they appeared to be snug and dry, so he decided to let them sleep. They were likely to have a long, hard day ahead of them, especially if the rain continued.

He saddled the horses, but waited to load the packhorses until Mary got up. She crawled out from under the canvas just as he finished pulling Toby's girth strap up tight. "Ugh," Mary muttered disdainfully, reached back under the canvas, pulled her hat out, and perched it upon her head. "Looks like you were right about the rain. I hope it isn't like this all day." She looked up at the dark clouds, then gazed around the campsite after a quick glance at the stack of gold dust under the branches. "It's a little early, isn't it?"

"Yes, ma'am," he answered. "I don't have a watch, so I don't know exactly what time it is, but it's a while before sunup. I figured we'd get an early start if you want to, and we'd eat some breakfast when we stop to rest the horses. You could make some coffee to get the sleep cobwebs outta your head, though, if you want to. I'll build you a fire in that little hollow under the side of the hill yonder." Having found ashes there, he figured the hollow had been used for fires in rainy weather before when they didn't want to use the stove inside the tent.

"That sounds like a good idea," she remarked. "I think I need it this morning. I can build the fire, though, and get the coffee on. You can go ahead and load the horses. I'll get the girls up whenever we're ready to go."

He hesitated briefly before Mary's fancy suitcases. "They're going," she informed him. "I'm not leaving them behind." She started to turn away, but paused. "And put some of that canvas over them."

"Yes, ma'am," he said, shaking his head as if bewildered.

By the time he had loaded the sacks of gold dust on the gray gelding, and covered them with pieces of the tent in an attempt to disguise them, a thin gleam of morning light crept under the heavy clouds that still enshrouded the mountaintops. Mary roused the girls out and Cam folded the remaining piece of canvas over the load on the sorrel packhorse, taking care that Mary's fancy luggage was protected from the rain. Seating Grace on the bay, and Emma up behind her, he looked around the camp to make sure he had left nothing behind. Mary, not waiting to be helped up, was in the saddle waiting for him to lead them back down the trail.

Checking behind him frequently to make sure his packs were riding all right, he guided Toby down the narrow trail that held closely to the stream. He would have preferred to ride around the camp where they had met Painter and Jones on the way up, but the only usable trail was the one they were on. When he entered the narrow gulch that ran close to their camp, he kept a sharp eye, but there was apparently no one about in the camp. He looked behind him at the girls on the bay and put a finger to his lips, signaling them to be quiet. They made no sound. Just below the camp, the gulch narrowed even more with high walls on each side. The rain let up a little at that point, now becoming more of a mistlike sprinkling, and then the silent morning was shattered by a burst of rifle fire.

Cam found himself in a hailstorm of bullets, the air filled with whining rifle slugs, ripping through the drizzle of rain to bury with a thud in the wall of the gulch. “Back up!” he yelled, and pulled Toby back to try to cover them. Mary responded at once, backing her horse to force the others to back as well. “Get down behind the horses!” he yelled again while trying to spot the location of the shooters. He knew for sure that it was the two miners who were out to murder them. And so far, he knew he and the girls were still alive because the two were frantically firing, cocking, and firing again, just as fast as they could instead of taking dead aim. He knew it was just a matter of time, however, because already there were a couple of holes in the yellow rain slicker he wore as the shots began to find their marks. In the next instant, he felt the impact of a slug on his leg. It was followed by a couple of shots he heard thudding against Toby’s side, and the horse faltered as it screamed with pain. It reared up on its hind legs and back on all fours again before stumbling toward the wall of the gulch. Realizing Toby was going down, Cam snatched his rifle from the scabbard and jumped from the saddle.

On the ground, he rolled over behind a fallen tree and searched the rim of the gulch above them. The firing stopped briefly. He figured they were reloading. “Mary! Are you all right?”

“Yes!” she answered. “We’re behind a rock!”

“Well, stay there. I think I see where they are. Just sit tight. They’ll be startin’ up again.”

Above them, at the edge of the gulch, Cecil and Everett fumbled frantically to reload, both men having emptied the magazines on their rifles. "I know we hit him a couple of times," Cecil exclaimed. "We had to, but I couldn't see what happened to him when he came off that horse. You reckon we killed him?"

"I don't know," Everett came back. "We throwed an awful lotta shots at him. We killed his horse. I know that." Neither man said anything about the woman and her daughters, and whether or not they were hit. Mary and the girls were spared in the ambush primarily because neither man wanted to carry the deed on his conscience, each hoping the other would shoot at the females.

"Well, we need to find out what's goin' on down there," Cecil said.

"Let's not get in too big a hurry. He might not be dead yet. He might be settin' down there waitin' for one of us to stick our head up." He was already sorry he and Cecil had decided to go through with the ambush. It had not been a simple squeeze-of-the-trigger-and-done that he had envisioned, and he feared that they had stirred a hornet's nest.

Below them, Everett's analogy was very close to being accurate, for Cam's anger was increasing with each plaintive whimper of pain from Toby, as the wounded horse leaned against the wall of the gulch. Finally, after waiting for several long minutes, with nothing from the ambush above them, Cam felt his patience run out. "You stay behind that rock," he ordered Mary, "and keep that pistol I gave you handy in case you need it." He rose slowly to his feet, watching the rim of the gulch intently.

"What are you going to do?" Mary asked, afraid when she saw him get up from behind the tree. "Where are you going?"

"They shot my horse," was all he offered as he pulled his rain slicker off, furious over the needless shooting of the only real friend he'd ever had. He ran through the stream to the other side of the gulch and began to climb up the twenty-foot side. Mary pleaded for him to come back, fearing he would be shot, but Cam's ire had been raised to a level that demanded severe retaliation.

Like an angry panther, Cam scaled the steep slope. Not sure what he would find when he reached the top, he dived over the edge, rolling over and over to come to a position on his belly with his rifle aimed at the two assailants some thirty yards away. Only then aware that the roles had been reversed and they were now under attack, both men threw a wild shot in Cam's direction, neither shot close. Taking deliberate care in his aim, Cam returned fire, his first shot catching Cecil in the shoulder and spinning him around to drop on the ground. Seeing his partner fall, Everett turned and ran. Cam got to his feet and started after him, but stopped after a few steps, took a solid stance, and aimed at the fleeing man. His shot, intentionally aimed low, hit Everett just below his hip, and caused him to collapse to the ground.

Still fuming over the loss of his horse, Cam strode toward Cecil, who was groaning in agony as he lay on the ground. Seeing Cam approaching, he tried to pull his rifle around but had to drop it when two quick shots from Cam's rifle hit terrifyingly close to his arm. "Don't kill me!" he pleaded pitifully as Cam walked up, picked up his rifle, and tossed it over the rim of the gulch.

"I ought to, you miserable son of a bitch," Cam growled. As angry as he still remained, he did not, however, have it in him to coldly execute the defenseless man. "You just sit there and don't move, or I'll blow your cowardly ass to hell," he threatened, then moved to deal with Everett, who was dragging himself along on the ground, still trying to escape. Cam walked up behind him and stopped his crawling with a foot in the middle of his back. He reached down and pulled the rifle out of his hand. Everett made no effort to resist.

"I'm bad hurt," Everett begged.

"You'll live," Cam said. "But you ain't got no right to. You two are the sorriest assassins I've ever seen. You shoulda stuck to pannin' for gold, instead of killin' for it."

"I didn't wanna do it," Everett whined between teeth clenched against the pain. "It was Cecil's idea."

"Is that a fact?" Cam replied in disgust. "Get on your feet."

"I can't," Everett complained. "I'm shot."

"You still got one good leg. Get up." He reached down and grabbed the collar of Everett's shirt and lifted him halfway off the ground until he could get his good leg under him. "Hold on to this tree." He left him standing there, supported by a young pine, while he went to get Cecil on his feet.

"I'm bleedin' like hell," Cecil complained when Cam told him to stand up.

"Ain't nothin' wrong with your legs. Stand up."

When Cecil got to his feet, Cam prodded him in the back with his rifle to get him moving to where Everett stood. "Now we're goin' back down by the stream to your camp," he told them. The slope by which they had come up was not as steep as the one where Cam had ascended, so he figured the two wounded men should be able to negotiate the descent. After yelling down to Mary that everything was okay and she should bring the horses along to the miners' camp, he gave the would-be assassins instructions. "You've got two good legs, so you can help your partner down the hill." Seeing their despairing expressions, he ejected all the cartridges from Everett's rifle and handed it to him. "Here, you can use this as a walking stick. Lean on him. Now get goin'." He prodded them with his rifle barrel and watched as the two hobbled down the hill; one limping cautiously on one leg, his arm across the shoulders of his partner, whose arm was dangling helplessly by his side. Both worried about what he intended to do with them.

When they got back down to their camp, Mary and the girls were waiting, staring wide-eyed at Cam marching his prisoners before him. He had only one word for her, a question. "Toby?"

Mary shook her head slowly.

A spark of anger flashed briefly in his eyes, and he turned to stare at the two remorseful bandits. "I've a good mind to shoot you down where you stand. The two of you together ain't worth half of that horse." Although the two men were afraid to make a sound, their eyes nevertheless screamed out their fear. Taking a coil of rope from the bay Grace and Emma rode, Cam tied his two prisoners to a tree. When Mary, who had been speechless to that point, asked why, he explained, "I've got things to do right now, and I don't wanna have to keep my eye on them." He went back upstream then to see about his horse.

It was only then that Mary noticed the hole in Cam's trousers, right about the thigh. Glancing down at his boots then, she saw the bloodstains on the arch and heel. "You've been shot!" she exclaimed.

"Yeah, but it don't seem too bad, just stiffenin' up a little. I'll take care of it when we get a chance to rest. Right now I've got to see about Toby. We can't waste any more time waitin' around here."

Toby was down. Cam counted three wounds in the unfortunate buckskin. Two of them might not have been fatal, but the other had evidently been a lung shot, and the horse was fading away fast. It was evidently in a lot of pain, so Cam knew what he had to do, and the thought of it almost made him cry. "I'm sorry, ol' partner," he said. "You're the best horse I'll ever have." He then took out his pistol and put Toby out of his misery. He couldn't help thinking that the buckskin was working to make his job easier right up to the end, because it had collapsed against the side of the gulch and the girth was not trapped under its weight. He pulled his saddle free with a minimum of trouble.

Back at the camp, he took one glance at his prisoners to make sure they were still secured to the tree before he walked over to a makeshift corral to look at the two horses inside. After examining both horses, he slipped his bridle on the dun and led it out. Informing Cecil and Everett, he said, "You killed my horse. This piece of dung ain't near the horse you shot, but it's the best you've got, so I'm takin' him." After he saddled the dun, he told Mary and the girls to get ready to ride. Turning back to the captives, he said, “I’m takin’ your other horse down the trail a ways, and then I’ll let him go. I’ll untie you so you don’t starve to death. Then I’m done with you. If I see you again, I’ll finish the job I started today.” He started to turn away but paused to say one more thing. “If you’ve got a lick of sense, you’ll move up to Raymond’s camp. If there’s any gold left on this mountain, that’s where it is.”

He climbed aboard the dun and led his little party of females down the narrow trail. They followed silently along behind him, still hardly able to believe the incident they had just been a party to. Mary was aware for the first time that her guide and protector had a temper if properly provoked. She couldn’t decide if that was a good thing or not, recalling the reckless determination he had displayed when he had charged up the side of the gulch after the men who had shot his horse. Luck had to be with him, for one of the men could easily have looked over the edge of the gulch and shot him. She knew one thing, however. When he was in a mood like this, it was best to keep your mouth shut and do what he told you to do.

He let Cecil and Everett’s other horse go after they had almost reached the foot of the mountain. There was a good chance that the horse would make its way back up to the camp. It didn’t make any difference to Cam if it did or not. He felt pretty sure that the two had no desire to come after him.

Chapter 6

The encounter with the would-be assassins caused a delay that Cam hadn't counted on, so he figured he'd better stop before long to allow the girls to have breakfast. He had planned to circle around Custer City, thinking it wise not to give anyone ideas about the heavy packs they carried, and then stop for breakfast somewhere beyond the town. When they arrived at the foot of the mountain, he wasn't given the opportunity to suggest a place to stop. Mary pushed her horse up beside his and informed him that she was ready to stop right where they were so the girls could have some breakfast and she could take a look at the wound in his leg. He couldn't help smiling, for she looked as though she was not going to argue the matter. "All right," he said. "I reckon you are the boss, but you just take care of breakfast. I'll take care of the doctorin' on my leg."

"I'm not sure you'll do a decent job of cleaning it up," she told him. "I want to see how bad that wound is. I notice you're limping a little bit."

"It ain't that bad," he insisted. "I can take care of it."

She had no doubt that his reluctance to have her look at it was simply because the wound was in his upper thigh, and he didn't want to take his pants off so she could see it. "You're just being silly," she said. "I was married for over eight years. I've seen a man with his pants down before." She had to smile then. "Besides, you're forgetting about when you were splashing about in that stream with nothing but a towel wrapped around you." Her smile took a wicked twist then. "That towel didn't hide as much as you thought." When he blushed visibly in response, she said, "We'll eat first. Then I'll look at that wound. I'm hiring you to take me to Fort Collins, so I want to make sure you're gonna be up to the task," she chided playfully. "It's the same as if one of the horses went lame."

After they had finished eating, she gestured toward the stream and ordered, "Here," and handed him the towel he had used before. "Sit down over there by the water and pull your pants down. You can cover yourself with this while I look at that leg."

Figuring it useless to argue further, he took the towel and proceeded to the stream bank. It would be his first opportunity to see how bad he was wounded, and he was a little concerned, because it was beginning to cause him some pain. When he had unbuckled his trousers and pushed them down to his knees, he draped the towel over his vital area and called out to her that he was ready. While she searched in her packs for some clean cloth and the bottle of medicinal whiskey she had carried all the way from Fort Collins, he wet his hand in the stream and tried to clean streaks of dried blood from his leg. It didn't appear that he had lost a great deal of blood, but there was enough that he could feel it in his boot. He was thinking that, had it been cooler weather, he would have been wearing his long underwear, and that would have helped soak up the blood before it got down in his boot.

"It looks a little puffy," she said upon her first examination of the small blue hole in his thigh. There was no exit wound, so she knew the bullet was still in there. When she felt around the wound, a slow trickle of blood appeared, so she took her hand away, afraid she might start a steady flow of blood again. "There's no telling how deep it is," she said. "It might help to pour some whiskey on it to clean it out."

Watching her studying the wound, he realized she had no idea what she should do. A bullet hole was a world's difference from the cuts and scratches she doctored on her husband and daughters. He reached down to his belt and pulled his skinning knife from its case. "Here, take this over to the fire and stick it in the coals till the blade starts to get red. We wanna get all the deer off it."

"What are you going to do?" she asked as she took the knife.

"I'm gonna see if I can get that bullet outta my leg," he answered.

"That doesn't seem like a good idea, to go digging around in there with that knife. You'll just make it a bigger wound."

"I can feel that bullet like it was a piece of rock in my leg, and I'd just as soon have it outta there, so go heat my knife please." She looked at him, then back at the knife, hesitating. "Please," he implored.

She shrugged and turned to do his bidding. "It's your leg," she said. After a few minutes, she returned. Holding the handle with just two fingers, she held it up before him and he took it, being careful not to touch the blade. He held it for a few minutes to let it cool down before he made his incision. Then he gently probed the wound, which resulted in a new flow of blood. "Ooh," she muttered, "I don't think I even want to watch this." She took a step backward, almost knocking her daughters over as they peered out from behind her. One glance and Grace turned away, just as her mother had. Emma, the precocious one, moved in closer to get a better view of the surgery.

"Back up a little bit, Skeeter. Your head's in the way. I can't see what I'm doin'." She gave him a step. "Here, you can hold this cloth." She took it eagerly, excited to be a part of the operation. Clenching his teeth, he made a thrust with the point of the blade, hoping to feel something metallic, but he met with nothing but bloody pulp. Emma's eyes got bigger and bigger and she moved in a little closer. He forced his knife in a little deeper, still with no resistance beyond that of the flesh and muscle. He wanted to yell out with the pain he felt, but he forced himself to remain silent in a show of bravery for the sake of impressing the little girl. Finally, when he felt he couldn't stand any further self-torture, he felt the tip of his knife strike the lead slug he searched for. Ignoring the pain at that point, so close to success, he worked the tip back and forth until the slug loosened slightly. Desperate, he dug into his leg with his fingers, into the hole that was larger by three times than the original, and pinched the bullet out. He released a great sigh of relief and held the bloody slug up triumphantly. Emma clapped delightedly. Mary said nothing, but stepped forward and poured whiskey in the wound. "Shit!" Cam blurted out before he could stop himself. It was the only sound he had made throughout the whole procedure. His face red again, he complained, "Tip me off next time you're fixin' to do that."

"I'm sorry," she said, unable to hide her smile. Both Grace and Emma giggled. "I'll wrap a bandage around your leg. You'll be lucky if it doesn't become infected. I hope you didn't do more damage than the bullet did in the first place."

"It'll heal up fine and proper," he assured her. "Won't it, Skeeter?" Emma nodded excitedly.

"You're the only one who would stand and help me," he told her.

As he had advised, they rode along the eastern edge of the valley, giving Custer City a wide berth. With plenty of venison as well as a supply of salt pork they already had before Cam killed the deer, there was nothing they needed in the town. Their first overnight camp was beside a creek near the south end of the valley. They were in good spirits, since the rest of that day had been without trouble. Even the rain had stopped before sundown, and for long periods of time he forgot that he was guarding a large quantity of gold. Every outlaw in the territory would be rawhiding his horse in an effort to find them if anyone found out about the fortune they were carrying. And Fort Collins in Colorado Territory was a long way away. He wasn't sure how far exactly, but he knew that Custer City was about two hundred and sixty miles from Cheyenne. And he would guess that Fort Collins was maybe another forty miles below Cheyenne. Ordinarily he would figure on about eight days without pushing Toby too hard. But Toby was gone, and he wasn't sure how the dun he was now riding would hold up. So far, the horse seemed stout enough. It didn't matter, anyway, for he found that Mary and the girls weren't up to riding forty miles or more a day when the trip of about eighty miles to Hat Creek took them two and a half days. So the total trip was most likely going to take them ten days, maybe more, for there was some rough going in parts of that country.

The first couple of days had been without a great deal of concern, for the most part because they had stayed clear of the stage road, choosing to parallel it. Running short of coffee and flour, they decided to stop at the Hat Creek Station to resupply. Mary wanted to take advantage of the opportunity to spend a night in the hotel there to get a good night's sleep for a change, as well as a hot bath for her and the girls. Her concern, however, was the gold, and how to protect it, especially since they didn't want anyone to know what they were carrying. Cam said he would sleep in the stable with their packs. The odds of getting held up in the station were not great, and as long as they didn't appear to be overcautious, probably their packs wouldn't attract attention. Mary decided to risk it. She had complete faith in Cam's honesty and his ability to protect her interest, although she felt a little guilty to take the comfort of a hotel room while he slept in the stable with the horses. He was not bothered by the accommodations, however, feeling perfectly comfortable with the prospect of a bed in the hay.

Traveling with a fortune in gold created unique problems, as they had already learned. Someone, preferably Cam, had to watch the packs at all times. So Mary found herself apologizing again when the subject of supper came about. The odds were slim that someone would bother their packs if they all went to supper together, but the possibility was always present. "When the girls and I finish eating, I can come out here and stand guard while you go to get your supper," Mary suggested, although she was not overly confident of her ability to protect the gold in the event of an attempted robbery.

Cam was equally leery, so he made a counter-suggestion. "Why don't you just have them make me up a plate and one of the girls can bring it out to me when you're done eatin'?"

"I'll bring it!" Emma immediately volunteered.

Cam smiled and said, "Maybe you and Grace could bring it." He glanced up at Mary. "Is that all right with you, ma'am?"

"When are you going to stop ma'aming me?" she responded. "You make me feel like I'm eighty years old. I'm not *that* much older than you. My name is Mary, and that's what I expect my friends to call me. And, yes, it's all right with me if the girls bring you your supper."

"Yes, ma'am, Mary," he replied, somewhat astonished that she had somehow had a fit of temper over something he must have said.

With the issue of supper finished, they pulled up to the hotel, where Mary and the girls dismounted. Cam untied Mary's two suitcases and set them down on the walkway. While they stood by the horses, he quickly carried the two bags inside and set them by the front desk. Outside again, he climbed aboard the dun and led the horses down the short street to the stables.

"Howdy," Bill Freed greeted the young man astride the dun and leading four horses, two of them loaded fairly heavily. "You lookin' to board them horses?"

"Yep," Cam replied. "I'd like to unload 'em and turn 'em out in the corral, but I'd like to put 'em inside for the night. I'll pay for a stall to keep my packs in, too, and I'll sleep in there with 'em. Is that all right with you?"

Freed shrugged. "Well, sure, that's all right with me, but there's a fine hotel up the street, unless you're worried about your belongin's. But I ain't never had no trouble with anythin' gettin' stole outta here, or the corral, either. I put 'em in the stalls at night, but I have left a couple of horses outside before, and there ain't nobody bothered 'em."

"We'll put my horses in the stalls tonight," Cam repeated. "And, like I said, I'll sleep here tonight."

"Suit yourself," Freed said. "I padlock both doors when I leave to go to the house tonight, about nine o'clock." He waited for a few moments and watched Cam as he led the horses down the center of the stable. "Want me to give you a hand pullin' off them saddles?"

"No, thanks just the same," Cam replied. "I 'preciate it, but I can take care of it." He continued on, past the tack room, toward the back stalls.

Freed watched him with a curious eye. *He sure is particular about his stuff,* he thought. The small hole in Cam's trousers would have been easy to miss, had it not been for the white bandage that showed through whenever the tall young man bent down to pick up a pack. It didn't take any imagination to identify the hole as one having come from a bullet. Wary, but unable to control his curiosity, he walked back to the rear stall where Cam had stacked the packs. "Looks like you got more saddles than you had when you led them horses in."

"I had 'em," Cam replied. "One of 'em was covered up—that one." He pointed to the saddle Rafer had used.

"That's a real fancy one. Musta cost a little money."

"Yeah, I reckon," Cam said. "But it ain't to my particular taste, too fancy to suit me."

"You ever think about sellin' it?"

"I don't know," Cam said, pausing as if considering the idea. "I might, if I was to get a fair price for it."

"I don't need a saddle myself," Freed said, "but if you're just lookin' to get rid of it, I'd give you twenty-five dollars for it."

Cam laughed. "I don't figure I'll give it away. I'll just keep it before I do that." He waited a few moments while Freed examined the hand-tooled saddle more closely. "Some fine handiwork on that saddle skirt, ain't it?" When Freed agreed that it was delicately done, Cam nodded slowly, as if making up his mind. "I'll tell you what, if you like that saddle, I'll let you have it for forty dollars, and that ain't even half what that saddle cost." When he saw Freed's eyes light up, he added, "Course, that's along with the bill for boardin' these horses overnight."

"Done!" Freed said, and extended his hand to seal the deal. Both men were pleased. Freed got the fancy saddle for a third of what he figured it was worth. Cam got rid of an extra saddle he didn't want. Now he could load their packs more efficiently with Rafer's saddle out of the way, and he had an extra forty dollars in his pocket.

It was still early in the evening when Grace and Emma came in the front door of the stable, looking for him. "Back here," he called out from his seat on a cushion of hay, his back against the wall of the stall. They hurried to him, Grace carrying a dinner pail filled with stew, and Emma holding a slab of corn bread wrapped in a checkered napkin. They sat down on either side of him while he ate.

He was only halfway finished when Mary appeared at the front entrance, carrying a cup of coffee. When she saw the three of them seated outside the stall in the back, she headed toward them, stepping carefully in an effort to avoid spilling the coffee.

"Ma'am," Bill Freed said when she passed by the open door of the tack room. Surprised, for he assumed she was looking for him, he stuck his head out the door to get another look. *Strange people,* he thought when it was obvious that she was looking for Cam and the two girls.

"Good evening," she tossed back at the stable owner, but kept walking. When she got to the back of the stable, she held out the coffee cup. "I know how you love your coffee," she said cheerfully. "I hope I didn't spill much of it. That street's pretty rough."

Cam smiled his appreciation. "I surely thank you for your trouble. You're right about that, I do truly love a cup of coffee." He took the cup, being careful not to spill any on Emma, who had snuggled up close to him.

Mary glanced down at her youngest, then back to Cam again. "I hope they're not too much of a bother to you."

He smiled. "No, ma'a—" he started, but caught himself. "No, they ain't a bother at all."

A wicked smile spread across Mary's face, and she was unable to resist telling him, "Well, you might be in more trouble than you realize. Emma told me she was going to marry you when she grew up."

"Mama!" Emma exclaimed, and jumped up, bumping Cam's coffee cup and causing him to splash some of it in his lap. "That was a secret. You weren't supposed to tell! I'm never telling you another secret." Thoroughly shamed, she went behind her mother to hide.

Cam grinned broadly. "Is that a fact?" he teased. "Well, that's all right with me, Skeeter. I'll wait for you." He looked up at Mary and winked. She answered with a smile. They were interrupted then by Bill Freed.

"If you folks don't' mind, I'm fixin' to lock up and go home a little early tonight. I hate to break up your little party, but I'm thinkin' right smart 'bout my own supper."

"Come on, girls," Mary said. "Let's let the man close up." Cam got to his feet to walk them to the front door. Mary paused briefly to say, "Thank you for guarding our future. I'm sorry you have to sleep in the stable."

"Honest, Mary, I don't mind one bit. You folks get a good night's sleep, and I'll see you in the mornin'."

Freed helped Cam move his horses inside before leaving him for the night. "If you have to go outside for any reason, you can get out by the hayloft. Just don't forget to leave that rope hangin' so you can get back in. I generally come in about five o'clock."

"Much obliged," Cam replied. "I doubt I'll wanna get out before you come back in the mornin'."

The night passed peacefully enough. Cam was aroused from sleep only when Freed unlocked the stable doors. He went to work right away, loading the horses and saddling the three to be ridden. When he was through, he shook hands with Bill Freed and led the horses down to tie them in front of the hotel dining room windows. When the dining room opened at six, he went in and seated himself facing the windows where he could keep an eye on the horses while he waited for Mary and the girls to appear. In a few minutes he saw the little Japanese woman, who always rendered Bob Allen tongue-tied, walk in from the kitchen. He remembered her name, Atsuko. She glanced his way as she carried a tray of clean coffee cups to place on a sideboard. Then remembering him, she looked again and gave him a smile.

She put the cups down, then came over to speak to him. "Good morning," she greeted him, a musical lilt in her voice. "You come in with Bob Allen before."

"That's right," he said, returning her smile. "Have you seen Bob lately?"

"Yesterday," she replied. "He drive stagecoach, heading north."

"Was Larry with him?"

"Yes, Larry with him." A mischievous smile appeared on her face. "Bob's getting up his nerve to talk to me. I think he wants me to leave this place and just cook for him." She giggled then. "Maybe I do it."

Cam laughed. "I think you're gonna have to tell him that. I don't think he'll ever get up the nerve to ask you."

"I think you right," she said, then changed the subject. "I see your lady friend and the two little girls last night. You wait for them?"

"Yep, I expect they'll show up sometime to get some breakfast."

"I'll get you some coffee," she said. "You want breakfast, or you gonna wait for them?"

"I'll wait on the breakfast," he answered. "Just bring me the coffee."

His wait was not as long as he had anticipated. In less than half an hour, Mary and the girls appeared in the doorway leading from the hotel's front parlor, she carrying the larger suitcase, Grace with the smaller one, and Emma carrying the carpetbag. They were apparently eager to get started. "Morning," Mary greeted him. She had a look of concern. "Are the horses still at the stable?"

"No, ma'am," he answered. "They're right

there." He pointed to the window. "Right where I can watch 'em."

She seemed relieved. "It looks like you loaded the packhorses differently."

"I sold that black saddle—made it a little better to rig up the packs." He unconsciously glanced around him before commenting, "I don't think you can tell what we're carryin' now. I doubt anybody'll take a second look at 'em."

They didn't linger long over breakfast, since both he and Mary were eager to escape the casual glances that might fall upon their little pack train. They decided to leave when two rough-looking men walked in to sit at a table next to them, obviously seeking to dispel the mental cobwebs left by a night of drinking. Both men looked Mary over thoroughly, averting their gazes only when Cam rose to his full height. Outside, after Mary insisted upon paying Atsuko for the meal, Cam tied the luggage onto the sorrel packhorse while Mary and the girls visited the outhouse.

They rode out of Hat Creek on the stage road, but with thoughts of the holdup they had experienced in the breaks about five miles south of there, Cam veered off the road after about a mile and took to the prairie. Behind them, the two men had watched them through the dining room window when they had taken the stage road toward Rawhide Buttes. "They had them horses loaded down, didn't they?" Leach commented.

An outlaw by profession, he was always interested in what other folks owned.

"Pilgrims, I reckon," Fuller replied. He got up from the table and walked over to stand by the window to get a better look. "You notice that one gray horse? Had a circle under his eye, like the horse Rafer Knoll rides. Rafer called him Evil Eye. That horse looked just like ol' Evil Eye."

"Damned if it didn't," Leach allowed, now that he thought about it. They were familiar with the notorious killer, having had the occasion to ride with him on one stagecoach holdup. They would have ridden with him again, but Rafer preferred to work alone. A meaner man neither Leach nor Fuller could recall, so it was doubtful anyone else could have come by that horse honestly. "I swear, that horse was a damn twin to Rafer's." The talk about horses prompted the pair to think about collecting theirs and starting out again on their way to the Black Hills. The pickings were easier there with miners staking out claims in all the gullies and gulches in the mountains. They had decided it unhealthy for them a few months before when they had to kill a man and his partner who didn't want to yield to their demand for their gold. A group of vigilantes out of Deadwood got on their trail, so they decided to leave the territory for a spell. Feeling that things had to have cooled down again by now, they were determined to give the territory another try.

Bill Freed was busy polishing the leather on his new saddle when Leach and Fuller walked into the stable. He looked up to greet them. "Well, I reckon you fellers have come to get your horses. I give 'em each a ration of oats, like you said. I guess you decided not to stay over another day or two."

"Nah," Leach said, "we drank up all the whiskey in town last night. We might as well get on our way." He and Freed laughed at the comment. When he turned toward Fuller, his partner was not laughing, staring instead at the saddle Freed was working on.

"Where'd you get that saddle?" Fuller asked.

"Why, I just bought it from a fellow who left his horses here last night," Freed replied. "Ain't it a fancy one? I didn't give him but forty dollars for it."

Fuller looked at Leach, who by then was staring at the saddle as well. There was no need to say anything. They were both thinking the same thought. Fuller turned back to the stable owner. "What's the feller's name who sold it to you?"

"I don't know," Freed replied, aware now that there was some reason for their interest. "I didn't ask him his name. Hell, I didn't ask you yours."

"How did he come by that saddle?" Leach asked. "Did he say?"

"No, he didn't," Freed said, concerned at this point by their attitude. "Now, listen, if you're thinkin' this saddle was stole, that ain't got nothin' to do with me. I paid him good money for this saddle, and gave him free board and oats to boot."

"This feller," Leach asked, "he the same feller with them packhorses, one of 'em gray?"

"One of his horses was gray," Freed said, still uncomfortable with the questions.

Ignoring Freed's apprehension, they settled their bill and saddled their horses, waiting until outside the stable before discussing the probabilities, based on the clues they had stumbled upon. "By God," Fuller stated, "that was Rafer's horse and Rafer's saddle. There ain't no doubt in my mind. The thing I'm wantin' to know is how that young feller with the woman and children came by 'em."

"That's a good question, all right," Leach said, "and I'm wonderin' somethin' else. What was in them packs they're haulin'? That packhorse was loaded down, and the other horses was carryin' a helluva lot of stuff to boot." He looked Fuller in the eye, raised an eyebrow, and said, "Rafer didn't do anythin' unless there was big money tied to it. I'd like to see what them folks are totin' on them horses."

"I would myself," Fuller agreed. "Deadwood can wait till we pay a visit to that little family party." The decision made, they climbed on their horses and rode past the hotel on the road to Rawhide Buttes.

Chapter 7

"We oughta caught up with them folks by now," Fuller complained as he reined his horse back. Leach followed suit and they let their tired horses walk for a while. "There ain't no way they coulda stayed ahead of us this long." The two outlaws had held their mounts to a steady lope all the way from Hat Creek, and they were going to have to let them rest before too much longer. Fuller looked down at the roadbed and remarked, "There's still pretty fresh tracks."

"Hell," Leach scoffed, "there's always fresh tracks on this road anymore." He leaned to the side and spat on the road for emphasis. "We just got bamboozled, that's all. They ain't stickin' to the road. We just missed the place they cut off. Fresh tracks, shit—you ain't no good at trackin', anyhow."

"I don't recollect that you're any better," Fuller retorted.

"I don't claim to be. That's the difference between me and you," Leach came back. "But if them folks didn't wanna travel on the stage road, that tells me they're totin' somethin' they're afraid of losin', scared of gettin' robbed, and I'm thinkin' I gotta have a look at it myself. So I say we turn around and go back till we find where they left the road. Maybe that'll give us an idea about where they're headin'."

"I expect they're headin' to Fort Laramie, or maybe on to Cheyenne," Fuller said. "Maybe we oughta push on ahead of 'em and wait for 'em."

"Maybe they ain't goin' to Fort Laramie or Cheyenne," Leach said, his tone heavy with sarcasm for his partner's reasoning. "And how in hell would we know where to wait for 'em if we don't know which way they're ridin'?"

"Oh," Fuller muttered. "I reckon we'd best go back and see if we can find where they cut off."

They were halfway back to Hat Creek when Fuller sang out, "I got 'em!" Leach pulled his horse over to that side of the road and both men dismounted to inspect the tracks.

"It'da been hard to miss these tracks if we'da had sense enough to look for 'em," Leach said with some disgust. Both men paused then to look in the direction the tracks led. "Looks like they're plannin' to stick close to them hills to the west of the road. They don't wanna meet up with nobody. I'm tellin' you, partner, I smell gold."

Fuller grinned, then had another thought. "What if these ain't their tracks? You reckon we oughta ride on back a little farther to make sure?"

"Hell," Leach insisted, "of course they're the right tracks. Look at 'em—four or five horses, fresh. Who else could it be?" He stepped back up in his saddle. "Let's get after 'em before they get any bigger head start, but we're gonna have to be more careful now, or we're liable to lose 'em."

More anxious than before to see what the two packhorses were carrying, they started out again at a brisk pace in spite of their obviously tiring horses. They had at least seven or eight miles to make up, but they were confident they could overtake their prey before very long, gambling on the idea that the woman and children would slow them down. Reluctantly they stopped to rest the horses when they came to a small stream running to join the Rawhide River. Fuller took a few moments to study the tracks left where the horses had crossed, double-checking to make sure they were the right ones, even though they were the only set of tracks heading that way. "Might as well make some coffee while we're settin' here twiddlin' our thumbs," he finally commented, and started looking around for enough twigs and limbs to start a fire.

"Their horses get tired, too," Leach said. "They're gonna have to stop, same as us."

Leach was correct. The people they trailed were stopped beside another stream some half a dozen miles ahead of them. While the horses rested, Cam helped Mary fashion a spit made from a green branch of a laurel bush to roast some of the smoked venison from their packs. For most of the morning, Cam had generally followed the course of the Rawhide River. His plan now, when the horses were rested enough to continue, was to veer away from the river and ride in a more westerly direction. He was still undecided if they should go into Fort Laramie or avoid it altogether. He leaned toward staying out of everybody's sight as much as possible.

"How much longer are we gonna ride before we stop for the night?" Grace asked her mother. "I'm tired of riding that horse. My bottom's sore."

Mary refrained from confessing that her bottom was getting a mite tender as well, not to mention a rather sensitive chaffing on the insides of her thighs. She had never spent much time astride a horse. When she set out from Fort Collins to find her husband, she anticipated traveling by stagecoach, not bouncing along on the back of a horse. She attempted to emulate Cam's easy motion on the dun gelding in front of her. He seemed to flow with the horse's motion almost as if he were a part of the animal, and never appeared to be surprised by any sudden changes in the horse's gait. She was unsuccessful in copying him, for it seemed that the black horse she rode was possessed of a gait in total contrast to her bottom's natural rhythm. So she could sympathize with Grace's complaint. Nothing, on the other hand, ever seemed to bother Emma. She bounced, just as her sister, but she never gave it a thought.

Mary wondered if she might even ride comfortably while standing on her head.

Looking up at the sun, Mary answered Grace's question. "We'll still ride for a few hours yet, honey. It's still early in the day. I'll get a blanket out of the packs and you can lay that across the saddle for a little padding. Maybe it won't be as bad with something soft to sit on." Her answer drew a frown of disappointment from her daughter's face.

Cam couldn't help overhearing the conversation between Grace and Mary, and he was sorry that he couldn't ease up on their day in the saddle. But to get to Fort Collins as quickly as they possibly could was foremost in his mind. He was riding shotgun on a gold shipment that would have called for an ironclad Concord coach and three messengers with rifles for protection. The responsibility weighed heavily on his mind. "Maybe it's just the horse you can't get used to," he told Grace. "If you wanna try it, I'll swap horses with you and Emma. I'll ride the bay, and you can try the dun."

They tried that for the rest of that day with little improvement in the state of Grace's bottom. In order to give the child some relief, Mary asked Cam to look for a campsite while there were still a couple of hours of sunlight left. Unaware of the two desperate men racing to catch up with them, Cam took the time to scout out a narrow creek that emerged from a notch in a line of hills almost barren of trees. Selecting a spot where the creek took a gentle turn around a group of cottonwoods, he called for Mary and the girls to follow him.

"Perfect," Mary said when she saw the spot he suggested. "The girls and I need to clean some of this dust off. We can go around those trees where the creek curves around."

"Ah, Mama," Emma immediately protested. "I don't feel dusty."

"We'll cook some supper first," Mary said, ignoring Emma's protest.

Cam gave the youngster a sympathetic grin and winked. "I'll get us a fire goin'," he volunteered. "Then I'll take care of the horses." He didn't express it, but he was in sympathy with Emma. He was sure he had never met a woman who was so strong on taking baths. *She's gonna rub the skin right off those young'uns,* he thought. The subject was forgotten for a time until they had eaten their supper, but while Cam prepared to have another cup of coffee, Mary made good on her threat. She got the towels and washcloths out of one of the packs and marched her daughters off around the bend. Cam gave Emma another wink when she looked back over her shoulder at him with a look of exasperation on her face. He filled his coffee cup, found a cottonwood to use as a backrest, and sat down, propping his rifle against the tree, where it would be handy.

She must have been afraid I was going to hear them, he thought, for he could hear no sounds of the girls or splashing in the water. *She's probably going to suggest that I go next,* he thought, and rubbed his chin. *I guess I could use a shave.* His rambling thoughts were suddenly brought back to the present when a couple of the horses whinnied. He was immediately alert, and reached for his rifle. There was no time to scramble behind the tree before he heard the voice.

"Ain't no need to grab a hold of that rifle," Leach said as he and Fuller walked out of the trees and into the clearing. "We was just makin' a neighborly visit—saw your fire as we was passin' by."

Cam looked quickly back and forth between the two men. He knew damn well that they hadn't just noticed his fire. He was certain the fire couldn't be seen outside the notch between the hills. They had to have been tracking them, and he berated himself for letting them walk right in on him before he was even suspicious of their presence. They were up to no good, that much he was sure of, for they had been careful to split up, with enough distance between them to make it difficult for him to defend against both of them. *I hope to hell Mary doesn't come walking in on this,* he thought. Playing along, he said, "Too bad you didn't drop in on us before we ate. And I just finished the last of the coffee."

"What's in them packs?" Leach asked, already through with beating around the bush.

"Nothin' but household goods," Cam replied.

"Why do I get the feelin' you're lyin' to me? Where's your wife and kids?" Leach asked, assuming it was a family they had been trailing.

"Well, right now she's standin' behind that biggest cottonwood at the bend of the creek, with a Winchester 73 aimed right at your back. She's a fair shot with that rifle—waitin' for you fellers to make your move, I reckon. We figured if you were plannin' on tryin' somethin', I'm quick enough to get one of you for sure and she'd take care of the other'n." He raised his voice then and called out, "You take the one wearin' the vest, honey. I'll take the other one." He had no idea where Mary was, and he knew for certain that she didn't have a rifle with her. If these two called his bluff, he could probably take one of them down, but the other one was bound to get at least one bullet into him before he could cock his rifle again. Knowing it was all or nothing, he cocked his rifle then, as if preparing to shoot.

"Whoa!" Leach yelled. "Hold on there, mister! You got the wrong idea. We didn't mean you no harm. No, sir, we'll just be on our way." Both men began backing away immediately, looking side to side cautiously. "Ain't no sense in anybody gettin' shot over a little misunderstandin'."

Cam got to his feet, his rifle before him ready to fire, and followed them as they retreated to their horses, tied in the trees. "Keep your rifle on 'em, Mary," he called out while Leach and Fuller got on their horses. He continued to walk behind them until they cleared the notch and rode out on the prairie.

"I don't have a rifle," Mary called out from behind him, frightened by what she and the girls had almost walked into.

"I know it," Cam replied, "but you did your part anyway. You and the girls hurry up and get packin'. We've got to get outta here before those two have time to figure out that I was bluffin'." He went at once to the saddles and packs to ready them for a quick departure.

"We were scared to death," Mary blurted breathlessly. "We hid under the creek bank. I wasn't much help, was I?"

"You did what I hoped you would do. Now let's get the hell outta here. I've got to get you someplace safer than this."

Everyone hurried to get ready to ride with no time to talk about being afraid. There were no complaints about having to break camp except one negative comment from Grace as Cam lifted her up on the saddle. "Oooh, here we go on my sore bottom again," she moaned.

With no time for patience, Mary said, "It's better than a robber's bullet in your bottom. Don't complain about it again." She didn't wait for Cam to help her up in the saddle.

When all were mounted and ready to go, Cam decided to follow the creek all the way through the notch and go out the other side of the hills. Once they were free of the hills, he turned south again, knowing he didn't have much time to find a campsite before the light faded away completely. There was another line of hills about a mile off to the right that looked to be larger than the ones they were leaving, so he veered farther west again.

By the time they reached the rugged breaks, it was already growing dark, so there was little time to make camp. There was no water, so they would have to be content to make a dry camp, making use of the water in their canteens. They were fortunate in that the horses had been watered just before they had evacuated their first campsite. Cam figured they would be all right until morning. He planned to leave early and they would water the horses again as soon as they struck a stream or creek. His objective at the moment was to find a place that might not be so easily seen and could be well defended. He selected a rugged ravine that led up the tallest of the hills. It was deep enough to hide their horses and their fire, and afforded him a good lookout post at the top of the hill. He was satisfied that anyone approaching the camp would have to come up the ravine, just as he had.

Cam rigged a rope between two scrubby pines across the floor of the ravine, and tied the horses to it for the night. He didn't want to take any chances that they might wander, even if he had hobbled them. There was no need to prepare food for the four of them. They had eaten just before the unexpected visit from the two outlaws, but Mary wanted to make coffee, so she got out her pot and coffee mill, filling the pot with water from the extra canteen. "You ever shoot a rifle?" Cam asked when he came back from tying the horses.

"Once," Mary replied. "I shot at a rabbit."

"Did you hit it?"

"No."

Cam nodded thoughtfully before asking, "Was it a rifle like this?" He held up the Winchester he carried.

"No," she said. "It was a smaller rifle, a .22 I think, and it was a single shot."

"I think it'd be a good idea if you learned to shoot a .44 Winchester. I've got a good one on the packhorse. That feller back at the Destiny camp left it for us, along with his horse and saddle." He thought it best not to mention the Sharps buffalo rifle Rafer had also carried, since it was the weapon used to kill her late husband. "I'm gonna climb up to the top of this ravine and take a little look around before it comes up a hard dark. Then I'll get out your rifle and show you how to shoot it."

"Good," she responded. "I was going to ask you if it wasn't about time you taught me to shoot a gun." It was her opinion that she had already waited far past the time when she should have developed that skill. Since venturing from Fort Collins, she had known nothing but attacks from every quarter, and she was tired of being dependent upon Cam for all of her and her daughters' protection.

As soon as they were out of sight of the camp by the creek, the two outlaws had pulled up to decide what to do since their plan had been foiled. "That son of a bitch was bluffin'," Leach said. "I know he was. There weren't nobody behind us in those trees. I know damn well they didn't hear us until I said somethin'. Where the hell was them two kids?"

"Hidin' somewhere, if he did know we were comin'. You might be right, though," Fuller said, "but I wasn't ready to call his bluff. He might notta been lyin'. He sure didn't look like he was worried about us."

"Well, his bluff mighta bought him a little more time, but that's all it bought him," Leach declared. "I know damn well they're carryin' gold in them packs, and I mean to have it. Hell, if they didn't have somethin' valuable, that woman and kids would most likely be ridin' on the stagecoach."

"We'll get 'em," Fuller declared. "Only next

time we'd best come in shootin'. It'll be a helluva lot easier searchin' those packs when ever'body's dead."

"You're sure right about that," Leach said, then paused a moment. "I don't recall as how I've ever shot any young'uns before."

"Don't make no difference to me," Fuller was quick to assure him. "They's just smaller targets is all. Now, the woman, we just might wanna save her till last."

"Might at that," Leach replied with a grin.

"What about ol' Rafer, though?" Fuller wondered. "You s'pose that jasper was the one that killed Rafer? That would take a real stud horse to get the best of Rafer. We might wanna be extra careful."

"Hell, he didn't look that mean to me," Leach said. "He probably bought Rafer's horse and saddle from the man who did the work, and that man most likely shot Rafer in the back."

"Well, whaddaya think we oughta do right now—crawl up the hill on the side of that notch and see if we can get a shot at 'em?"

"Might as well try it," Leach said, "maybe split up. You go up one hill, and I'll go up the one on the other side. One of us oughta get a clear shot. We're gonna have to get movin', though. It's gonna be dark pretty damn quick."

Agreed on their plan, they wheeled their horses and headed back toward the notch in the hills, unaware that the people they were planning to attack had already left their camp and ridden out the other end of the notch. They were gone by the time the two outlaws got in position to fire down into the camp.

The girls complained when Mary roused them out of their blankets the next morning. It was still an hour or so before sunrise and it looked to be in the middle of the night down in the ravine where they were camped. Cam had suggested that they should leave earlier than usual. His reason was unnecessary to explain to Mary, so she was alert as soon as he had gently touched her on the shoulder, on her feet, and readying herself to ride. They intended to get in the saddle immediately, not planning to stop for breakfast until watering and resting the horses. Mary got the girls ready while Cam saddled the horses. Remembering what he had suggested to Grace, he threw his saddle on the bay and let her and Emma try the dun he had been riding. When all were ready, he led them out of the ravine and started out along the base of the hills until reaching the southernmost end. Then he changed their course to a more southwest direction toward a range of mountains in the distance, barely visible in the darkness of the early morning light.

It was well over an hour before the sun made an appearance on the eastern horizon, and there had still been no sign of water. Finally, after a few miles more, the course of a small creek was spotted, outlined by the sparse bushes and infrequent trees along its banks. Horses and children were more than ready to stop and rest, and grown-ups were suffering for a cup of coffee. They found a place where a group of pines had formed a half circle around a little patch of grass, so they unloaded the horses there. While Mary and the girls went about building a fire and preparing breakfast, Cam walked seventy-five yards to a low mesa where he could take a long look back over the way they had come. There was no evidence of the two men who had been following them, but he lingered a while longer, searching the horizon, half expecting to see two tiny specks pop up at any moment. Satisfied that they were in no danger for the time it might take to rest the horses, he returned to the creek. He would check on their back trail again after he'd had some coffee. Although there was no sign of the outlaws now, he was convinced that they had not seen the last of them. He figured that he and the girls had gotten a head start, but he was not ready to believe that they had lost the two men. He knew for certain that he could follow the trail they had left, and if he could, so could they. There was nothing they could do but keep running, so that was what he planned.

Mary decided to make some pan bread, even

though she didn't have enough time to let it rise properly. It mattered little, however, for she was cooking for a hungry crowd, and the bread was received with gracious approval. It was a welcome addition to the last of the smoked venison. There was no time to be spared for Cam to go hunting for fresh meat, so she would go back into the salt pork they had packed after this. "Maybe I'll have time to soak some of the dried beans when we stop for supper," she said.

When they were ready to start out again, Cam made one more trip to the mesa and stood for a few minutes, studying the distant horizon. It appeared they were still clear of their pursuers, so he turned to return to the creek, only to stop suddenly when a tiny dot caught his eye. At first, he thought it was a spot of sagebrush, almost too tiny to have noticed before. But then the spot separated into two specks, and he knew he had spotted that which he had hoped not to. He watched for a minute more, to confirm that the specks were moving. There was no doubt. It was them. He estimated them to be at least an hour behind him, maybe more. It was difficult to guess with nothing but prairie between them. At any rate, there was no time to lose, so he ran back to the creek to tell Mary the news and get everyone mounted and ready to go.

As he led his little party away from the creek, he mulled over the decisions posed before him.

The path they were on had been toward a range of mountains to the southwest. Knowing that sooner or later he was going to have to turn in a more southerly direction if they were ever going to get back on a path that would take them to Cheyenne, he had planned to turn south before reaching the mountains. Now he wondered if they should continue into those mountains in hopes of losing the outlaws, which would result in taking that much more time to get to someplace to put Mary's gold safely away. "Damn," he swore, not sure, but changed his direction slightly in a more southern swing anyway.

With only a general knowledge of the territory he was riding in, he was somewhat surprised when they approached a river after riding about ten more miles. It was a wide river and didn't appear to be very deep at the point they struck it. It then occurred to him that it had to be the North Platte, and from the course they had followed, he figured they were somewhere to the west of Fort Laramie. With this much he felt fairly certain of, he figured it was time to talk it over with Mary, so he reined back until she caught up with him. He told her what he figured to be their options, but the decision was very much hers to make. "We can follow this river back east to Fort Laramie if you want to. Oughta be able to find someplace there to keep your gold safe, but nothin' would keep these buzzards followin' us from waitin' around there for us to start out again."

"We could tell the soldiers that these men have been following us, and they could arrest them," Mary suggested.

"Maybe," Cam replied. "I ain't sure the army might not say they ain't got no reason to arrest 'em, since they ain't really done nothin' but visit our camp."

"Yes, but what about the fact that they're trailing us?"

"I don't know if they can arrest 'em for ridin' the same trail we're ridin'," he answered. "And I don't know what anybody can do about them layin' around watchin' us."

"Well, what are our other options?" Mary asked, somewhat exasperated.

"For one thing, I think it's worth a try to see if we can't lose 'em here in the river. We need to try that no matter which direction we head in. The water close to the bank doesn't look too deep. I think we oughta go in the water and stay in it for a mile or two before we come out. And if I had to guess what those two behind us will think, I'd say they'd figure we headed back toward Fort Laramie, so if we want a better chance of losing 'em, we oughta head the other way."

She thought about it for a few moments before deciding. "Let's go with your instincts, and ride in the opposite direction from Fort Laramie. I don't want to sit around that fort like a bird with two tomcats waiting for me to come out."

"Yes, ma'am," he said. He then told Grace and Emma what they were going to do and the importance of staying behind him in the water. When they both assured him that they understood, into the water they went, staying as far from the bank as possible without forcing the horses to swim. He silently hoped he had made a fair estimate of the distance between them and the outlaws, and that there was ample time for the bottom to settle again so as not to leave any clues in the water.

After what he figured to be about a mile, he signaled them to stop while he crossed over to the other side. "Come on," he called back over his shoulder, "ride right where I did. It ain't too deep right here and I don't wanna see if those horses can swim with those packs." Once the horses were safely across, he kept them in the shallow water close to the opposite bank. Then he began looking for a place to leave the river. After another hundred yards paralleling the bank, they came to a place where it sloped down from a grassy knoll. "This looks about as good as we're likely to find," he told them, so he pointed the bay gelding at the spot and climbed out of the water. With the peaks of the Laramie Mountains on the right, they started out again, holding close to foothills dotted with pine and cedar and odd outcroppings of rock. They rode for over an hour before coming upon a small stream, where they stopped to eat and rest the horses.

After their belated midday meal, Mary walked over and sat down beside Cam while the girls played by the water. "Do you think we've lost them?" she asked.

The serious expression on her face told him of her concern. He felt that she deserved his unpolished opinion of their circumstances. "I don't know," he answered honestly. "But I reckon we'll find out soon enough. It looked to me like they were gainin' ground on us. Maybe we'll lose 'em here at the river. I sure hope so, but if we don't, then I reckon we're gonna have to stand and fight before it's over with. And I don't know how desperate these men are, whether they're just set on robbin' us, or if they mean to leave no witnesses. This is sure as hell not my line of work. I know horses and cattle, and that's about it, but I'll do my best to try to protect you and the girls. That's all I can promise you."

She nodded slowly, thinking how grateful she was that he had shown up in her life. She hoped with all her heart that they could somehow avoid having to take a defensive stand somewhere out there in the rugged hills where there would be no one to know if she and her two daughters were brutally murdered. There would not even be anyone to care enough to look for them. She then turned her thoughts to Cam again. "I know you will protect us, Cam, and I guess I haven't told you enough how much I appreciate it. You could have left us at any time, even taken the gold for yourself, and I couldn't stop you. So thank you for your loyalty. I certainly plan to repay you if we find our way safely back to Fort Collins."

"Well, you're welcome, I guess," he replied, somewhat surprised that she had harbored thoughts that he could have run off with her gold and left them stranded. "The only pay I'm lookin' for is that forty dollars we agreed on, and the only way I figure to collect on that is if I get you and your gold to Fort Collins."

My God, she thought, *is there that much honesty in any man?* She couldn't help wondering if his demands might change when they were all safely in Colorado. As soon as she thought it, she wanted to bite her tongue for thinking it.

They pushed on, extending their time in the saddle until Cam thought the horses had traveled enough for the day. The time coincided with their arrival at the North Laramie River. Thinking the spot too much in the open for his liking, for there were no trees along the stretch of river they had reached, he looked toward the hills to the west. "We'll push 'em a little bit farther," he said, "follow the river back up there where it comes outta that pass. We'll be better off makin' camp there, where there are some trees and rocks to hide us."

• • •

"Hell, they musta gone the other way," Leach called out to his partner, who was searching along the other side of the North Platte. "We've gone at least a mile, maybe more. They woulda come outta the water by now."

"I reckon you're right," Fuller called back. "I ain't seen the first track. Maybe they ain't thinkin' about headin' to Fort Laramie. You reckon they're goin' to old Fort Fetterman? What the hell would they wanna go there for?"

Leach wheeled his horse and started back the way he had just ridden. "No, they ain't goin' to Fort Fetterman," he said. "They're just tryin' to lose us."

"They must know we're followin' 'em."

"I expect they must," Leach replied. "That feller's slick enough to know we ain't likely to give up on that gold that easy." He proceeded up the river, passing the point on the north bank where Cam and the girls had entered the water, his eyes never leaving the edge of the water. They had ridden almost as far as they had searched in the other direction when Fuller called out.

"Here they are," he shouted. "I almost rode past 'em. They came out on this bank of grass, right up through these rocks."

Leach quickly crossed over to the south side of the river to see for himself. "Yep," he gloated, "that ol' boy's pretty slick, all right, but he's gotta be slicker'n that to throw us off for very long.

There better be a good load of dust in them packs, 'cause he's puttin' us to a helluva lot of trouble."

Fuller, who fancied himself an expert tracker, dismounted and studied the tracks carefully. "We ain't that far behind 'em, Leach. Look at where they stomped down the grass here. Half of it ain't sprung back up yet."

"Our horses ain't in that bad a shape," Leach decided. "We'd be smart to push 'em on past dark, catch up with them folks tonight."

"Sounds like a good idea to me," Fuller replied. "They've been ridin' mostly in a straight line for the last few miles." He glanced up at a clear sky overhead. "And if there's a moon tonight, shouldn't be no trouble a'tall to follow 'em."

They hesitated for only a few seconds more to follow the direction of the tracks with their eyes before starting out after them again. Both men sensed the end of the hunt and the excitement of the kill, for they felt their prey was at hand.

Chapter 8

The spot they picked for their camp seemed to offer some protection from two sides, with a gulch formed by a huge column of rocks on each side of the river. Not a wide river in the open prairie, the North Laramie was compressed even more as it was squeezed through the narrow pass. There was grass for the horses just beyond the pass and a good sheltered spot to build a fire on the narrow riverbank. It was doubtful anyone could see the camp from the lower prairie below them. The travelers were tired, so little time was wasted as Cam took care of the horses and Mary busied herself with preparing something for their supper. Since there was not a great deal of room between the river and the rocks on the side, they laid their bedrolls in a line, with Cam's closest to the path they had ridden into the gulch. "Looks like a snug little camp, doesn't it?" Cam commented when they finished just as Mary announced that supper was ready.

"I'll be so glad when I can fix a meal like a normal human being," she remarked as she spooned the boiled beans onto each plate. "I'm really beginning to wonder if that day will ever come."

"I hope you invite me to supper when it does come," Cam remarked. The meal he was eating was more like what he was accustomed to, beans and bacon, unless he had had an opportunity to kill some fresh game. He nudged Emma, who was sitting close to him as usual. "These beans are pretty good, though. Ain't they, Skeeter?"

She wrinkled her nose to make a face. "I don't like beans," she complained. "When we get back home, I'm never gonna eat another bean."

"I like beans," Grace announced, and stuck another spoonful in her mouth.

"Grace knows," Cam told Emma. "Beans make you strong."

"I still don't like beans," Emma said as she chewed on a piece of bacon.

Cam chuckled at the precocious child's protest. Mary sat quietly eating, listening to the wordplay between Cam and her daughters. She knew what he was doing. The girls were showing the strain of their flight, and he was attempting to take their minds off the hardships of the last few days. She appreciated his efforts, but she was not convinced they would do much good. They still had so far to go, and there was the constant worry about the two outlaws who might or might not be right behind them. She shook her head to rid her mind of the negative thoughts and told herself she would sleep close with her children tonight and trust the Lord would see them through to another dawn—and hope Cam knew what he was doing. Later, when the girls had crawled under a single blanket to sleep, Cam built up the fire while Mary washed the dishes in the river.

"You remember how to use that rifle?" he asked when she came up from the river. She nodded. "Good. I hope you don't have to, but it can't hurt to know how just in case."

Two riders approached the North Laramie River under a bright three-quarter moon. The tracks of five horses were easily seen on the bank. "What did I tell you, Leach? They're still ridin' in a straight line, and look at them tracks. Might as well be in the middle of the day." He nudged his horse and entered the water; however, he reined back on the horse upon reaching the other side. "Uh-oh, lookee here. There's tracks on this side, but they turned and followed the river up yonder way." He pointed toward the narrow gulch through a hill covered with scrub pines and a lot of rocky outcroppings.

"Looks like they were fixin' to make camp," Leach said. "It'd be about the right time when they got here, and they'd likely camp by the river." He looked upstream and down. "If they know we're trailin' 'em, they mighta tried to throw us off. They coulda started out that way, and then gone in the water and turned around." He stared downstream again. "They wouldn't likely camp out in the open. They'd be lookin' for someplace they could hide. I'd bet they rode up toward those hills there." He pointed upstream.

"Yeah," Fuller replied, a wicked grin on his face. "I expect you might be right. We mighta run 'em to ground. Let's take a look in them hills."

They followed the obvious tracks along the river, watching carefully to make sure the tracks didn't lead back into the water, as Leach had speculated. When within fifty yards of the rocks that stood like columns on each side of the river, they dismounted. Leaving their horses tied to some bushes near the water's edge, they proceeded on foot, carefully. "They picked a good place to camp, if they're in that gulch," Fuller whispered. "We can't hardly walk in there without them seein' us."

"Yeah," Leach answered, also in a whisper, "if they're in there. They mighta just rode right on through, followin' the river."

"They're in there," Fuller remarked confidently, and pointed toward the darkened shadows in the gulf where a few sparks from a campfire drifted up to become invisible again in the bright moonlight above the gulch.

Since walking straight in along the narrow confines of the gulch was a bit too risky, even if chances were good that the camp was asleep at this late hour, they paused to study the sides. Two small hills with rocky outcroppings protected the camp from sight, but there was no reason why they couldn't climb up and see if the camp was visible from the top. The way the gulch was formed, it gave the impression that it had been one big hill in the beginning. The river might have carved a notch right through the middle, leaving cliffs next to the water, but gentle slopes on either end. That appeared to be the easiest option, so they went back for their horses. Leach rode up one side and Fuller the other. Their thinking was that one of them had to have a shot.

Leach rode partway up the relatively gentle

slope of the hill on the east side of the river before dismounting and going the rest of the way on foot. From the top, it was a more difficult task to make his way back down through a maze of boulders facing the river in an effort to find a place near the edge. Working his way farther down the face of the clifflike side of the gulch, being careful not to dislodge any smaller rocks, he finally reached a point where he could see the camp below him. He looked toward the other side of the gulch and saw that Fuller had also reached a vantage point. As he returned his gaze to the sleeping camp, a slow smile crept across his face. Owing to the tight confines of the gulch, his victims had been forced to make their beds along the narrow river-bank. *All lined up in a row,* he thought. It was almost too pretty a picture to disturb, he was thinking, and he took another moment to antici-pate the pleasure it was about to bring. But his eagerness to open the packs lying beyond the bodies quickly overcame his desire to savor the moment. On the opposite side, Fuller, evidently even more eager to begin the massacre, opened fire.

Before splitting up, the two assassins had agreed on the order of execution. The primary target was, of course, the man, quickly followed by the woman. The two little girls were not as important, and could come last. "That'll add a little sport to it," Fuller had remarked. "If them two young'uns get to runnin' around half crazy like chickens, it'll give you some target practice." As he and Leach discovered, they had given them better targets than they expected. The girls were bundled up in one blanket, with the daddy and the mama close on each side, providing the assassins with easy targets, all within a small space.

As soon as Fuller opened fire, the narrow gulch was ablaze with rifle fire coming down from above, the sleeping targets soon riddled with bullet holes, and no chance to run for cover. "Whoo, mercy!" Fuller cried out in the excitement of the massacre. The victims had had no opportunity to move a muscle before all hell rained down upon them, much less return fire. Such was the volume of rifle fire between the rock walls that the silence that suddenly followed was nearly as devastating as the uproar that preceded it until broken by Fuller's shout. "I'm goin' down! They're done for!"

Every bit as anxious as Fuller to rip open the packs that had tantalized them for days, Leach scrambled down the rocky slope, sliding over the loose gravel, half the time on the seat of his pants, while grappling with his rifle to keep from losing it. It soon turned into a competition between the two of them to see who could get to the packs first. It was almost a tie, with both partners reaching the river bank at virtually the same time. The edge went to Leach because

Fuller had to cross over to his side of the river.

With no interest in the dead at that moment, Leach hurried straight toward the packs stacked one upon the other against the wall of the gulch. Dripping wet from the chest down, Fuller ran to catch up, almost colliding with him when Leach suddenly stopped dead in his tracks and dropped to one knee. "What—" was as far as he got before the report of the Winchester and Fuller doubled over and dropped, shot in the stomach. Leach got only a glimpse of the rifle lying across the top of the packs and protruding between two fancy suitcases before the next shot ripped into his chest, knocking him over backward. Stunned, but still able to get on his feet, he opened fire on the packs, cranking the lever on his rifle as fast as he could, while backing slowly away.

Cam levered another cartridge into the chamber of the Winchester, but Leach had backed far enough to hinder his line of sight. He pushed the packs away to give him enough room to get out of the hole he had carved out of the gravel between two large rocks, and stepped out in the open to be met with a rifle slug low in the shoulder. Unwilling to go down, he returned the fire as rapidly as he could manage, but his accuracy was impaired by the painful wound, and he was not able to prevent Leach from escaping.

Cursing himself for the carelessness that caused him to get shot, he ignored the pain and the loss of blood to warily approach the body left writhing in agony on the ground. Fuller was gut-shot and had little chance of surviving. The burning pain in his innards was scalding his insides to the point of desperation. When he opened his tightly closed eyes to see Cam standing over him, he cursed. "Damn you! Finish it, damn it. Don't leave me gut-shot." Cam cocked his rifle and held it over the suffering man. Fuller looked up at him, his eyes pleading. He spoke once more before Cam sent him to hell. "There was gold in them packs. I gotta know."

"Yes, there was," Cam answered, "a lot of it."

"I knew it," he gasped, seeming to relax just as the Winchester spoke.

Cam continued to stare down at him for a moment longer, before taking a few steps back to drop to one knee. He looked toward the mouth of the gulch where Leach had fled, but there was no sign of the would-be assassin. Feeling that the threat was over, Cam called out to Mary, "You can come out now. It's over. Might be a good idea to keep the girls there for a few minutes till I do somethin' with this body." She got to her feet then and left the girls where Cam had told the three of them to stay, in the grass of the bank, surrounded by the horses. He had stressed that she was not to come out until he told her it was all right. She carried the rifle he had shown her how to use, and as he had instructed, she had not fired it. He had insisted that she was to shoot it only in the event the two men got by him and came for her. There were not many places she could have hidden, but he had been convinced that the killers would not likely shoot at the horses. They were worth money.

"I'm gonna have to buy some new blankets," Mary said when she walked up to him. She then stopped abruptly when she saw that his shirt was soaked in blood. "Cam!" she blurted. "You're wounded!" She hurried to him then. "Oh my God! How bad is it?"

"Well, I ain't sure. I mean, I guess I'll live. It smarts a good bit, and I don't feel like I could run up that cliff right now." He remained on one knee while she tried to see how bad the damage was.

"I don't know how you can stay upright," she said, worrying over the wound. "You've lost so much blood, you need to be lying down. Once again, you've been wounded saving me and my daughters," she said, thinking it her duty to express her thanks. "I can't say how grateful I feel that you have taken it upon yourself to protect us."

"You're welcome," he said, "but right now we need to get ourselves outta this open space. I don't know for certain how bad that other fellow is wounded. I hit him in the chest, and I wouldn't give him much odds of makin' it, the way he was staggerin' when he left here. But he might be climbin' back up on that hill to take another shot at us."

"They weren't going to just rob us. They came to kill us," she said when the sobering thought struck her. Looking at him, she feared that they might have succeeded in killing him. There was so much blood. "What will we do?" she asked.

He remembered how flustered she had been over the wound now healing in his thigh, so he expected even less from her on one he knew was far more serious. *Damn my carelessness,* he thought again. "Right off, I need a rag or somethin' to stuff in this hole to see if I can slow this bleedin' down. Then we need to find us a hole we can all get in, 'cause I don't think I can get us all packed up to head outta here right now."

He was interrupted then by a plaintive wail from Emma. "How much longer do we have to stay here? They're gonna step on us with their big feet."

"I'd best drag that body outta here before they see it," Cam said, and struggled to his feet.

"I can do that," Mary insisted, and quickly jumped to the task. Not without a great deal of effort, she managed to drag the deadweight over to a gully and rolled it in. Then she hurried back to help steady Cam as he made his way back to where the horses were tied.

With little choice but to find a place he and Mary could defend, Cam selected the first reasonable spot and pulled their bedding and packs back to form a barricade. Trying to move as fast as he could while he still had the strength, he helped Mary move the horses over closer to them. "We might be doin' all this for nothin'," he told Mary between grimaces of pain, " 'cause I'm pretty sure he's in worse shape than I am. But I don't wanna take the chance. We can't hide the horses in this gulch, but we can sure as hell shoot anybody that tries to steal 'em." When he was satisfied that they were well protected, with his and Mary's rifles ready, only then would he permit her to bandage his shoulder.

No one got much sleep the rest of that night. Although caught up in the frightening chaos of the assault, Grace and Emma eventually succumbed to the urge to drift off. Mary's nerves were still struggling to deal with the wanton slaughter, and she thought back on the days since leaving Fort Collins. She might have gained a fortune in gold, but at an extremely high price—not only the wounds Cam suffered, but also the loss of her husband and the exposure to a violence she never dreamed existed. The evil man could inflict upon his fellow man was difficult to imagine, and the small value placed upon the life of a human being in this untamed territory was enough to make a person question the sense of it all. She looked at Cam as he sat there trying to keep his eyes open with Emma snuggled close against his side. She wondered if he now regretted ever having crossed paths with her and all the trouble it had brought down upon his seemingly carefree life. She wondered if he had ever killed a man before his fateful meeting with her and how the killing he had done since was affecting his mind. Realizing she was getting too deeply engrossed in her sense of right and wrong, she reminded herself that the two men had come to kill her and her children as well. *Cam had to kill them, and I would have killed them if they had gotten by him,* she thought. *So stop fretting over things that had to be done.*

Like probing fingers of light searching the darkened gulch, the first rays of the morning sun began to search out the huddled party. In a few minutes more, it looked directly into the gulch to find all members asleep. Cam opened his eyes and glanced at Mary, sound asleep, still holding on to her rifle, although it had slid off the pack to settle in her lap. Beside them, the horses were snuffling the sparse bits of grass within their reach. *We're still here,* he thought, and tried to rouse himself after gently moving Emma back against the river-bank. The sharp pain that resulted reminded him of his wound. He made a couple more attempts to get to his feet before he was successful. After a few uncertain steps, he held on to a small bush to steady himself until his head stopped spinning. Then when he was sure he was going to make it, he walked back toward their abandoned camp to see if anything had changed. He decided that the other outlaw had either died or run for a doctor. *Good,* he thought, *because I'm in no shape to fight anybody.*

When he came back to the girls, Mary was awake and already looking for wood to make a fire. She looked up when he approached. "I'm glad to see you on your feet. I was afraid we were going to lose you during the night. How do you feel?"

"Not worth a damn," he said, and meant it.

"It looks like there's no one here but us," she said. "So we can thank God for that. And Cam Sutton," she added. A grunt was his only response. "I'll make some coffee and find something for us to eat. You look like you need a lot more than what we've got in the packs. You lost so much blood."

"If a deer comes running right up to us, maybe I'll shoot it," he said drolly.

Coffee and breakfast helped to the point where he felt that he could do what was necessary to get them on the move again, although Mary was not so sure. Determined to prove her wrong, he forced his body to do his bidding, loading and saddling the horses with Mary's help. Then, remembering the deceased outlaw lying in the gully had a horse outside the gulch somewhere, he climbed into the saddle and rode out to look for it.

Not more than fifty yards downstream from where the river exited the gulch, Cam found the horse down by the water's edge. A sorrel, it lifted its head and looked at him curiously as he approached. He looked it over thoroughly, and after going through the saddlebags to take everything of value to him and his charges, he took another look at the saddle. It was in decent shape, and would be worth a little money if he got an opportunity to sell it. On the other hand, leading a horse with an empty saddle might attract too much speculation from anyone who happened to see them. Reluctant to simply throw a good saddle away, however, he decided to keep it.

They only traveled a distance of ten miles that day until striking the Laramie River. It was obvious that Cam needed rest, and since Mary had managed only an hour or two of sleep, she was ready to stop as well. She told him that she might have elected to stay there on the North Laramie, but she felt it better to leave the scene of such violent action. She admitted that both she and her daughters preferred to rest somewhere away from the body she had dumped in a gully.

With no reason to believe they were being followed by anyone, Cam decided it was safe to leave the girls while he rode toward the mountains in hope of finding a deer. Mary argued against the insanity of a seriously wounded man insisting on trying to ignore his condition. "You're just trying to kill yourself," she charged.

With a little show of impatience, he fired back,

"We need meat, all of us. I need meat to build my blood up, and I'm the only one liable to get it. A man can't build his blood up on salt pork."

"Go, then," Mary said, still exasperated, "but, Cam, for goodness' sake, be careful." She could see that he was determined to go.

Emma begged to go with him, and he tried to convince her that he would feel better if she remained in camp to look after her mother. She argued that Grace was the elder and would be better at taking care of Mary. "It might take us a while to find some game," he told her, still hoping to discourage her. "We might not find anythin' at all." She said nothing, but continued to gaze up at him with pleading eyes. "You can't talk when you're tryin' to get close to a deer," he said. "You'd have to be quiet."

"Quiet as a mouse," she promised, her steady gaze constant.

He found that he couldn't bring himself to disappoint her. "All right," he finally surrendered, "just this one time, but you've got to promise me you'll be quiet and do like I tell you." He was rewarded with a gracious smile that reached from ear to ear. Cam looked at Mary and commented, "She shoulda been a boy."

"Don't I know it?" Mary replied. She stood and watched the two of them ride away. *A child and one who thinks like a child,* she thought. *I pray God they'll be all right.*

• • •

Cam grunted as he dismounted to examine some droppings that appeared to be fresh as he followed a game trail that led into the foothills. Not to be left out of anything, Emma scrambled down after him. "Is it deer doo-doo?" she asked in a whisper.

"I reckon that's one name for it," Cam replied quietly. "Looks like this one has been eatin' some berries, and I'd guess he left this for us this mornin'." He looked down the trail toward what appeared to be a small valley, or maybe only a pass, that looked as though there might be a creek or stream. "From the looks of this trail, there might be a regular waterin' hole down at the bottom of this hill," he told her. The possibility seemed likely because it was a frequently used game trail by all indications. "We'll leave the horse here and walk on down the hill."

His hunch proved to be accurate, for there was an abundance of deer sign as they made their way down the trail, with Emma trying her best to walk in his footsteps. He cursed under his breath when the wound in his shoulder began a constant throbbing, and he scolded himself once more for being careless. He had no choice, however. He had to find some game, if it was no more than a rabbit.

Just before reaching the bottom, he saw the stream winding its way out of a pass that appeared to lead between the two mountains ahead of them. “We’ll wait here a bit,” he told Emma, and guided her to a stand of short pines from which he could watch the watering hole for a while. Nothing moved in the bushes lining the stream, so it appeared that the deer that had left the droppings on the trail behind them had long since passed through here. He continued to wait and watch for a while, already aware of the fidgeting of the impatient child close beside him. Suddenly there was movement in the leaves of the high laurel bushes on the other side of the stream. He looked down at Emma and whispered, “Don’t make a sound.” She nodded vigorously and clamped both hands over her mouth as if to prevent any sound from accidentally escaping. He grimaced with the pain caused when he raised his rifle and trained the front sight on the edge of the bushes. *Don’t take too long,* he thought, *I can’t hold this rifle up much longer*. In a moment he saw the muzzle of a young buck appear, so he rested his finger gently on the trigger and waited for the deer to push out of the bushes.

As he was about to apply pressure to the trigger, he was suddenly startled by the blast of a shotgun from the other side of the stream. “What the . . .” he muttered, and dropped the barrel of his rifle while he tried to see the shooter. The buck bolted from the brush and jumped the stream, wounded, but apparently not enough to slow him down. Since it was now coming directly toward them,

Cam quickly pulled his rifle up and dropped the wounded animal. Too late now to consider if it had been a wise decision to shoot, he ejected the spent cartridge, placing another in the chamber to be ready for whatever was to follow. All went silent in the pass, with no indication of another soul around. If it was an Indian hunting party, they were evidently not well armed if they were hunting deer with what sounded to be a light-gauge shotgun, and there were no arrows in the carcass that he could see from that distance. After what seemed to be a lengthy pause, he heard a voice.

"Are you gonna eat that deer?"

He wasn't sure how to answer, since it was beginning to appear that there was going to be a question as to who had first claim on the animal. So he said nothing for a moment, holding Emma back when she tried to inch forward to see what was going on. The voice sounded like a woman's, and in another moment, she stepped out of the pines on the other side of the stream. Astonished, Cam eased the hammer back on his rifle, hardly able to believe his eyes. A short, solidly built woman, wearing a man's shirt and trousers and boots that almost reached her knees, walked boldly out on the trail and stood there waiting for a reply. Cam got up from his kneeling position and walked out of the clump of bushes he had hidden in, Emma close behind him.

"I was just fixin' to squeeze the trigger when you fired that shotgun," Cam said, and made his way down the path to the stream where she waited, shotgun propped by her side. "I reckon there's plenty of deer in these mountains, judgin' by the sign I've seen. Looks like you had first claim on this one. I just thought I'd stop him, since that shotgun wasn't up to the job." He could see her more closely now, a gnomelike woman, her face tanned and wrinkled by the sun, her yellowish gray hair rolled up in a bun behind her head, supporting the weathered flat-brim hat she wore. There seemed to be no malice in the face he saw, and no evidence of fear at all, only an expression of surprised curiosity to see a man obviously shot by the look of his shirt. Then, catching sight of Emma holding on to the back of Cam's trouser leg, the face blossomed into a rosy smile.

"Well, lookee what we got here," she exclaimed delightedly. "Hey, darlin', you helpin' your daddy hunt?"

Emma came out from behind Cam long enough to take a good look at the strange woman, and did not answer until she decided it was all right. "This is Cam," she informed the woman. "He's not my daddy. My daddy's dead."

"Well, bless your heart. I declare, it's been a heap of years since I saw a little one like you. I'd ask you for a hug, but I reckon you might be too shy right off." She turned abruptly to Cam. "My name's Ardella Swift. I reckon I wasted a shell tryin' to kill that deer. This shotgun is all I've got to hunt with, and it's all right for birds and squirrels and rabbits. But you have to get so close to a deer to kill it that you'd do just as well beatin' him over the head with it. But I still can't resist takin' a shot at one when he ends up right in my lap. Lucky you and little missy here came along when you did. I'da had to walk all over these hills to try to see if he mighta been wounded enough to die. I ain't et deer meat in quite a spell."

"Well, there ain't no reason you can't eat some now," Cam said. "My name's Cam Sutton, and I reckon that deer's yours. You got the first shot in him."

"Well, that's mighty sportin' of you, Cam," Ardella said. "But it was your kill."

"Why don't we just split it down the middle?" Cam suggested, looking at the two-point buck. "Looks like plenty of meat for everybody." He could tell by her expression that the suggestion pleased her. "How much family you gotta provide for?" he asked.

"Just me," she replied. "Ain't nobody but me."

Surprised, Cam asked, "You're just huntin' for yourself? You livin' somewhere hereabouts alone?"

His questions drew a chuckle from Ardella. "Huntin' by myself, livin' by myself, everythin' by myself," she answered. "I got a cabin 'bout two miles back up near that highest peak yonder." Without turning around, she pointed back toward the west.

"How'd you wind up here, alone in these mountains? You musta had some family, a husband, or somebody."

"Oh, I had a husband," she replied with a nostalgic smile. "Long Sam Swift, he was a helluva trapper and a helluva man—had hands big enough to crush a coyote's head." Her smile broadened a bit. "You remind me of him." She sighed. "Lord in heaven, I was lucky to have been married to that man." Changing the subject abruptly, she gave Emma a smile. "What might your name be, missy?"

"Emma," the little girl replied, still gazing wide-eyed at the strange-talking woman.

"Emma," Ardella repeated. "Why, that's a dandy name—suits you."

Still finding it hard to accept the fact that this elderly woman, though obviously tough as nails, could be living alone out in the rugged mountains of Wyoming, Cam had more questions. "How long ago did your husband pass away?"

"Let's see," she said, thinking hard. "I make it eighteen years come spring."

"Eighteen years?" Cam responded, amazed.

"Yep," she confirmed with a single nod of her head. "He was kilt by a Pawnee war party on the

South Platte. They jumped us on our way back from South Pass. He made me hide under the bank while he went to try to talk peace with 'em, but they jumped him. It took four of 'em to take him down, and only two of 'em got up again when it was over." She paused to sigh again. "Damn, he was a man."

A woman alone in this wilderness for eighteen years was hard for him to believe, but she seemed bright enough and in command of her senses. "Didn't you ever think about goin' back to where other folks were?"

"At first," she admitted, "but I didn't have no horse or nothin'. The damn Pawnee took the horse and Long Sam's rifle. The only thing I did have was the cabin Long Sam built for us back up the mountain, so after a while, I just said I'd stay where I was. You see, back about that time, the Sioux and Cheyenne was causing a lot of trouble. I figured it best to stay where I was till things calmed down. Then, by the time they did, I'd been here so long without nobody botherin' me, I decided to just stay till I forgot to wake up one mornin'."

He couldn't help wondering, so he had to ask to satisfy his curiosity. "Livin' alone up here all that time, how'd you come by those clothes? They don't look like you've been wearin' 'em eighteen years."

Ardella laughed. "I didn't say I ain't never been

out of the mountains in all that time. Bein' married to a trapper for thirty years, I learned somethin' about takin' pelts. After Long Sam was gone for about a year, I knew I had to do some tradin' or start wearin' hides like the Injuns. So about once or twice a year I'll go out to John Sartain's tradin' post up on the South Platte." She had to laugh again. "No, these duds ain't eighteen years old. If they was, I couldn't get in 'em. I was a lot skinnier then." There was a long pause in the conversation at that point with Ardella still eyeing him intently. Finally she said what puzzled her most. "You know, I reckon that you're walkin' around with a hole in your shoulder. You ain't said nothin' about it. Don't look like somethin' that would slip a body's mind. I sure hope it don't have nothin' to do with this little girl's daddy bein' dead."

"No," Cam said, "nothin' to do with that."

"How'd you get shot?" Ardella finally put it to him straight out, after deciding he was never going to explain.

"This little girl's mama and her sister are camped back at the river. We got jumped by a couple of outlaws last night. I killed one of 'em and wounded the other'n, but I got hit in the shoulder before he took off."

His story sounded believable, but Ardella was inclined to verify what he said. She reached down and patted Emma's head. "You poor little darlin', that musta been pretty scary when those men started shootin' at you."

"Yes, ma'am," Emma replied. "They tried to sneak up on us when we were asleep, but Cam made us hide before we went to bed, and they couldn't shoot us."

Ardella nodded thoughtfully, satisfied that if there was another version to the story, the child would most likely have told it. She then turned her attention back to Cam. "Well, it don't look like you're takin' care of that wound worth a toot. Let me take a look at it."

Cam hesitated but couldn't think of a reason why he should mind her examination, so he shrugged his consent.

"Unbutton your shirt so I can pull it back a little," she instructed. She pulled it back, exposing the bandage over the wound and the wad of blood-soaked cloth stuffed against it. After a brief look, she told him, "Cam, that thing's still bleedin', and it looks like it wants to fester. You must be a helluva man to still be walkin' around huntin' deer and such, instead of lettin' nature heal it. Nature needs quiet and rest to heal somethin' properly. Did you try to get that bullet outta there?" He shook his head. "Well, sometimes a bullet just heals right over, but that wound looks like that bullet wants outta there. You keep workin' that shoulder and it's gonna fester for certain, and in a day or so, you ain't gonna be able to get around without feelin' sick."

"I was fixin' to take care of it," Cam claimed lamely, "but we needed fresh meat, so I had to take care of that first."

Ardella studied the young man's face for a long moment, trying to make a decision. "How 'bout this other feller you shot? Is he still comin' after you?"

"Can't say," Cam answered. "I don't know how bad he's hurt."

"Where was you folks headin', Fort Laramie?"

"No, we thought it best to go around Fort Laramie. We're headin' for Cheyenne, and then on to Fort Collins, down in Colorado Territory."

She took another moment to consider that. "Sounds to me like you must be packin' somethin' that attracts outlaws."

"I reckon," Cam replied, seeing no reason to tell her otherwise.

"Well, I expect I need to take care of that wound for you," she decided. "I can't remember the number of rifle balls and arrowheads I've cut outta Long Sam, but it has been a while. I reckon I ain't lost my touch, though. Why don't we go on back to your camp and butcher this buck, and I'll fix you up while I'm there?"

It was a hard offer to pass up. He thought again of the last time Mary tried to doctor his leg wound, and the uncertain look on her face when she applied the dressing on his shoulder. Ardella talked a pretty confident talk, and he tended to believe she could do what she claimed. "I'd be obliged," he told her, "and I'll carry your half of the deer back to your place for you."

"Mama," Grace sang out, "they're back, and they brought somebody with them."

Mary turned to look in the direction Grace pointed out, relieved to hear Cam was returning. She had not permitted herself to be separated from her rifle for much of the time since he and Emma had left. She placed her hand over her eyes to shade them from the sun while she stared in an effort to see if Grace had really seen someone else. Her daughter was right. Walking along beside Emma was a stubby character Mary assumed was a man. The two of them were walking beside Cam, who was on the horse, and there was a deer carcass riding across his horse's withers.

When they were closer, Emma ran ahead to announce the news. "Mama," she exclaimed, "we shot a deer, and Ardella's come to have dinner with us!"

"Is that so?" Mary replied. She waited, curious to learn how Cam happened upon someone in these rugged mountains, not realizing it was a woman until they were within a few yards.

"My name's Ardella Swift," the stumpy woman announced enthusiastically, and strode forward to shake Mary's hand. "Me and Cam was huntin' the same buck, so we brung it back here to skin and butcher it." She shifted her gaze to Grace, who was standing gaping next to her mother. "And this is Emma's sister," she announced. "Grace, ain't it?" She extended her hand to Grace as well. Grace hesitated, but shook it after a moment. "Two fine-lookin' little girls you have here." With Mary hardly able to respond, Ardella turned away to help Cam dismount when she heard him grunt as he threw the buck's carcass off the horse. "Cam here is startin' to feel poorly. I think the poison from that bullet is startin' to work on him." She smiled then. "But we'll take care of that, won't we, Cam?"

"I reckon," Cam mumbled when his feet were planted firmly on the ground. "First, I'll see about butcherin' this deer, before we go to do any doctorin'."

"You go set down before you fall down," Ardella ordered. "I'll skin this deer and butcher him. Won't be no time at all we'll have fresh meat roastin' over that fire." Looking at Mary, she suggested, "If you'll see about building your fire up a little bigger, I'll handle the rest."

"Well, maybe I can help you with the deer," Mary offered, feeling that she should do something to help this whirlwind who had seemingly taken over her camp.

"Ain't necessary at all," Ardella assured her.

"I've skinned and butchered so many deer, I don't hardly think about it. It comes natural now, I reckon. Although it's been a while, I've skinned elk, antelope, even buffalo. Course I don't even count little critters like rabbits and squirrels and such. You'd just be gettin' in my way." She flashed a wide grin at Mary. "You could make us some coffee, if you got any." Ardella's boast was hardly an exaggeration, for she had the deer skinned and butchered in a short time. Soon there were strips of venison roasting over the fire.

When everyone had eaten their fill, Cam sat on a log while Ardella turned her attention toward his wounded shoulder. "I expect that's gettin' a mite sore, ain't it? I'm gonna heat up this knife and we'll see if we can't get that piece of lead outta there." She winked at Mary. "Long Sam used to call me Dr. Ardella."

She probed the wound with the same skinning knife she had just used to cut up the deer, going deeper and deeper until she finally found what she was looking for. Cam made not a sound, but his tightly clenched teeth and deep grimace were enough to betray his attempt to hide the pain. When she finally picked the bullet from the wound and held it up for all to see, especially Emma, whose nose was practically in between doctor and patient, Cam relaxed, unaware his body had been so tense until then. Ardella looked at Mary and said, "You can slap a bandage on there now, if you've got anythin' to use for one." She got up and went to the edge of the river to clean her knife.

When Ardella returned from the water's edge, she took a moment to look around at the temporary camp, noticing the packs stacked nearby and the horses grazing on the grass along the bank. "Cam ain't gonna feel much like travelin' for a day or two, and this ain't no fittin' place for you folks to wait around. I think you'd be better off if you'd come with me up to my cabin on the mountain. I've got some things in my garden that'll help Cam's wound heal quicker. I'll make him up a poultice of costmary and sage. It'll help that wound heal a heap quicker."

Undecided at first, Mary looked at Cam for his reaction to Ardella's invitation. At that moment, however, his attention was focused on the wound left throbbing as a result of Ardella's knife. She looked back at the expectant face of the smiling woman, who was waiting for her response. "That's a very generous offer," she finally said. "I guess it's up to Cam, though."

"It might not be a bad idea," Cam said. "I ain't too sure how much good I'll be till this shoulder gets a little better."

"Then I guess we'll go with you," Mary said to Ardella. "If we won't be too much trouble for you," she added.

"Good," Ardella responded cheerfully. "You won't be no trouble for me. Hell, I'm tickled to have some company. Matter of fact, you'll be the first folks I've ever had to my cabin."

Chapter 9

As she was inclined to do with most anything, a trait Mary attributed to the colorful woman living so many years alone, Ardella took over the move from the camp by the Laramie River. When Cam insisted that he should take charge of the horses and the packing, she yielded only a little, picking up a saddle and asking, "Which one gets this one?"

Realizing there was no arguing with the woman, Cam pointed to the sorrel that had been ridden by the dead outlaw. "That one," he said.

"It's been a while, but I've saddled a horse before," Ardella informed him. "I had a pretty little pinto till we met up with those Pawnee." She paused a moment then, obviously thinking back. "Damn Injuns cost me a lot." As soon as she uttered the thought, she immediately released it to return to her cheerful disposition. "You can check the girth straps to see if they're as tight as you like 'em."

When Ardella picked up another saddle and looked at Cam for directions, he pointed and said,

"That one goes on the bay. Grace and Emma ride together." Grace had expressed a desire to return to the bay after trying out the dun. She said the bay was hard on her bottom, but no worse than the dun. "Your bottom will toughen up," he had assured her.

Ardella paused to look at Cam, then Mary, then the girls. "How come you got an extra saddle without a fanny settin' in it?" she asked.

Cam smiled. "We were savin' that one for you to replace that pinto the Pawnee took." He glanced at Mary and she smiled and nodded her approval. "Sorry we didn't have a pinto."

"You mean it?" Ardella exclaimed, her air of authority temporarily replaced by childlike excitement. She, too, turned to look in Mary's direction for confirmation.

"It's the least we can do for taking us in till Cam gets well enough to go on," Mary said.

"Glory be," Ardella exclaimed, scarcely able to believe it, "a horse and saddle! What a lucky day for me when I decided to take a shot at that deer." She gave them all a great big grin and a grateful squeeze to Emma, who was standing next to her. "Well, I reckon I'd best do a good job of takin' care of you folks."

When it came time to load the packhorses, Mary tried to lend a hand, feeling she was not pulling her share of the work. But she found that she was almost run over in the bustle Ardella created in her effort to get the party on the trail. Pausing to stand before the packs, hands on hips as she surveyed the many bullet holes in the canvas coverings, Ardella seemed at a loss for words for a change. Of particular interest were the two suitcases on top with several bullet holes through the colorful fabric. Finally she voiced the thought running through her mind. "Looks like somebody didn't care much for your packs. They plumb shot 'em up good. You must be totin' somethin' somebody wants for themselves."

"I guess you could say that," Mary said. "Of course, none of those outlaws knew what we were carrying in our packs—mostly household goods. They would have just robbed us of anything, I expect."

"Lookin' at them bullet holes, it looks like they thought it was worth killin' you." She gave Mary a little smile. "I expect you might wanna sew a patch on that bag there, 'cause it looks like some of your household goods is leakin' out."

Mary looked to see what Ardella was referring to, and immediately hurried to fix it. Some of the sacks of gold dust had become exposed when Cam began to load the packhorses. One had been pierced by a bullet and there was now a thin trickle of dust from the hole, making a small pile of dust on the packs under the bag. She quickly turned the sack on its side to stop the loss of fortune. It was no bigger than an ounce, but realizing this represented twenty or twenty-one dollars, she carefully brushed it off into her hand.

"Want me to untie that sack so you can put it back?" Ardella asked. Seeing the obvious confusion in Mary's face, she sought to reassure her. "Mary, it ain't none of my business what you folks are totin' in them packs. I ain't surprised it's gold. I kinda had my suspicions when there was folks after you with killin' on their minds. That's why I thought you oughta get to someplace where other folks can't find you till Cam gets hisself in better shape. And you ain't got to worry 'bout me, if that's botherin' you. I'm too damn old to worry about stealin' somebody's gold. Besides, you already gave me the only thing I was missin'—a horse—and I'm tickled to death with that."

Completely flustered now, Mary tried to apologize. "I didn't mean to even insinuate that you can't be trusted," she started. "It's just that—"

That was as far as she got before Ardella interrupted. "You got no need to explain nothin' to me. Hell, you didn't know me from Adam's house cat before today. I don't blame you for not showin' your hole cards. I wouldn't. But, Mary, you ain't got nothin' to worry about with me, and if you ain't comfortable goin' to my cabin, I'll leave you be and go on back by myself."

Reading sincerity in the woman's eyes, and in need of someone to trust, Mary stopped her from going further. "No, let's go to your cabin. I believe you're an honest woman, and I'm sorry if it seemed I didn't trust you. Just believe me when I tell you that what we have, we came by honestly. My late husband and his brother mined this gold. Others have found out about it, unfortunately, and Cam is doing his best to take me and my daughters back to Fort Collins safely."

"He looks like he can do the job if we can keep him patched up. Nothin' more needs to be said about the gold," Ardella assured her. "We'll finish up here and get on up to my place. We've got meat enough to last for more'n a few days. By the time we need some more, Cam oughta be in better shape."

At that point Cam walked up, leading the other packhorse. Ardella looked at him and said, "You keep workin' that shoulder and you're gonna bleed out. Set yourself down over there out of the way. Me and Mary and the girls will finish this up and get started up the mountain."

"Roach!" Ben Cheney yelled. "Don't shoot! It's me." He reined his horse back, waiting to make sure Roach had heard him before riding down into the ravine where his partner spent much of his time of late.

Cotton Roach cast a grimace in Cheney's direction and yelled back, "Well, come on." He returned his attention to the five tin cans lined up on the side of the narrow ravine. Setting his feet squarely about shoulder width apart, he hesitated for a few seconds. Then he suddenly reached across his waist with his left hand, pulled the Colt .44 from its holster, and methodically sent all five cans flying, one at a time. When the last can flew up against the side of the ravine, he turned, aimed the pistol at Cheney as he rode up, and pulled the trigger. Cheney ducked to one side, almost coming out of the saddle, before hearing the metallic click of the hammer on an empty chamber.

"Damn you, Roach!" Cheney complained. "One of these days you're gonna forget to leave an empty chamber in that damn gun." He had counted the five shots and knew the weapon should be empty, but Roach had been acting strange ever since his right hand had been injured.

Roach smirked while he reloaded the .44. "Hell, I wouldn't lose nothin' but you."

"You don't wanna lose me," Cheney said. "Won't nobody else ride with you." The two outlaws had been holed up for the past four days at Bill Foley's place on Chugwater Creek. Bill called it a trading post, but he sold more liquor than anything else, and most of his profit came from outlaws on the run.

"I don't need nobody to ride with me," Roach said. With the double-action Colt reloaded, he held it up and looked at it. "Damned if I don't think I'm better with my left hand than I used to be with my right."

"Maybe you oughta be thankin' that feller that shot your right hand, then," Cheney remarked with a chuckle.

Roach's face immediately became twisted with anger, the usual reaction any time someone mentioned the man who had crippled his right hand. "One of these days I'll find that son of a bitch. Then I'll thank him." He held his right hand up before his face. The withered fingers were bound tightly with a rawhide strap to hold them in place. It was the only way he could hold the butt of his rifle against his shoulder and pull the trigger with a clawing action of his middle finger. It was clumsy, but he could never hit anything when trying to fire the rifle as a left-handed man would. Lately, he spent most of his time practicing with his pistol to compensate for his weakness with his rifle. He scowled and dropped his hand again. "What are you doin' out here, Cheney?"

"I got tired of drinkin' by myself, and I didn't have nothin' else to do." He shrugged. "Matter of fact, I'm tired of hangin' around here. When are we gonna get on the road again? I've drunk so much whiskey till that ol' sow Foley's married to was startin' to look good." Before he gave Roach room to comment, he asked, "You remember a feller named Leach, used to ride with that feller outta Texas, Fuller was his name?"

"I reckon. What about him?"

"He rode into Foley's a little while ago with a hole in his chest, 'bout half-dead—said Fuller was dead. Foley was cussin' him out, scared he'd bring the law after him." The mention of the law captured Roach's attention and Cheney continued. "Leach said it weren't the law that was after him. There weren't nobody after him, he just needed a doctor." Cheney paused to chuckle. "Foley told him he weren't no doctor, and Leach said he didn't have no other place to go. Foley told him he could lie up there for a while and see if he could make it or not."

"Huh," Roach scoffed, "I'm surprised Foley didn't tell him to go somewhere else to die. He must be gettin' soft in his old age."

"I don't know," Cheney said. "It wouldn'ta been the first time Foley's took a bullet outta somebody's hide. More'n likely he's figurin' on Leach's horse and saddle if he cashes in. And from the looks of Leach, ol' Foley might have pretty good odds at that."

Cheney's assessment of Leach's condition proved to be fairly accurate. When he and Roach returned to the saloon, Foley told them that he had fixed Leach a bed in his smokehouse. "I told him I'd feed him," Foley said. "I'd even dig around in that wound to see if I could get the bullet out of him, but he said he wanted to wait it out for a spell to see if he might get a little stronger. Might be a good thing if he does, 'cause that wound looked mighty bad."

"Who shot him?" Roach asked. "Cheney said it weren't the law."

"I don't know," Foley replied. "He said somethin' about trailin' somebody sneakin' a load of gold outta the Black Hills, and him and Fuller comin' out on the short end of a shoot-out."

The comment piqued Roach's interest. "A load of gold, huh? Maybe we oughta pay a visit to poor ol' Leach. Might cheer him up a little."

Not sure what kind of reception they might meet with, Roach and Cheney stopped outside the smokehouse door, and Roach announced loudly, "Leach! It's me, Cotton Roach, and Ben Cheney. We've come to see how you're doin'." When there was no reply, Roach pushed the door ajar and peered inside, making sure Leach wasn't sitting up with a gun on the door. Leach wasn't sitting up. He was lying on his side, with his back against the back wall of the smokehouse. At first, they thought he was dead, but in the darkness of the smokehouse, the open door providing the only light, they saw his eyes open and blink at the sunlight. "Damn, Leach, you look like hell."

"I feel worse than I look," Leach struggled to reply.

"Well, you're still talkin'," Cheney commented,

"so maybe you're gonna make it all right."

"I don't know," Leach replied weakly. "I can't lay any way but on my side. That's the only way that don't hurt like hell. That damn bullet is in deep. I can feel it, like it's tryin' to burn a hole in me." He had to pause when he began to cough, bringing a trickle of blood that ran out of the corner of his mouth and dripped down on the sleeve of his shirt.

Noticing the spreading stain of blood on the shirt, Roach glanced at Cheney and raised an eyebrow. Cheney nodded. Roach went on. "Hear tell you was trackin' some folks outta the Black Hills. Looks like you caught up with 'em—musta had you and Fuller outnumbered."

Leach didn't reply right away while he reached up to wipe some more blood from his chin. "Wasn't but one man, a woman, and two young'uns," he managed to mutter.

"One man?" Cheney questioned. "One man against you and Fuller? He musta bushwhacked you."

"He did," Leach grunted, "him and his rifle—cut us down before we knew he was there."

Leach's statement struck a chord in Roach's brain, especially when he mentioned the woman and two children. That would be too much of a coincidence. Still, he proceeded to press for information. "That woman with the two kids, were they two little girls?"

"Yeah, two little girls."

"How 'bout the man with the rifle, was he a kinda tall young feller?"

"I reckon," Leach replied, and groaned when he tried to shift his position against the wall.

"Wore a bright red bandanna around his neck?"

"That sounds like the man. You know him?"

"I might," Roach replied, thinking hard now, a feeling of cold hate suddenly gripping his spine. It was possible, he thought. It very well could be his tall young rifleman with the red bandanna. With emotions of revenge swirling in his brain, he had to calm himself, because he needed more information out of Leach. And he had to be careful how he asked the questions, or Leach might clam up. "Say they was packin' a big load of gold outta there, huh?"

"I didn't say that," Leach muttered.

You just did, Roach thought, more convinced than ever that he and the man who had crippled his hand had crossed paths again. "What you need is a couple more men to go with you after that bastard. Whaddaya say me and Cheney wait around here till you get well enough to ride, and then we'll all three go after the son of a bitch? We got nothin' on our minds right now. We might as well join up." In an effort to talk it up, he turned to Cheney and asked, "Whaddaya say, Cheney? We can help him catch this bastard. We can wait till he gets well enough to ride, can't we?"

"Why, hell yeah," Cheney answered, aware of what Roach was trying to do. "We'll see if that jasper is as tough against three of us. Whaddaya say, Leach? Wanna give him a dose of what he gave you?"

Leach didn't answer, so Roach continued to press. "Where'd you and Fuller tangle with this feller? On the stage road?"

Leach wasn't sure he could trust them, but he feared he was going to need some help if he did survive the wound. "No," he finally answered, "on the North Laramie."

"What in the world were they doin' up there?" Roach asked. "Was they in the mountains?"

"Nah," Leach forced painfully, his insides hurting so badly that he didn't care whether he told them or not, " 'bout ten miles west of the fork with the Laramie." That was as much as he planned to share, so he pretended to lose consciousness.

"Leach!" Roach prodded. "Can you hear me?" When there was no sign of a response of any kind, he turned to Cheney. "I reckon we'd better go get Foley. I think he's done for."

"Looks that way," Cheney agreed. "Foley might be able to do somethin', but I doubt it."

Back in the saloon side of Foley's trading post, they told him that the dying man in the smokehouse looked as though he was halfway there. "Well, I told him I'd try to dig that bullet outta him if he didn't get no better. I'll go see what I can do." He walked to the back door and called his wife to come watch the bar while he was gone. Roach told him he needn't bother because he and Cheney were riding out right away.

"Where the hell are we goin'?" Cheney wanted to know when they headed for the door.

" 'Bout ten miles east of the fork of the Laramie and the North Laramie," Roach answered. He looked back over his shoulder to see Foley go out the back door, then stepped to the bar, reached over, and quickly grabbed a bottle of whiskey before Foley's wife, Mabel, came in. He then continued toward the front door. "I'm gonna need somethin' to celebrate with tonight. I just found that son of a bitch that ruined my hand."

"Hell," Cheney responded. "Is that what you're thinkin'? There's about a fart's chance in a dust storm that the feller who shot Leach is the same one that shot you."

"Too many things add up that says it's the man, and I got a feelin' to boot. It's him. I knew I'd pick up his trail one of these days." He kept walking, straight to Foley's small barn where their bedrolls were, Cheney right beside him, shaking his head the entire way.

"That feller is long gone from there by now," Cheney insisted.

"Listen, Cheney, if you don't wanna go with me, just stay here, but Leach and Fuller were tailin' those people 'cause they was haulin' gold on their packhorses. That right there is enough reason for me to take a little ride up that way and see if I can pick up a trail. Hell, if they weren't tryin' to stay outta sight from ever'body, they'da been on the stage road."

"I swear, maybe you're right," Cheney said, allowing for the possibility that Leach and Fuller might have been onto something that promised a big payday. What Roach was saying was beginning to make sense, even though at high odds. "Hell, I'll go with you just so you don't have to drink that whole bottle of likker you just stole by yourself." They were saddled up and riding out the path from Foley's Place in a few minutes' time, anxious to eat up some of the distance before dark.

Behind them, Foley prepared to perform surgery on the hapless Leach. "Take another slug of whiskey if you can hold some more," he instructed his patient. Leach, who had opened his eyes as soon as his two visitors had left, tilted the bottle back with a shaky hand and gulped as the fiery liquid scalded his throat. It came back up almost immediately. "You ready?" Foley asked when Leach stopped retching, his skinning knife poised over the suffering man.

"Go to it," Leach replied gamely, then arched his back up sharply when he felt the knife probe into the swollen wound.

Foley recoiled from the rotten smell that escaped from the incision he had just made, but continued to probe deeper and deeper, thinking he was bound to find the bullet if he kept going. Leach screamed in pain, arched his back again, then fainted dead away. Finding it easier with Leach's body relaxed, Foley prodded first one way, then another, but could feel nothing that felt like a piece of lead. His patience soon began to run out, so he withdrew the knife, pulled Leach's chin up, and with one firm stroke, neatly slit his throat. "You was gonna die anyway," he said, thinking now of the horse and saddle he had just gained.

Mabel came to the smokehouse door then. "How's he doin'?" she asked, with little interest one way or the other.

"He didn't make it," Foley answered. "Now I'm gonna have to dig a hole for him." He cleaned his knife blade on Leach's shirt. "I reckon it's worth it, though. I got a right fine-lookin' horse, and I'll take a look in his saddlebags and see if there's anythin' else."

"You gonna want your supper now?" she asked in the bored tone that was typical of her manner of speech.

"Nah, I'm gonna plant him in the ground first, so I'll be a while."

Chapter 10

How much they could trust Leach's testimony was hard to say, but it was Roach's opinion that the encounter with the man with the red bandanna more than likely had occurred on the North Laramie River as he claimed. Exactly where was the hard part, but it had to be somewhere between the fork with the Laramie and the mountains to the west. Leach could have been truthful in saying it was about ten miles from the fork. It made sense that it would have been in that general area if, in fact, these people were traveling south while trying to avoid seeing anyone on the stage road. Roach was convinced that it was the same man who had crippled his hand, so he started his search at the fork of the river with himself on one side and Cheney on the other.

By the time they had ridden what Roach estimated to be about ten miles, it was time to stop to rest the horses. There had been no sign of any activity along the banks, save for a few places where single, and sometimes two or three, riders had crossed over the river. But there was nothing that would indicate a gunfight had occurred, and they were rapidly approaching the foothills. "That lyin' bastard, Leach," Cheney complained as he filled the coffeepot at the water's edge. "He sent us off chasin' our tails."

"Maybe," Roach allowed, "but I ain't ready to give up yet."

There were two good reasons to keep going—the chance to even the score with Red Bandanna and the prospect of gaining a large amount of gold. His resolve proved to be valuable, for they continued on, following the river into the hills, and soon reached a section where it split one high hill in the middle, forming a narrow gulch. It was in this gulch that they found the sign they had searched for. "Now, by God, I reckon you'll see I know what I'm talkin' about," Roach boasted while the two looked at the obvious evidence of a major confrontation. The many hoofprints and other tracks told of the activity of people and horses moving around.

"This look like Fuller?" Cheney asked when he stopped to stare down into a gully running parallel to the gulch.

Roach walked over to look at the corpse lying in the bottom. "Yep," he replied, "best as I recall." He snorted a chuckle. "He looked a little better the last time I saw him, though."

They didn't spend much time looking around the site of the gunfight, for there was nothing else they needed to learn there. An obvious trail led away from the river to the south, tracks left by at least half a dozen horses. Roach easily pictured

Red Bandanna, the woman, and the two little girls riding away from the scene of the shoot-out, leading a couple of packhorses loaded down with gold dust that was his for the taking.

It was late in the afternoon when the two outlaws reached the banks of the Laramie and another obvious campsite of the people they followed. "They didn't ride very far from their last camp, did they?" Cheney remarked. Both men dismounted.

"Looks like they stayed here awhile," Roach said, after walking a dozen yards away from the remains of a campfire and finding the head and the few remains of a deer the scavengers had not finished.

"They got fresh meat," Cheney said, when joining his partner at the edge of the gully. "Wish to hell we had some."

"Well, there's a little bit of gristle left around that head," Roach japed. "Help yourself."

Upon a thorough search on both sides of the river, they could find only one trail out of the camp and that was to the west, into the mountains. It was puzzling to Roach, for he figured they would continue south. "What the hell would they be headin' that way for?" he asked aloud.

"I don't know," Cheney answered him. "Maybe they changed their mind about where they're goin'." He turned his head to spit a stream of tobacco juice at a lizard, but missed. The lizard was unmoved by the attempt, so Cheney worked his chew up again and fired another stream of brown tobacco juice at the insolent reptile. When he missed for the second time, he lost interest and returned to the discussion. "One thing for sure, though, there ain't no other tracks outta here." Roach had to agree, so the next morning they followed the only trail left for them and headed up into the mountains.

On the second morning after reaching Ardella's cabin high up near the top of a mountain, Cam awoke after a full night's sleep. For a few minutes, he didn't move, unsure if moving was going to bring pain, and for the moment, he was comfortable except for the incessant reminder of nature's call. Knowing he was going to have to answer that call before very much longer, he reached over and felt the bandage on his shoulder. The wound was sensitive to his fingertips, causing him to use a more gentle touch, so he took his hand away. He remembered then that he was in a bed instead of his bedroll. Since there was only one bed in the tiny cabin Long Sam Swift had built for Ardella and himself, Cam immediately felt guilty for driving Ardella out of her bed. It had not been his intent to do so, but Ardella and Mary had practically forced him to lie down on the bed after he suffered a dizzy spell and could hardly stand alone. Ardella was sure it was from the loss of blood.

He pushed himself up to a sitting position and looked around him. Two large quilts had been hung up on a line to form a wall for his bedroom, and the voices on the other side were almost in whispers, in order not to bother him, he figured. He swung his feet over on the dirt floor and his head started spinning at once, causing him to grasp the blanket, fearful that he might fall over on the floor. He sat perfectly still for a time, hoping his head would settle itself. Ardella had mixed up a potion the night before and insisted that he should drink it. Whatever the ingredients were, it had certainly knocked him out for the entire night. He knew it was a good part whiskey, but she wouldn't tell what else it contained.

In a little while, his head stopped spinning, so he decided he could make it to his feet without falling through the quilt curtain. It was evidently not without noise, for the curtain was pulled back at one side, just enough for someone to peek in. "Well, goodness' sake, he's already up." Ardella pulled the quilts aside. He was greeted immediately by an instant burst of loud conversation, a result no doubt of having to have been so quiet for such a long time. "You feel like you could handle some coffee?" Ardella asked.

"That'd be mighty good right now," Cam answered, "but first I've got a powerful need to make some room for it." He headed toward the door. Still unsteady on his feet, he lurched to one side, catching himself on the doorjamb to keep from falling.

"Here, lemme help you," Ardella said, "before you fall in the stream outside." She dived under his good arm and straightened up again, supporting his weight on her shoulder. "Now, let's go."

"Cam," Emma said, "Ardella doesn't have an outhouse. You have to go in the woods."

Cam managed a smile for her as he replied, "I reckon that's what the woods are for, Skeeter." Outside the door, however, he told Ardella, "I can make it by myself now."

"Horse feathers," she replied. "I'd end up right back here pickin' you up off the ground. I'll walk you over to that pine tree yonder, and you can hold on to it while you get your business done." He started to protest further, but she cut him off. "My goodness alive," she told him, "I'm old enough to be your mama. I ain't gonna look, anyway. I'll turn the other way till you're done."

With her only feet away, it took him a minute or two to convince his bashful bladder that it was all right to release its contents. "Don't look this way," he warned her once when she took a quick peek in his direction.

"I was just checkin' to make sure you ain't fell down," she laughed. "I didn't wanna see you lyin' flat on your back, peeing straight up in the air." Chuckling to herself, she murmured, "Damned if you ain't the shy one." Reasonably sure he was not going to fall, she turned and headed back to the cabin. "I pulled out an old shirt of Long Sam's," she called back to him. "It might be a little big on you, but not too much, and that bloody shirt of your'n is about ruined."

Cam was a strong man. He didn't remain an invalid for long. After that first night, he insisted on returning to his bedroll and surrendering the bed to Ardella. She embarrassed him by remarking that she might not wash the bedclothes for a while, because it had been so long since she had the scent of a man in her bed. "Ha!" Mary blurted, unable to contain her delight upon seeing Cam blush. "I can understand that right enough." Both women enjoyed a laugh, causing him to retreat from the cabin.

"I'd best go see about the horses," he mumbled as he went out the door.

Another day found him rapidly getting his strength back, bringing a comment from Ardella that he must be building his blood back up. "Long Sam was like you," she remarked, a wistful look in her eye. "He could come back from a wound or injury faster'n any man I ever saw. I remember one time he went huntin' the day after he got caught between a mama bear and her cubs, and she damn near mauled him to death."

"Well, that's what I'm fixin' to do," Cam said. "I think I'll walk back down the mountain a piece and see if there's a chance to add to our meat supply."

"Are you sure you're ready to do that?" Mary asked. "You might not be as strong as you think."

"Can I go with you?" Emma asked at once.

"Not this time, Skeeter," Cam told her. "The last time I took you huntin', I came close to shootin' Ardella." He hated to disappoint her, but in truth, he felt as if he needed some time alone. Emma screwed her face into a pout, but Mary told her she wanted her to stay close to the cabin.

Cam picked up his rifle and went out to check on the horses before he left. The small patch of grass around Ardella's cabin was soon going to be grazed bare, so he knew he was going to have to move them before another day or two, and look for some grass somewhere else. *Maybe tomorrow,* he thought as he walked toward the path that led down the mountain. It would be handy if he ran up on a deer, but he really didn't expect to see one. The mountain offered very little to attract any kind of game—gaunt, hard-looking heights with trees on very few slopes. He was surprised to find game trails in some of the more barren stretches. His real purpose was to get away from the four females for a little while. His life had changed so drastically since meeting Mary and the girls, from one of a loner to one constantly in female company. It was good to get out on the mountain alone.

He had made his way a fair distance down the narrow game trail when it occurred to him that he might have gone far enough, for he reminded himself that he was going to have to climb back up the steep incline, and he was a long way from being fit again. The path wound through a belt of scattered pines at that point, still some one hundred feet or more above the foot of the mountain. He decided to walk over to a large outcropping of rocks that would give him a view of the valley below and the way he and the women had approached the mountain on their way to the cabin. It would be nice, he thought, if he spotted a herd of deer moving through the valley, even though he knew he was in no position or physical shape to go after them. But there was nothing moving in the valley—until he started to return to the path. "Damn!" he uttered, for two men on horseback suddenly appeared at the mouth of a wide ravine.

He remained there, watching the progress of the two riders, for as he could best remember, they seemed to be riding the same trail Ardella had chosen to lead them to her mountain. He knew for sure they had ridden up the middle of that same ravine. There was no doubt in his mind, after watching the way the men studied the ground before them, that they were tracking his party. Conflicting thoughts raced through his mind as he continued to watch their progress. From that distance, he couldn't tell much about their features. He could only tell that one of them rode a black horse, the other a paint. It mattered little, for he was convinced they were coming after him, and for the same reason the others had. Stand and fight, lie in ambush, or clear out before they found them? He was not sure which would place the women and children in more danger. The last ambush had resulted in the wound he was now trying to recover from. *I'll stand and fight,* he thought, but first, he must protect Mary and Ardella and the girls. His next thought was to get back to the cabin to warn his people while there was still a little time to prepare.

As he hurried back up the mountain, he couldn't help feelings of regret that they had now pulled Ardella into their problems. The tiny game trail that led to her cabin had been free of tracks from deer or any other game before they came. There was now evidence of hoofprints and not from deer, but from half a dozen horses. They would be found. As he approached the cabin, his lungs heaving from the exertion he had placed upon himself, he studied the situation as the two men would see it. The cabin was nestled back in the mouth of a ravine and hard to see. But that also made it hard to defend because of its vulnerability on three sides, and the steep ravine behind. It would afford the attackers possession of the high ground on two sides of the cabin. He didn't like the setup. He would prefer to have the high ground. The next thing that struck him as he neared the cabin was the fact that his horses were all bunched there in front of the cabin. *This ain't worth a damn,* he decided, but there was no place else to take them within a reasonable distance from the cabin. There were too many signs that told him their best chance was to run.

"Mary! Ardella!" he shouted as he ran up to the door. His shouts emptied the cabin at once, as everyone responded to his frantic alert, immediately alarmed. "We've got to get outta here!" he told them. "There's two riders trackin' us, and I don't think we've got much more than forty-five minutes' or an hour's head start on 'em." Accustomed to quick escapes by now, Mary reacted immediately and returned inside to gather up her belongings and those of her daughters.

Ardella moved to help with the horses, and started saddling Mary's horse while hurriedly giving Cam instructions. "You and the girls go down the ravine back of the cabin. It don't look like a trail, but you can make it if you do just like I tell you. And it'll lead you to another game trail that leads to the other side of the mountain. Long Sam moved some of the rocks that were there. He said it was our back door, if we ever had to make a run for it. They'll have to look pretty damn hard to find it."

"You, too, Ardella," Cam said. "You're goin' with us."

It had not entered the stocky woman's mind that she would run with them. "Me?" she responded. "Hell, I ain't leavin' my place here. This is my cabin. They'll have to go through me to get to you folks. Besides, they ain't lookin' for me. I'll tell 'em you've already gone."

"Ardella, these men are killers. Every one of 'em that's come after us has come with murderin' in mind. They'll kill you without askin' the first question. So get whatever you just can't do without and let's get goin'." She still hesitated, causing him to lose his patience. "You're goin'. I ain't havin' you on my conscience. So get movin'. I'll saddle the horses." She hesitated a moment longer but decided he might be right, so she ran to get her belongings.

When all were ready, Ardella led them into the ravine behind her cabin. "We'll have to walk and lead the horses," she told them. "It's pretty steep right off and we might go head over heels if we try to ride down this ravine. But if you walk where I walk, we'll make it all right, and maybe won't cause a landslide."

Her precautions proved to be legitimate, for the horses slid and skidded as they descended the steep ravine. Cam, leading the packhorses as well as his dun, had all he could do to keep from being caught up in an avalanche of horseflesh, and it looked as if Mary's fortune in gold was in danger of being spread over the rocky trough. Somehow they managed to reach a wide rock ledge that gave them a nearly level footing, but still not to the extent they could climb in the saddle. The ledge looked to become even wider as it extended to their right, and Cam started to lead his horses that way until Ardella stopped him. "Go this way," she said, pointing in the opposite direction to a narrow rock ledge.

"This way looks a helluva lot easier," Cam replied.

"That way leads halfway around the mountain to a cliff," Ardella told him, "and there ain't no way down from there."

"You lead, I'll follow," Cam said, and made no more suggestions till they reached the bottom.

Finally they came out on a game trail that led down the mountain, and they were able to climb onto the horses at that point. They continued a slow descent until reaching an open meadow near the bottom. Grace, who had been looking back, exclaimed, "Look!" The others turned to see where the child was pointing. High up near the top of the mountain, a dark column of smoke rose above the rocky defile.

"That's where my cabin is," Ardella blurted, "or was." She looked at the sympathetic faces turned to her then, none knowing what to say. "That's all I had," she said. "Now what the hell am I gonna do?"

Mary didn't hesitate. "You're coming with us. You don't want to end your days up there on that mountain alone, anyway." She glanced in Cam's direction when she added, "If you don't mind taking your chances with us. But I warn you, so far we haven't had an easy time of it."

Never one to harbor negative thoughts for long, Ardella brightened and asked, "You mean it?"

"Of course we do, Aunt Ardella," Grace answered for her mother. "We wouldn't leave you up there on that mountain by yourself."

"Well, let's go, then," Ardella exclaimed, "before those scoundrels up there find out which way we went." She pointed the way to Cam. "Follow this trail. It'll take us to the other side of the mountain from the way they went up to my place." They wasted no more time looking at Ardella's past eighteen years going up in smoke. "*Aunt* Ardella," she murmured to herself. "I kinda like that."

Under way again, they paused when the report of two gunshots, high above them, rang out. Too far away to hear more than a muffled sound, they could only speculate on its purpose. It was a pistol, Cam felt. It was too far to be aimed at them, and it was not followed up by other shots, so they wasted no time worrying about it. Once they reached the floor of the valley, they set out in a southeastern direction, with no real idea where they might be heading. Their only thought was to get as far away from the men following them as possible. They held the horses to a comfortable lope for a good while before easing up on them. At this point Ardella was more familiar than Cam with the country they traveled, and she soon proved it, while leading them through some unlikely looking passes and draws until finally coming to a river. “It’s the Laramie,” she told them.

“I reckon we’d better rest the horses for a spell,” Cam said. “They were workin’ pretty hard back there.” They rode along the river a bit farther, looking for the best place to ford. Cam decided to stop to rest on the other side, preferring to have the two men chasing them confronted with crossing the river to get to them. This was in case they were that close behind and caught up while they were still resting the horses. It was merely a precaution, for he didn’t see how their pursuers could possibly catch up to them this quickly, especially considering the several blind passes through which Ardella had led them.

“I don’t know ’bout you folks, but I think I could use a cup of strong coffee,” Ardella announced. “Maybe chew on a little piece of that jerky we smoked the other day.” When she saw Mary’s look of concern, she told her, “Them two ain’t gonna catch up with us for a while yet, if they trail us at all.” She was confident that they would have a great deal of difficulty finding their way down the rocky ravine right behind her cabin. Then if they managed to make it to the rock ledge without tumbling, she would bet they would choose the wrong way to go, just as Cam almost had done. And that would cost them some more time when they had to backtrack from the cliff. She winked at Grace and said, "How 'bout helpin' your aunt Ardella find some wood for a fire?"

"That sounds like a good idea," Mary said, a little less anxious since Ardella seemed so at ease. She went to the packs to get her coffeepot and coffee mill. "We're running low on a few things. I hope we'll get to someplace where I can get some things."

"We need to decide where we're goin' from here," Cam said. He turned to Ardella. "Where will this lead us if we keep goin' in this direction?"

"Well"—she took only a second to remember—"if we keep going, we'll strike Chugwater Creek, but I don't remember how far it is from here. It's been a while since I went that far. I don't usually come over on the east side of the mountains."

That was country Cam was a little more familiar with. "If we hit the Chugwater, we can follow it on down to where it takes a turn toward Laramie, then keep ridin' south till we get to Cheyenne," he said. "If we're lucky, we might lose those two behind us, and I'm thinkin' you might wanna put your gold in the bank there. I reckon they've got one big enough to take it."

"Big enough to take it?" Ardella echoed. She was sitting by the fire, inspecting the repeating rifle she had gained with the horse and rig that had once belonged to Jed Fuller. "How much gold have you got?" As soon as it left her mouth, she wished she had the question back. "Ain't none of my business, though."

"I've got enough to take care of you," Mary said. She felt a strong obligation to Ardella for disrupting her entire existence, and putting her in danger. She shifted her attention to the statement Cam had just made. "I don't know what's best. Maybe you're right. I know I'm sick and tired of running all over this wilderness, trying to keep myself and my daughters from being murdered."

"Cheyenne's on the way to Fort Collins, anyway," Cam said. "But from what you told me about Fort Collins, it ain't hardly as big as Cheyenne. Ain't that right?" She nodded. "So I figure they might have a better bank, and maybe some kind of law." She seemed to be giving the matter serious thought, so he said, "First thing, though, is to see if we lost our two friends."

After the horses were rested, they pushed on straight east. Cam stood on the bank of the river for a long time before they rode away, scanning the valley behind them, searching for some sign of two riders. There was none, thanks to Ardella's knowledge of her mountains, he figured.

• • •

Ardella's guess about their pursuers' probability of trouble behind her cabin turned out to be a near-fatal prophecy for the two bandits. When they found the tracks leading up the mountain on the old game trail, Roach was certain he had his quarry treed. The mountain was so steep that he was sure there would be no place for them to run, and the odds looked even more in his favor the higher they climbed. When they had finally reached the cabin, it was so well hidden they almost rode right up to the front door before Cheney suddenly reined his horse back sharply.

"Damn!" Cheney cursed. "Cabin!" They backed the horses away. "I damn near rode right in the door."

"There ain't nobody here," Roach said, "or they'da shot at us." He looked hurriedly around the small clearing in front of the crude structure. "Where are the horses?" Furious and frustrated after having been sure he had caught up with Red Bandanna, he gave his horse a kick and rode up before the cabin. "Where is he?" he demanded loudly, his fingers itching to pull a trigger. "They ain't been gone long," he said, pointing to the dying embers of a cook fire on the ground. Dismounting, he then walked up to the door and kicked it open, his pistol in hand, only to confirm what he had already surmised. There was no one there. Enraged, he walked in and began to throw what little furniture there was against the wall, turned the table upside down, and kicked the small stove over, leaving the stovepipe dangling from the roof.

Cheney walked in behind him, disappointed, but a great deal calmer. "Somebody's been livin' here," he said, stating the obvious. "But they're gone now."

Cheney's innocuous statement only served to add fuel to Roach's fury. "Where the hell did they go?" he demanded again. He stormed back outside and turned around in a circle, searching for an obvious way out. "There ain't any way outta this hole but to go back the way we came up."

When Cheney came out to join him, he again stated the obvious. "Unless they went out the back," he said. They walked around to the back to look down the steep, rocky ravine. "That's where they went," Cheney said, pointing to the hoofprints at the edge of the opening. "Don't look very safe to me."

Roach took a closer look at the tracks. There seemed to be enough tracks to indicate that all the horses had descended into the ravine. "Hell, if they can do it, we can do it," he said, and went back to the cabin. Inside, he picked up everything he could find that would burn and piled it up in the middle of the room. With some still-glowing pieces of limbs from the cook fire outside, he ignited the pile of broken furniture. After pausing a few moments to make sure his fire was going to live, he went to his horse, climbed into the saddle, and returned. "You comin'?" he asked when he pulled up beside Cheney.

"I reckon," Cheney replied reluctantly, and went to fetch his horse.

Both horses hesitated at the brink of the rocky slide, but Roach kicked his repeatedly until the cautious gelding started down the ravine. Cheney followed. The first few yards were rough, but past that the horses' hooves began to slide on the loose shale, and they were struggling to remain upright. Both riders were leaning until their backs were almost flat against their horses' croups and their stirrups straight out before them. When Cheney's horse lost control and almost crashed into Roach's, Cheney frantically pulled the frightened animal's head around, trying to wind up beside Roach instead of on top of him. In its effort to turn, Cheney's horse stumbled on a loose rock and went down, breaking a leg. The horse screamed and tumbled, tossing Cheney out of the saddle. Unable to stop his fall, he bounced from one boulder to the next, grunting painfully with his impact against each one, until finally coming to a stop beside his dying horse on the rock ledge.

Trying to avoid the same fate that Cheney had come to, Roach took one foot out of the stirrup when he felt his horse beginning to stumble. When the horse started to slide, Roach rolled off the saddle, landing amid some smaller rocks, receiving some cuts and bruises, but nothing of a crippling nature. When he was able to get to his feet and find he was not seriously hurt, he couldn't contain his rage, and he roared his frustration out over the rock ledge where he found Cheney and his horse lying still. His own horse had escaped the fatal mishap that claimed Cheney's. In all appearances, Cheney himself had met the same fate as his horse on the treacherous rock slide, but then Roach heard a painful whimper emanate from Cheney's lips. "I thought you was dead," Roach said unemotionally.

"I'm afraid to move," Cheney gasped. "I think I'm broke up inside. How 'bout my horse?"

"Looks dead to me," Roach said. "Might as well be, even if he ain't. He's got a broke leg." Realizing then that his pistol was no longer in its holster, he started looking around for it among the rocks. "They tricked us," he said, still fuming. "They never went down these rocks, and now we let 'em get away again."

"Roach," Cheney pleaded, "you're gonna have to help me. Somethin's broke and I'm afraid to try to move."

"I lost my damn gun," Roach replied. "I gotta find my pistol first." He climbed back up the slope partway, looking right and left among the rocks. "Go on and see if you can get on your feet," he called back to Cheney. "That's the only way you'll know. One thing for sure, you can't lay there forever." A moment later, he heard a cry of pain from his partner as he attempted to get up on his knees. He looked back to see Cheney on hands and knees, unable to get any farther. "There it is," Roach sang out when he caught a glimpse of metal down between two rocks. He reached down and picked it up and examined it for damage. When he was satisfied that there was no harm done, he put it back in his holster and said, "I'da played hell if I'd busted up my .44."

With pain racking his spine now, Cheney cried out again, "Roach, help me."

All that was on Roach's mind at that moment was the fact that the man he hated more than anybody or anything else on earth was gaining distance on him. Cheney had been a pretty good partner, but now he was a liability. Roach made his way back down to the suffering man and stood over him for a few moments. "You got up on your knees. See if you can get on up the rest of the way. That son of a bitch is gettin' away. We've got to get goin'."

Cheney tried, but each time he tried to pull a leg up under him to lift himself up, the pain was enough to almost make him faint. "I can't do it, Roach. I can't move." He realized how desperate his situation was and he began to beg. "Roach, you gotta pick me up and put me on your horse. I can't do it by myself."

"Shit, partner, I can't pick you up. Besides, my horse can't carry double down this mountain. I'd never catch up with that bastard." He shook his head as if in deep concern. "I can't stay around here. I've got to get ridin'."

"What about me?" Cheney exclaimed, seeing the handwriting on the wall. "You can't leave me like this!" When Roach did not reply, he cried, "Roach! You wouldn't ride off and leave me here to die!"

"No, sir," Roach told him, "I wouldn't do that." In one swift move, he reached across and drew the .44 and placed a bullet in the back of Cheney's head. "There, now you ain't got nothin' to worry about." Pausing then to decide whether to waste another bullet, he shrugged and put the injured horse out of its misery. He studied the pistol for a moment before holstering it. "I swear I'm faster with my left hand than I ever was with my right." That thought brought his mind back to the urgency he felt to catch the man who had ruined his right hand. *I've got to get moving,* he thought, and wasted no further thought on his damaged hand.

He turned Cheney over and quickly went through his pockets to take the little bit of money his late partner had managed to save. The small amount of cash caused him to grunt his disappointment. "By God, you wasn't lyin' when you said you was about to run outta money," he told the corpse. "Well, your six-gun and belt are worth more'n you are right now." He pulled the belt from around the body, then went to Cheney's horse and searched the saddlebags before pulling the rifle from its scabbard. When he had taken everything he thought worth something, he took his horse's reins and started walking along the ledge where it widened as it led around the mountain. "It was nice knowin' you, partner," he called back over his shoulder facetiously. "I'm sorry I can't take that saddle with me, but I know where it is if I ever wanna come back to get it. I doubt anybody'll stumble on it."

After following the ledge almost all the way around the mountain, he reached the end of it and stood glaring down at a sheer drop of several hundred feet. Cursing his luck again, he yelled out over the empty space before him, "What'd they do, fly off this damn mountain?" With no option but to reverse his path and go back the way he had come, he continued to fume, still convinced that the people he chased, with women and children and heavily loaded packhorses, could not have come down the way he had.

Chapter 11

They had hoped to strike the Chugwater by nightfall, but because of their late start from Ardella's and the difficult country they crossed, darkness found them short of their destination. They were fortunate to come across a small stream that ran along beside a line of low, treeless hills, so they stopped to make camp there. Several times during the long day, Cam had waited while the others continued on, watching to see any sign of the two outlaws. And at the end of the day, he was halfway convinced that they had managed to lose them. Still, he climbed up the hill beside the stream to keep watch for as long as there was enough light to see anyone approaching. When supper was ready, Emma climbed the hill to bring him a plate of beans and sowbelly, and sat with him while he ate. She had attempted to bring him coffee as well, but barely half of it made the trip up the hill successfully.

"Cam," the little girl said after a long moment studying his eating, "you know, I don't have a daddy anymore."

"I know, Skeeter, but you've got a fine mama and now you've got an aunt Ardella, so you'll be all right."

She paused to consider that, then continued

with what was on her mind. "You know, you could be my daddy," she said.

He chuckled. "I don't know about that. I think it'd work out better if I was your uncle Cam. How 'bout that? That'd be all right, wouldn't it?"

"I suppose," she replied, disappointed that he didn't accept the job she was interviewing him for.

"You never can tell what's gonna happen down the road," he said. "Your mama ain't that old. You might have a new daddy one day."

"Do you like my mama?"

Cam chuckled again. "Sure, I like your mama—got no reason not to. We're good friends." The precocious little miss didn't say anything more, but Cam laughed to himself, thinking that marrying Mary was maybe the last thing on his mind. In fact, he seriously doubted that he would ever settle down with a wife. *Foolish thoughts,* he told himself, and let them go. *I wonder how old she really is*. It was hard to tell.

When it became too dark to see farther than the base of the hill he was sitting on, he decided that there were going to be no visitors that night, and he went back down the hill, where Mary and Ardella were sitting by the fire. "I bet you're ready for some more coffee," Ardella said. "You ain't had but one cup."

"I didn't get but about half of that one," he said. "Emma pretty much sprayed the side of the hill with most of it."

"I told her not to hurry up that hill carrying that cup," Mary said.

"Don't matter none," Cam said. "She thought she was helpin' out, and I got a little bit of coffee, anyway." He looked around to see if the girls were about, but Mary said they had gone to bed.

"I declare, she's a caution, that young'un," Ardella remarked, and changed the subject abruptly. "You think we're clear of those two murderers?"

"I don't wanna speak too soon," Cam told her, "but we've either lost 'em for good or they're way to hell behind us. I think that you guidin' us through those rough parts of the mountain is what shook 'em off our trail."

There was a definite sense of relief in the camp that night when they decided to turn in. However, Cam slept very lightly, waking several times to listen to the horses and take a quick look around the perimeter of their camp. When morning brought no threat of attack, the mood of the travelers was almost cheerful as they set out again to find the Chugwater. They were not in the saddle long before they reached the creek and turned to follow it south.

Shortly after noon they came upon a log cabin of sorts that, at a distance, appeared to be a farm or ranch house, for there was a small barn and what was probably a smokehouse close beside it. However, there were no fields or pastures, although there was a small garden beyond the barn. "Don't look much like a homestead," Cam speculated. "Could be a tradin' post."

"Oh, I hope it is," Mary said. "We really need some things."

"I'll ride on ahead and take a look," Cam said. He nudged the dun gelding with his heels and departed at a lope.

There was a short path leading from the creek to the cabin, and it was not until he had turned the dun onto it that he saw the roughly carved sign by the front step, FOLEY'S PLACE. It appeared that Mary's wishes might have been answered. *I'd better take a look inside to make sure it's not just a saloon,* he thought, and rode on in. There appeared to be no one about as he stepped down from the saddle and looped his reins over a short hitching post, stepped up on the low stoop, and pushed the door open. There was no one inside, but he found that the large room consisted of a bar at one end and what appeared to be a general store at the other. "Howdy," a voice came from behind him, and he turned to find a woman following him up the one step from the stoop. She carried a bucket with a handful of string beans in it. "I saw you ride up," she said. "I was in the garden, pickin' the last of these summer beans. They didn't do much this year, not like last year's crop." She pushed by him to walk toward the counter. "You lookin' for Foley?"

"Ah, no, ma'am," Cam replied. "I don't believe I know Foley. I was lookin' to see if you sold supplies like flour and coffee and such. The rest of my folks are coming along behind me."

"Oh," Mabel Foley responded. "You've got some other folks with you. I thought you were wantin' a drink of whiskey."

"No, ma'am," Cam replied politely.

"Well, sure, we've got flour and coffee beans, and some other staples—be glad to help you out. You've got family with you?" she asked.

"I guess you could say that," he said. "Anyway, I'll signal my folks to come on in. We weren't sure this wasn't a homestead—didn't see the sign till I got to your front door."

"Most people around here know we're here," Mabel said. "I've told Foley he oughta put a sign at the head of the path, up by the creek. I expect there's been other folks that mighta thought the same as you did."

The small talk finished, Cam went back outside and rode up to the creek to signal Ardella and Mary. Then he waited for them to catch up to him. "It's a store, all right," he announced when they rode up. "Looks like a saloon and a store, but this time of day the saloon half is empty, so I reckon it's all right for you ladies to go in and buy what you need to."

When Cam had left to get the rest of his party, Mabel went into the back where her husband was sleeping off a drunk incurred the night before in a contest with two of his regular customers. He raised himself up on one elbow when his wife walked in the room. "Who is it?" he groaned.

"Nobody you need to worry about," she told him. "Just some folks passin' by and needin' some supplies."

"Hell, I was gcttin' up anyway," hc said with a groan. "I can't stay in this bed all day." He sat on the side of his bed and started coughing violently. Since this was the usual reaction after a night of heavy drinking, Mabel walked over to the other side of the bed to fetch the chamber pot. She set it down beside his feet, then left him to deal with his demons.

Back in the store, she walked to the front door and looked out to see the party of one man, two women, and two children. The man was now leading two heavily loaded packhorses, one of them carrying two colorful suitcases on top of the load. She didn't notice until they pulled up to tie their horses that the suitcases had what appeared to be several bullet holes. She didn't give it a great deal of thought; she was accustomed to an assortment of odd people following the trail along the Chugwater. "How do, ladies?" she greeted them, and nodded toward Cam. "He says you might be needin' some supplies."

"That's right," Mary replied. "I surely hope

you've got some flour. I haven't been able to bake any bread for a while now."

"We could sure use some grain for the horses," Cam said. "You got any of that?"

"Sure do, young feller." Cam turned to see Bill Foley entering the store, having won another round in his battle with the whiskey demons. "I can let you have as much as you want, at a reasonable price, too. How you folks figurin' on payin'? Paper? Gold?"

"Dust," Cam answered, "if that's all right with you."

"Yes, sir," Foley answered without hesitation. "That'll be just fine. I've got an accurate scale." His attention now fully captured, he offered Cam a drink of whiskey while the ladies did their shopping. When Cam declined, saying it was a little too early in the day for him to partake of any strong spirits, Foley said he was going to need a little hair of the dog that bit him. "I'll go out to the barn and fetch a sack of grain," he said, while walking to the bar at the opposite end of the room. He poured himself two shots of whiskey, then went out the front door. Cam remained with the ladies as they called out the things they needed, while Grace and Emma searched the counter in vain for the hard candy they usually found in most general stores. Watching them, Cam decided that Foley's Place most likely did only a small part of their business on that end of the store.

Outside, Foley came from the barn with a sack of oats on his shoulder. Not having paid much attention to his customers' horses on his way to get the grain, he paused a moment now to consider their load. Like his wife, he noticed the bullet holes in the suitcases and thought, *They must dearly love them suitcases. I believe I'da already throwed them away. Them horses are loaded down pretty good.* His mind was beginning to come out of the fog induced by the alcohol, and he started adding up coincidences. *They're paying with gold dust,* he thought. He stared at the canvas covering the major portion of the packs as if trying to penetrate it. Then the facts started adding up more quickly, and he thought of Leach's tale of the man who shot him and killed Jed Fuller. They were after a man and woman with two small children. The only difference from his story was there were two women in this party, instead of just one, but everything else pointed to its being the same party Leach and Fuller were after. And Leach was convinced that these folks were riding out of the Black Hills with a substantial load of gold dust. He and Fuller caught up with them, but ran into an ambush. "Glory be," he exclaimed. "That's the folks Cheney and Roach took outta here after." They had not shared that information with him, but it had not been hard to figure out. "And they wind up right on my doorstep," he whispered, unable to suppress a chuckle for the irony of it. *I wonder how much gold they're toting,* he thought, unable to guess just by looking at their packs. Convinced that he had a fortune in gold sitting out front, he went back in the store.

"I got your grain outside," he announced as he went in the door. "Where you gonna put it?"

"Up behind the saddle on the black," Cam answered. "I'll take care of it." He figured that next to Grace and Emma's bay, Mary's horse was carrying the lightest load. He would tie what supplies Mary bought onto his and Ardella's horses.

When Mary and Ardella had finished with the shopping, Mary took a small pouch from inside her jacket and watched closely while Mabel weighed out the payment in dust. Foley helped Cam carry the sacks of supplies Mary was paying for. "You know you folks are welcome to camp here for the night," Foley said as he watched Cam tie a sack behind Ardella's saddle. "There's a dandy little place on the other side of the barn on a little stream that runs into the Chugwater. We don't get many women visitors, and I know Mabel would be tickled to death to have some female company for a change."

"Thanks just the same," Cam said, "but I expect we'll get on our way."

"It's already past noon," Foley pressed. "Don't look like you'll make many more miles today, anyway. You could rest up them horses."

"We're kinda in a hurry," Cam said, "but 'preciate the offer."

Inside the store, while Cam was talking to Foley, Ardella was asking for information from Foley's wife. "Where would we end up if we keep followin' the Chugwater?" she asked.

"Keep followin' Chugwater and it'll take you to Laramie," Mabel told her.

"Laramie," Ardella echoed. "We don't wanna go to Laramie, do we, Mary?" Mary shook her head.

Not realizing that her husband was outside, trying to convince Cam to stay overnight, Mabel was free with information for customers who had made such a substantial purchase. "Well," she offered, "if you follow the creek for about twenty miles, you'll come to a place where it kinda loops around more to the west. The Chugwater Stage Station is there, so you can't hardly miss it. Easiest thing to do then is to just follow the stage road south to Cheyenne." She could tell by the expressions on both women's faces that Cheyenne was more what they had in mind, although neither expressed it. "You'll know it when you get there. They built an inn and a store there."

Ardella thanked her as she and Mary herded the girls outside, where they ran to Cam to be lifted and placed aboard their horse. Ardella hopped up in the saddle, surprisingly sprightly for a woman her size, while Mary allowed Cam to give her a helping hand. When Cam stepped up in the saddle, Mabel noticed a look of anxiety in her husband's eyes, approaching panic. She favored him with a bored look of disgust, naturally thinking he was still feeling the results of a wasted night of drinking and would no doubt run for the outhouse any minute. Had she any notion of the real cause of his feeling of helplessness, she would have endeavored to persuade them to stay over, with no concern or conscience for what might happen to them during the night.

As for her husband, Foley's mind was whirling with wild thoughts about making some attempt to stop them from leaving. If he had guessed correctly, and he was almost dead certain he had, he was helplessly watching a millionaire's fortune ride away from his front door. There were no witnesses to see what might happen here, but he was held back by the memory of Leach lying in his smokehouse, and his telling of the man with the rifle who did for both him and Fuller. *Red Bandanna!* The thought leaped to his mind then. Leach had muttered something about the gunman wearing a red bandanna. And this fellow had a red bandanna tied around his neck! He had no doubt now that it was the same man. Seeing the tall man in person, and the way he checked his rifle to see if it was resting easy in the saddle sling, Foley was not confident in his ability to go up against him. It didn't help his courage when he looked at the rawhide-tough woman on the sorrel with a .44 strapped around her waist. Had he known that Cam was still healing from a serious gunshot wound, he still might not have had the courage to make a move against Ardella.

"What is it, Bill?" Mabel asked when their guests rode up the path. "You look like you're about to turn green. Go on and throw up and get it over with. You oughta had better sense than try to outdrink them boys last night."

He stood there fidgeting nervously, like a dog at the end of a rope, watching helplessly as a golden opportunity rode out of sight. "It was them!" he finally exclaimed.

"Who?" Mabel asked.

"Them," Foley responded impatiently. "Them folks with the gold that Leach was chasin', and Roach and Cheney went after. And I had to stand here and watch 'em ride right outta here, pretty as you please."

Mabel's mouth dropped open and she turned to stare after the party of three adults and two children, now almost to the end of the path. "Well, I'll be . . ." she muttered. "How do you know that?"

"Can't be nobody else," he exclaimed.

She took another look at the departing horses. "I coulda charged that woman a helluva lot more for them supplies, if I'd knowed that."

"Charge 'em more?" Foley replied, astounded by his wife's witless remark. "We coulda had enough gold to live like kings and queens if we coulda just talked 'em into stayin' here for the night. If I coulda got that stud horse to drinkin' some of that rye whiskey that damn near done me in last night, I'll bet it woulda been no trouble a'tall to slit his throat while he was tryin' to sleep it off. The rest of 'em wouldn'ta been no trouble if we took care of him first."

"I don't know about that," Mabel said. "That one ol' woman looked like she was part she-bear." Still stunned by what Foley was telling her, Mabel was trying hard to decide if her husband was serious or had simply lost his mind. "You talkin' 'bout killin' women and children?" she asked.

"I'm talkin' 'bout two packhorses loaded with gold, enough gold to take care of us in style for the rest of our lives—instead of sellin' a little bit of whiskey to every low-down outlaw that comes through here, and scratchin' in the dirt for every dollar we can cheat 'em out of. That's what I'm talkin' 'bout. They just rode right in here and fell in our laps. Yeah, I'm talkin' 'bout killin' women and children. A man's gotta take what's dangled in front of his nose. That gully out back's deep enough to hold the lot of 'em. Ol' Leach won't mind sharin' it with 'em."

Mabel was somewhat dazed. Her husband's wild ranting did not horrify her; far from it. She knew he was capable of any degree of foul play, and it would not have been the first time she played a part in it. "Well, what are you aimin' to do about it?" she asked, thinking of the things that a vast fortune could buy. "I mean, they're just gettin' farther away, but ever'body that's tried to take that gold away from those folks is dead, maybe even Roach and Cheney, too."

"I don't know," Foley answered honestly. "That ain't my line of work to go up against that son of a bitch riding guard over that gold. But I swear, I'm thinkin' it couldn't hurt to trail them folks and just take a little look at their camp tonight. As late as they started out, I'll bet they don't get all the way to Chugwater Station tonight. I'm a fair shot with a rifle, if I was to get a shot at him while they're asleep, and maybe one at that ol' she-bear. I might not have to kill the younger woman and them two little ones. I could just ride off with the gold and there wouldn't be nothin' she could do about it."

"Maybe show up here with a U.S. marshal," Mabel countered, "or a troop of soldiers."

"Not if I'm wearin' a mask," Foley said, warming up to the idea. "As far as she knew, I'd just be one of them road agents that rob the passengers ridin' the stagecoach. She wouldn't have no reason to think it's me. Besides, you and me would hightail it outta this damn hole before anybody knew we was gone."

As Foley had stated, armed robbery was not his

line of work, and he was a bit too old to start, but he was rapidly talking himself into giving it a try. The stakes were high enough to warrant it. Mabel reminded him again of the fate of Leach and Fuller, but he assured her that he intended to be very careful. And if he couldn't get a safe opportunity to assassinate Cam and Ardella, he had no plans to take them on face-to-face. She followed him out to the barn and talked to him while he saddled his horse, cautioning him to be careful. "Don't leave me here by myself for too long," she said.

"If I get the chance I'm countin' on," he assured her, "it'll be tonight when they camp. I just hope they don't go a long way before they decide to stop. I'll be back before mornin'. You oughta be all right for that long. Just keep that shotgun where you can get to it quick."

"Don't forget to tie that bandanna over your face," she reminded him, "and pull your hat down low. Make sure that woman don't recognize you."

"She won't," Foley assured her. "I'm takin' my rain slicker, so I'll put that on before I walk into the camp to take the gold." He climbed up into the saddle. "I'd best be goin'. I don't want 'em to get too far ahead."

She stepped back when he turned his horse toward the path, and stood watching him until he reached the trail by the creek and disappeared from her sight. *That old fool,* she thought. *He ain't got no business going after a man as handy with a rifle as the gunman riding with those women.* She turned to look back at the store with their living quarters behind, and it suddenly struck her that it was a lonely place, maybe the loneliest place in Wyoming Territory. "I hope to hell he makes it back, with or without that gold." For she never really thought he'd get up enough nerve to go through with the plan. It was just talk.

Overcome with the frustration of not being able to find a trail left by six horses, all carrying riders or packs, Cotton Roach reined his horse to a stop and looked left and right at the mountains before him. "Damn it, they couldn't just disappear!" he complained aloud. It was bad enough to know that he had wasted so much time back on the mountain when Cheney had fooled around and broken his neck or whatever it was. Then on top of that, he had followed a ledge that only led him to a cliff. He was still convinced that the people he stalked had taken some other trail down that mountain, and he was concerned that it might have increased their lead on him even more. Whoever joined them at that cabin must know every inch of these mountains, he thought, for he had spent the rest of the day searching every pass and draw he could find with no results. And now he was faced with rapidly approaching darkness. He was going to be forced to make camp, so he had to forget the search for the day and try to find some water if he could.

He found a small trickle coming down from a mountain before darkness set in. It was the first piece of good luck that had struck him all day, and his mood was hardly lifted by it. At it again early the next morning, he worked his way back to the eastern side of the mountains he had left the night before. Around noon, he finally admitted defeat, knowing he could not possibly search every ravine and gully in the whole mountain range, looking for a trail that was getting older as each hour passed. Cursing his luck, he decided to head back to Foley's, for want of a better idea. It was a bitter pill to swallow, after having come so close to finding Red Bandanna, to have to admit defeat. He would find him again, he swore it. He would show up again, *and this time maybe I'll be there*. After resting his horse, he set out for the Chugwater.

With no more than four or five miles left to go, Roach was reluctant to stop for the night, even though it was already getting dark. His horse was in need of rest, but he decided to push on in to Foley's, feeling in need of something to eat and a stiff drink to go with it. He had downed the last swallow from the bottle he had stolen from Foley while resting his horse that afternoon. He and Cheney had done most of the damage to it before finding that game trail up to the cabin.

When at last he struck Chugwater Creek, he guided the weary horse along the trail that led to the trading post. It was somewhere around nine or ten o'clock by the time he turned down the path and rode up to the store. There was no light in the store or the rooms behind it, but Roach did not hesitate to pound on the door until a light from a candle appeared in a small window in the living quarters. "Open up!" Roach shouted.

"Who is it?" Mabel called back.

"Cotton Roach," he answered. "I need somethin' to eat. What the hell are you all locked up for?" He had never known Foley to go to bed early.

"Foley ain't here," Mabel answered. When there was no immediate reply to that statement, saying he'd come back in the morning, hopefully, she said, "Wait till I get my robe on and I'll let you in. I reckon I can find you somethin' to eat. Go around to the front of the store." With a tired sigh, she put her candle down long enough to pull a robe around her and tie the sash. She was not happy to see Roach show up again now that Foley was making a move on that gold. If Roach found out what her husband was up to, he was going to insist that he be made a partner. If Foley was successful and returned with the gold, it was going to be difficult to deny Roach a share. He was too dangerous to fight over it. The result might very well be that she and her husband would end up with nothing.

"Where's Foley?" Roach asked as soon as she unbarred the door.

She looked past him while she formulated an answer she thought he might believe, then answered with a question since she saw only one horse behind him. "Cheney ain't with you?"

"Nah, Cheney's dead, broke his neck in a rock slide," Roach replied. "Where's Foley?"

"He's gone lookin' for some horses," she answered. It was all she could think of at that moment.

"Lookin' for some horses," he repeated, "in the middle of the night? What the hell's he doin' lookin' for horses? What's Foley gonna do with horses?"

She tried to make her story as believable as she could. "A feller told him about some wild horses on the other side of the creek, and he went to see if he could find them."

"Foley don't know nothin' about horses," Roach said. "What's he gonna do, try to sell 'em?" She nodded. It sounded pretty strange to him, but he wasn't interested enough to pursue it, especially when his belly was running on empty rumbles. "You reckon you could rustle me up some coffee and a little somethin' to eat? I ain't had much all day."

"I reckon," she said. "There's still a little bit of coals in the stove. I can warm up some biscuits left over from supper. If you need more'n that, it'll take a little time."

"That'll do," he said. "I'll go take care of my horse while you're doin' that." He went out the door and led his horse down to the barn, pulled his saddle off, and fed the horse a healthy portion of Foley's oats. By the time he returned to the store, the coffee had boiled and was sitting on the corner of Mabel's iron stove. She placed a plate of warmed-over biscuits she had heated in the oven with some dried apple slices on a table in the corner of the room, then poured two cups of coffee.

"Might as well have a cup myself," she said, and sat down at the table across from him. "I don't reckon you caught up with them folks totin' the gold."

"Who said me and Cheney was goin' after somebody?" She shrugged in answer to the question. He thought about it a second before deciding it made little difference now if she knew what they had left there to do. "Nah," he said, "they got away, just seemed to vanish to someplace. I couldn't find 'em." That reminded him. "Where's Leach? Is he still here?"

"No, he didn't make it," she replied. "Foley tried to save him, but he was shot pretty bad." She watched him eat for a few minutes before asking, "What are you gonna do now?"

"I don't know," he said, then paused to take a sip of the hot coffee. "Ain't nothin' changed. I'm still gonna track that son of a bitch down." He raised his right hand and stared at the rawhide binding holding his fingers in a cupped position. "I'll get him." He studied the crippled hand a few moments longer before abruptly changing the subject. "So Foley's gone chasin' wild horses in the middle of the night?"

"Yep, don't know when he'll be back."

"Left you all by yourself. You interested in makin' a little extra money, doin' somethin' besides cookin'?"

"Reckon not." It was not that she was above such doings. It was more the eerie feeling she got when looking at the sinister-looking man, what with his long white hair and those crazy eyes.

"Thought I'd ask. How about a drink of whiskey, then?" He wasn't especially attracted to the weary-looking, matronly woman, so he was not overly disappointed. But it was worth a try, he figured. She got to her feet and went over to the bar to get a bottle and a glass. She poured him a drink and left the bottle on the table, thinking it might be a good idea if he drank himself into a sleepy stupor, all the while wondering what kind of situation her husband might be facing.

At that particular moment, Bill Foley was crawling up the side of a low rise on all fours, dragging his rifle behind him, aware of his heart-beat pounding inside his chest. So far, everything had gone just the way he had told Mabel it would. They had stopped after riding no more than ten miles. He had followed a fresh trail left by the horses carrying Cam and the females, and had almost ridden right in on them until he caught sight of the horses hobbled in the trees beside the creek. Stopping just in time, he backed slowly away and guided his horse over behind a sizable swale back some distance from the creek bank. There he left the horse and crawled up to the top to see if he could look into the camp from that position. He found that he couldn't get a clean look at the entire camp because they had pitched their bedding behind a stand of cottonwoods. He moved several feet from side to side, trying to find an unobstructed view of the camp. In his thinking, it was mandatory that he should be able to pick two clear shots. He was afraid of getting Cam and missing Ardella. He had to have two clear shots. If he didn't, he wasn't going to risk a shot.

Perplexed, he looked at a stand of high shrubs a good twenty yards closer to the creek bank. From that spot, he should be able to see into the side of the clearing beneath the cottonwoods, but he was not willing to risk moving across a small clearing between his present position and the shrubs until they had gone to bed. So he waited. Although he could hear voices muffled by the trees, he could not get a clear view of everyone in the camp.

After what seemed a long time, he could still

hear voices but felt that surely the camp must be settling down for the night, so he told himself that it was time to move. Feeling his heart pounding again, he forced himself to leave the relative safety of the swale. With his rain slicker rustling with every movement he made, he ran to the clump of shrubs, sliding to a stop on his knees in the sparse grass. The thought flashed through his mind that he had no business trying to do this, and in spite of the cool of the evening, he was perspiring heavily under his arms. He could already feel the dampness, causing his shirt to cling in that spot. He had been right about the new position, however, because he could now see the entire camp from a side perspective. The little girls were already tucked away in their blankets, and he could see their mother kneeling by the fire, tending something in a frying pan. He lifted his rifle and slid the barrel through the leaves as he sighted on the other woman who just then appeared, coming up from the water's edge. She paused to say something to the woman by the fire, giving Foley a stationary target. His finger nervously brushed the trigger, but he hesitated, knowing that when he pulled that trigger there would be no turning back. All hell would break loose, and he'd have to finish what he started. He decided it might be unwise to take the shot until he knew where Cam was, and the broad-shouldered rifleman was nowhere in sight. It was then he felt the light tapping of a rifle barrel upon the crown of his hat.

Foley went ice cold inside, his body freezing in a helpless paralysis as Cam reached over him and grabbed his rifle barrel, forcing it upward until Foley could no longer hold on to it. "Doin' a little huntin', Foley?" Cam asked softly.

Terrified, the would-be assassin crumbled into a quivering mass, trying to think of some plausible excuse for his presence there, while knowing there was none. "I wasn't gonna . . ." he started, unable to finish his explanation. "I was just gonna . . ." he tried again but could find no words that would explain what he was doing there with a rifle aimed at the camp. He quickly abandoned the notion of trying to think of a believable explanation for his presence in their camp in the middle of the night, instead made a simple but sincere plea for his life. "Please don't kill me," he cried. "I admit it, I thought about it, but I wouldn't never have gone through with it. I swear."

"I find that hard to believe, Foley," Cam calmly replied. "It don't take much for a man to pull a trigger." Although there was no evidence of indecision in his tone, Cam was not sure what he wanted to do about the attempted assault on his camp. The man quivering fearfully before him was such a pitiful sight, it seemed a cruel thing to execute him. He wasn't sure Foley would have had the nerve to do it if he had not been stopped.

By this time, the altercation in the shrubs was discovered by the rest of the camp.

"Cam!" Ardella called, already moving toward the clump of bushes, her pistol drawn. "You all right?" Mary picked up her rifle and moved to stand before her children.

"Yeah," Cam answered her. "I'm all right. We got a visitor."

Ardella strode up to find Foley cowering at Cam's feet. "What the hell?" she exclaimed. "Foley?" She took a quick look around then. "Anybody else with him?"

"No," Cam said. "I don't think so. Is that right, Foley?"

"No," Foley sputtered. "There ain't nobody else. I swear there ain't, and I was fixin' to turn around and leave. I couldn't bring myself to do you folks no harm." With eyes pleading for mercy, he looked up into the stoic face of the formidable man standing above him.

"You believe that, Ardella?" Cam asked.

"Shit no, I don't believe it," she answered at once. "The cowardly little bastard was sneakin' up on us, fixin' to kill us in our beds. I say let's kill him right now." She was struck with the same indecision that Cam felt, but she maintained the same bluster that Cam was displaying, unsure what action he had in mind.

"Maybe you're right," Cam said. "He was fixin' to cut down on us."

That brought a frantic plea for mercy from the trapped man. "Oh Lordy, please don't kill me. I swear I'll run from here and you won't never see me again. I wasn't really fixin' to shoot anybody. Please, I got a wife that won't have nobody to take care of her. I need to get back to her."

Cam's stoic expression never changed as he looked into the eyes of the desperate man. He almost wished Foley had shot at him. Then he would have felt no hesitation or conscience about reacting to the attack, returning fire, and killing him. But somehow he couldn't bring himself to brutally execute him. "Get on your feet," he finally ordered. Foley, convinced that he was about to meet his Maker, struggled up to stand on unsteady feet. "You got any other weapons with you?"

"No, just this rifle is all," Foley answered, his voice quivering.

"Start walkin'," Cam commanded, and prodded him in the back with his rifle, heading him toward the swale where he had first watched the camp. Cam handed Foley's rifle to Ardella and walked Foley back over the rise to his horse. When they reached the horse, Cam took a quick search in his saddlebags to make sure Foley had no additional weapons. "Get on," Cam said, motioning toward the saddle. Foley did as he was told, not sure what was about to happen. "All right, you miserable bastard," Cam told him, "I'm lettin' you go back to that wife of yours, but if you show up around my camp again, you're a dead man." Foley's body, having been locked in rigid anticipation of the fatal bullet, almost turned to liquid in his relief. Cam, still holding the horse's bridle, had one last thing to tell him. "Listen, Foley, somebody has been feedin' you a big story about a lot of gold. There ain't no gold but that in that little pouch you saw Mary pay you out of. Everything else we're totin' is stuff to set up house with. It ain't worth killin' nobody for. You understand?"

"Yes, sir," Foley quickly replied. "You won't never see me again."

Cam released his bridle. "And, Foley," Ardella said, "we don't never sleep. One of us is always awake."

"Yes, ma'am," Foley said, gave his horse a sharp kick, and was off at a gallop.

"I didn't think you was that softhearted," Ardella said as they watched Foley disappear in the dark.

"You think he believed that story about the gold?" Cam asked.

"I don't know, maybe, maybe not, but I don't think we'll see him again tonight," she said. "He's got too far to ride to get another gun. But we need to be gone from here in the mornin' in case he gets his nerve up again." She walked with him back to the camp. "That little weasel would have shot at us if you hadn't caught him in time.

How'd you know to look for him? I didn't see you slip outta the camp."

Cam shrugged. "I don't know. I heard the horses makin' some noise like they heard somethin', so I just thought I'd go take a look around. I guess I'm just touchy when it comes to hearin' noises that don't belong."

"Out here on the prairie, that's a good way to be," Ardella said. "Long Sam was like that. He could hear a mouse fart in a dust storm." She paused, as if recalling something. "Except that one time on the Powder when them damn Sioux jumped us. It cost him his life."

Cam thought about her comment for a moment, then decided to question her. "I thought you said you and your husband got jumped on the Platte by Pawnee."

"Damn," she replied without hesitation, "so it was. I swear, sometimes I think my mind is startin' to rot. I guess I'm gettin' too old to remember anythin' the way it was."

Chapter 12

Foley feared his troubles were not at an end. The sun was rising behind him by the time his exhausted horse walked slowly down the path to his store. There was a horse in the small corral next to the barn, and it looked like the one Roach rode. He preferred not to arouse anyone until he had a chance to talk to his wife and find out why Roach was back. So he pulled the saddle off his horse and left it on the top rail of the corral. Then as quietly as he could manage, he opened the gate and let his horse inside. After closing the gate, he tiptoed inside the barn to peek over the side of the back stall to see if Roach was there. He was met with a Colt .44 looking at him as Roach sat up from his blanket.

"That's a damn good way to get yourself shot," Roach growled, "sneakin' up on a man like that."

"I wasn't sure that was you in there," Foley said, still trying to recover from the second time he had been staring into a gun barrel in the last few hours. "When did you get back?"

"Last night," Roach answered as he released the hammer and put his gun back in the holster. "Where's the horses?"

"How's that?" Foley replied. "The horses?"

"Yeah, Mabel said you was out last night chasin' some wild horses."

"Oh," Foley said, baffled until it occurred to him that Mabel had made up a tale for Roach. "Yeah, I'll tell you about it over some breakfast. Let me get in the house and get Mabel up." Then it occurred to him. "Where's Cheney?"

"Dead," Roach answered. "We can talk about that over breakfast, too." He threw his blanket back. “Tell Mabel to get some coffee on the stove. I’m gonna need some this mornin’.”

“I’ll do it,” Foley said, and left immediately before Roach might decide to ask him about catchin’ wild horses again.

Mabel was already out of bed and pulling on her clothes by the time Foley rapped on the back door. “That you, Bill?” she asked before removing the bar. When he bolted into thc room, she asked excitedly, “What happened? Did you do it?”

“No, dammit, they was set up in ambush,” he lied, unwilling to admit his failure. “There weren’t no way I could get to where I could take a shot at ’em.” Her face drooped immediately with her disappointment. “I was ready,” he told her, “but I just couldn’t get close enough without them seein’ me. What about Roach?” he asked, anxious to change the subject. “What’s he doin’ here?” He told her about seeing him in the barn.

She told him of Roach’s failure to catch up with Cam and the women, and of Cheney’s death from a rock slide. “Rock slide, huh?” Foley remarked. “More’n likely Roach shot him. Did you tell him that them folks was here?”

She shook her head and said, “No, I didn’t wanna tell him that you’d gone after ’em.”

“Good. I’ll build up the fire in the stove. He’s already wantin’ some coffee, and you’d best tell me what kinda story you told him about me huntin’ wild horses.”

"I expect he's gonna want some eggs and a slice of that side meat, too, but I'm gonna have to go to the barn to get the eggs," she said.

"Well, he looked like he was fixin' to get up when I left," Foley said.

"All right," she decided, "go ahead and get that fire going and I'll look for some eggs." She went out the back door.

When she got to the barn, Roach was not there, so she went into the back stall where the chickens nested to look for eggs. Finding four, she held the two corners of her apron together to form a pocket to hold them. *Well, there's enough for him,* she thought. *Bill and I will have to get by on bacon and coffee.* She was on her way out the barn door when she met Roach on his way back from answering an early call from Mother Nature. He hadn't bothered to pull on his pants yet.

Grinning at her, he said, "I reckon you ain't never seen a real man in his long johns before, have you?"

"I still ain't," she replied, and continued out the door.

As they had learned to expect from earlier visits, Cotton Roach made very little conversation when he sat down at the table to eat. Helping himself to several slices of salt pork, and raking all four eggs onto his plate, he dived in with both hands, either unaware or unconcerned that there were no eggs left for Foley and his wife. He finished them just as the biscuits came out of the oven, so he used one of them to sop up the remains of egg and bacon grease on his plate. Content, he pushed his plate away and held his cup up for a refill. Mabel got up and got the pot from the stove. "Now," Roach said, "what's this about you goin' after some wild horses yesterday?" He sat back, sipped his coffee, and listened while Foley made up a tale about someone stopping by and telling him about a herd of mustangs on the other side of Chugwater Creek. He said he just rode over that way to see if he could find them.

Roach didn't say anything until Foley was finished. Then he commented, "Foley, you're about the worst liar I ever heard. What in hell would you do with a bunch of wild horses even if you was to catch any? You don't know nothin' about breakin' horses. How was you gonna catch 'em? I saw your saddle settin' on the corral rail, and you didn't even have a rope on it." Seeing the obvious fluster in Foley's face in the wake of the avalanche of questions, Roach was suspicious that the simple storekeeper had been up to something he didn't want to share with anyone. And that made Roach determined to find out what it was. "Why don't you come on out with it and tell me what you was really up to?"

"Why, nothin', Roach," Foley stammered. "Ain't nothin' goin' on."

"The hell there ain't," Roach countered, impatient now with the charade. "Whatever you got goin' for yourself, I want a piece of it."

Growing impatient as well, and ready to be done with it, Mabel spoke out. "Hell, why don't you go ahead and tell him, Bill? You found out you can't do nothin' about that gold, anyway. Might as well tell him."

"Yeah, Bill, maybe you'd better tell me," Roach said. There was a definite hint of a threat in his tone after a mention of gold in Mabel's comment.

Foley didn't say anything for a long moment. With his eyes on the table right in front of him, he could still feel the intimidating stare coming his way from Roach. What had possessed Mabel to put him in a spot like that? Another moment passed with Roach still staring, until Foley decided Mabel was right. He had already had his chance and he wasn't able to cash in on it. He might as well confess and let Roach go for it.

"He was here!" Roach roared out in rage when Foley told him of their recent visitors. "The son of a bitch was here?" In his frustration to strike out at something, he raked his coffee cup off the table with his bound right hand, sending it crashing against the wall. "I've been chasin' that bastard all over the Laramie Mountains, and he was here!" He turned on Foley then. "He was right here, and you let them ride out alive?"

"We didn't know it was the same folks you've

been trailin’,” Foley pleaded. “They were already ridin’ out of the yard when I figured it out, ’cause there was two women, and you said you was chasin’ a bunch with only one woman. There wasn’t nothin’ I could do about it by then, but I trailed ’em to their first camp last night. Like I told Mabel, though, I couldn’t get close enough to get a shot at ’em. If I coulda, we’da split whatever they had, but to tell you the truth, them folks ain’t carryin’ a big load of gold, just household goods.”

“How the hell do you know that?” Roach demanded.

Foley realized too late that maybe he shouldn’t have said that. “Uh, I heard one of ’em say that.”

“You tellin’ me you got close enough to hear them talkin’, but you was too far away to shoot?” Roach demanded, growing more irate by the moment. No longer able to control his rage, he reached over and grabbed Foley by the collar. “Which way did they go?”

“South,” Foley choked out. “They followed the Chugwater south.”

“Well, by God, that son of a bitch thinks he’s got clear of me, but he ain’t, not by a long shot!” He gave Foley a look of disgust and asked, “Where are they headin’ to? When you was close enough to hear ’em talkin’, but not close enough to shoot, did you hear where they were goin’?”

“No,” Foley said.

"Cheyenne," Mabel said.

Roach jerked his head around to stare at her. "Cheyenne? How do you know that?"

"One of the women told me," Mabel answered.

"Well, I'll be . . ." Roach started, disgusted with the both of them now. "You two have cost me time, time I coulda been using to catch up with that bastard." He paused for a moment, thinking about the things he needed to get in the saddle without delaying longer. Then he shot another question at Foley. "Red bandanna, was he wearin' a red bandanna?"

"I don't know," Foley stammered, "I didn't take no notice."

"He was wearin' a red bandanna," Mabel said.

"Damn," Roach cursed, certain without a doubt that it was the man he sought, so he brought his attention back to getting under way as soon as possible. He was low on every kind of supplies, as well as ammunition, and he wanted enough to last however long it might take him to track the rifleman down. He was also out of money. His share of the money stolen in the stage holdup at Hat Creek was all gone—a good portion of it spent right there at Foley's. But the lack of money didn't bother him at the moment, because he wasn't planning to pay for anything. "What else did they tell you?" he asked Mabel.

"Nothin'," she answered.

He nodded slowly, trying to determine if there was anything else they could tell him. When nothing came to mind, he reached over and drew his pistol. Foley watched with only a smidgen of curiosity as Roach casually pulled the hammer back. One moment later, his bored expression changed to one of stunned horror as the gun was turned on him, and he carried the shocked expression to eternity when the pistol discharged.

Mabel dropped her coffee cup and screamed, not a piercing scream, more akin to the uncontrolled yelp a dog would make, and she backed away from the smirking outlaw. He watched her, apparently in no need of haste, until her back came up against the wall. Her brain was unable to make sense of what had just happened. She could not speak as she stared down at her husband's body, halfway expecting him to get up again. "What did you do?" she finally blurted out in horror.

He found the question somewhat amusing. "Kinda speaks for itself, don't it?" he answered while watching her closely for any sign of retribution. When she continued to press her body against the log wall, he said, "I'm gonna need a slew of supplies and ammunition, and that horse of yours to tote it. And I'm fresh outta money right now."

Gradually recovering her ability to speak, she cried, "You didn't have no need to shoot Bill.

You coulda just robbed us and run, like the coyote you are, instead of leavin' me a widow out here alone."

"You're right. I wasn't thinkin' about you bein' left here alone. You might as well go with Foley." The pistol discharged a second time and she crumpled against the wall. He got up from the table and walked over to see if she was dead. Finding that she was still breathing, he put a bullet in her forehead. "I reckon that makes us even for you and that damn husband of yours trying to cut me outta my share of that gold."

Aware that time was once again his enemy, he went through the shelves in the store, pulling out everything he thought he might need for an extended period of time. There was no telling how long this chase was going to take, but he was determined to hunt Red Bandanna down, if it took a lifetime. The gold would be icing on the cake. When he had a pile of goods stacked in the middle of the floor of the size he figured a horse could carry, he went down to the barn to get his and Foley's horses. In the tack room, he found a rigging for a packsaddle that Foley had evidently used at some time to haul goods back to his store. It looked as if it had not been used recently, and it struck him that Foley had only one horse. "Maybe he *was* out chasin' wild mustangs," Roach said, and laughed at his joke.

• • •

They had gotten an early start in the morning, planning to reach Chugwater Station before noontime. "Provided Mabel Foley knew what she was talkin' about when she told you and Ardella how far it is," Cam had said. "We can rest the horses there, and you can spend a little of your money and eat at the inn she said was there. Course, that's up to you. I'm gettin' by just fine on your cookin'."

"Is that so?" Mary replied playfully. "Well, I'd like to have someone fix me a good dinner for a change." The thought of sleeping in a real bed again was very appealing as well. It would make for another short day if she decided to stay over for the night, but she felt like treating them all, since there seemed no longer to be a threat of being attacked at any moment. "We'll see when we get to the stage stop," she decided.

"Yes, ma'am, boss lady," Cam responded, feeling the pressure of predators less as well. After sending Foley running for home without his rifle, he felt there would be no others to deal with, having apparently lost the two who had been following them back in the Laramie Mountains. There should be no threat upon them while they were resting at Chugwater Station.

Pushing on through the morning, riding through barren, treeless country littered with odd-shaped piles of earth and sandstone that resembled ruins of ancient structures, the small party of females and guide seemed to be as a small ship upon a vast sea of sand and clay. Toward midday, they sighted yellow bluffs ahead as they descended into the valley of the Chug, for which the creek was named. There was grass now, a striking contrast to the territory they had traveled since leaving Foley's Place, and Cam remembered having been told that the valley, some one hundred miles long, was a favorite wintering place for cattle. Upon reaching Chugwater Stage Station, Mary and the girls were thrilled to see trees again. Willow, box elders, and cottonwoods grew along the creek banks, and as Mabel Foley had told them, there was a working ranch as well as what appeared to be an inn for stagecoach passengers. Mary didn't wait for Cam to lead; she headed straight for the inn.

Ardella pulled up beside Cam, who had paused to look the place over before riding in. "I believe Mary's had enough of the saddle," she said with a chuckle. "Looks like we made it all right. I expect we lost our two friends for good."

"Looks that way," Cam said, and nudged his horse to follow Mary and the girls.

Mary supposed the Chugwater Inn could be classified as a hotel of sorts by a most generous appraiser, but it looked good to her after her adventures on the high plains. Perhaps it would be better described as a boardinghouse with a couple of extra rooms built onto the rear. These two rooms were seldom used since there were ample accommodations for stage passengers in the main house. But it was these two rooms that Mary requested, because they were handy when it came to unloading the packhorses and transferring the load they carried to the rooms. “You folks could have your pick of the rooms,” Sarah Kelly told Mary. “There ain’t nobody in ’em right now. The only time we rent ’em is when the stage lays over here for the night, and that’ll be tonight when the stage pulls in from the north. We ain’t but about fifty miles from Cheyenne, so they only stop overnight on their way back from Deadwood.”

“Why is that,” Ardella couldn’t resist asking, “if it ain’t but fifty miles?”

“Because the stage doesn’t usually get here until late in the afternoon,” Sarah answered.

“I shoulda figured that out,” Ardella said.

“We’ll take the two rooms out back,” Mary told Sarah. “They’ll do just fine.”

“Yes, ma’am,” Sarah replied. “The rooms in the main house are a little bit nicer, but I reckon it’ll be a lot easier for your husband to carry some of your things off your packhorses into those two on the ground floor.”

“He’s not my husband,” Mary was quick to correct her. “The rooms are for us and my daughters—and they’ll be nice enough after sleeping on the ground for so many days. He'll be sleeping in the barn with the horses." When Sarah raised her eyebrows in response to that remark, Mary said, "It's his idea."

"He's just like Long Sam," Ardella offered, "worried more about the horses than the folks ridin' 'em."

Cam was always concerned about the horses, but not at this station. In fact, he was somewhat relieved of the worry about Mary's gold, thinking there was very little danger of being robbed at this point. No one knew what they were carrying on the packhorses. There had been no one around to see them unloading the packs into the rooms. The simple reason he had not insisted on a room for himself was that he didn't see the sense in paying for a room when he could sleep in the stable for nothing—or for twenty-five cents at the most. In fact, he was giving some thought toward loading Mary, Ardella, and the girls on the stage to Cheyenne when it came through. With no tipoff to anyone that there would be over a hundred pounds of gold dust on board, he seriously doubted there was much danger of a holdup. Most of the worry about holdups was in the territory between the Black Hills and Hat Creek. There was always a risk, but not a very big one, he figured. He would talk it over with Mary. The question he had not settled on, if they did take the stage to Cheyenne, was whether he should go with them or bring the horses along after them as quickly as he could. He could not escape his feeling of responsibility toward not only Mary's safety, but also the safe delivery of her gold. *Too much thinking will give me a headache,* he thought. *I'll see what she has to say about it.*

Supper that evening found the ladies in good spirits, Mary because of a semblance of normal living with a roof over her head and four walls surrounding her. Ardella, on the other hand, was always in high spirits, and would have been had she been bunking in the stable with Cam. When Cam walked into the dining room, Emma immediately summoned him to sit beside her, which he did. They had seated themselves around one end of a table long enough to handle a dozen or more. The food was good, although not fancy, but to this party fresh off the plains, it bordered on exotic, with beef, fried potatoes, field peas, and biscuits, with a slice of honey cake for dessert.

After Grace and Emma asked to be excused, and Mary told them not to wander away from the inn's front porch, the adults remained at the table to drink coffee and consider what they should do from this point on. Mary was very much in favor of taking the stage in to Cheyenne, but there was still some concern about the safety of her fortune without Cam on hand to watch over it. They had come so far, and overcome so many dangers, that she felt that she would be devastated if she lost it this close to a major town and a place to secure her deposit. She had still not decided when they were interrupted by the sound of the southbound stage thundering into the station. They got up to witness the arrival, for usually the drivers liked to give the folks in the towns and changeover stations a big show by whipping up the horses to a gallop before dragging them to a sliding halt.

Out on the front porch, they looked up the lane to the stage road to see the horses racing into the station with two familiar figures on the seat. Larry Bacon bent over the reins, driving the weary horses with the slap of his reins, while Bob Allen yelled encouragement in a singsong manner. The horses were pulled to a stop in front of the inn and Bob called out, "Chugwater Station! We'll be stayin' overnight. Step right on inside and Mrs. Kelly will fix you up with a room and some supper." He climbed down and opened the coach door, holding it while the passengers disembarked. When the last one stepped down from the coach, he stuck his head inside to make sure he hadn't missed anyone before closing the door. Glancing up toward the porch then, he stopped and muttered, "Well, I'll be. . . . Larry, lookee here."

Larry looked over to see the smiling faces of Cam, Mary, and the two little girls, plus another grinning lady he didn't recall seeing before.

"Well, I'll be . . ." he echoed. He hopped down to join Bob on the ground to help passengers with their luggage. "Didn't know if we'd ever see you folks again," he called out.

After taking care of the passengers, they moved over to shake hands with Cam and give Mary a courteous nod of the head. "What are you folks doin' here?" Bob asked, surprised that Cam was still accompanying Mary and her two daughters. "Did you find your brother-in-law?"

"We found him," Mary answered, then introduced Ardella. "This is a friend of ours," she said, "Ardella, this is Bob Allen and Larry Bacon. They drove the stage we were on coming up from Cheyenne."

"The one that got held up?" Ardella asked.

"That's the one," Bob replied, "and if it hadn'ta been for ol' Cam here we'da all been bleachin' our bones out on the prairie now." He looked at Cam and grinned. "Which way you folks headin' now?"

"Cheyenne," Cam answered. "Mary's thinkin' 'bout takin' the stage on in. You run into any road agents between here and Cheyenne lately?"

"No," Bob said, "not for a long time, not since the army started sendin' regular patrols along the road." There was no further comment from either Cam or Mary, so Bob asked, "You folks goin' inside for supper?"

"We've already eaten," Mary replied, "but we

can go in with you and have some more coffee, and we'll tell you what we've been doing since we saw you last."

"That sounds good," Larry remarked. "I'll join you as soon as I drive the horses down to the barn."

"My Lord in heaven," Bob Allen remarked after he had heard about all that had happened to them since they had said good-bye at Custer City. He gave Cam a shake of his head. "So you're still healin' up from that bullet you took, huh? Well, you look spunky as ever. Don't he, Larry?" Larry answered with a grin. Bob then turned his attention to Ardella and commented, "And you lost your cabin and everythin'. I know that smarts some, but you're hooked up with some fine folks now."

"Ardella's going to help me run a boarding-house in Fort Collins," Mary said. "We're going to build a brand-new building, have a big kitchen to feed our boarders, and everything."

"That sounds mighty nice," Bob said, then turned to Ardella. "Are you gonna do the cookin'?"

"Lord no," she replied. "We wouldn't wanna run the customers off. I ain't much of a cook. Long Sam, that was my husband's name, Long Sam Swift, he used to say he'd et road apples better'n my biscuits."

Bob's eyes lit up and looked back at Mary. "I know where you can hire a jim-dandy cook, a Chinese woman—"

"Japanese," Larry interrupted.

"Japanese," Bob repeated. "And she's one helluva cook." Then he remembered. "You've et her cookin' before, at Hat Creek."

"Atsuko," Mary said, remembering the name. "You're right, she's a good cook, but what makes you think she wants to leave Hat Creek?"

"Just from talkin' to her," Bob said. "She's ready to live somewhere closer to a town."

"He's fixin' to ask her to marry him," Larry said with a chuckle. "That's why she might be leavin' Hat Creek." He prodded Bob on the shoulder. "But you're tryin' to get her to go to Cheyenne. You don't want her to go to Fort Collins in Colorado Territory."

"Maybe we'll talk about it later on when we're farther along with our plans," Mary said, but the idea intrigued her. Atsuko's cooking could be a strong draw for customers.

The conversation turned to other things then, and continued long after supper was finished. When it was time to put the children to bed, the party broke up. While Mary and Ardella took the girls back to their rooms, Cam let himself be persuaded to go with Larry and Bob to the small saloon at the front corner of the dining room. "Cam," Ardella called after him, "wouldn't be a bad idea for you to stop by the room and let's take a look at that wound, if you ain't gonna be too late. I ain't gonna wait up for you."

"All right," Cam said. "I'm just gonna take time for one drink."

"Now I know you'd best watch your step," Bob baited him when they were out of earshot of the others. "That ol' gal there might demand more'n you're holdin'." He and Larry laughed at the picture that inspired. Cam just shook his head as if exasperated.

Bob's question regarding the cooking caused Ardella's mind to question. Exactly what did Mary have in mind for her? Was she thinking of her as a possible cook? How long would Mary be willing to take her in? She wasn't getting any younger. There had been no discussion about her role in Mary's plans, and now that the immediate threat of danger was past, maybe things would be different. If Mary knew the real story about her marriage to Long Sam Swift, would she still want her to help run her boardinghouse? In the quiet of her room, she let her mind go back through the years, as she had done so many times before.

Long Sam Swift did cut a rather impressive figure of a man when they were married. But Ardella was an innocent girl of fourteen, and Long Sam was a mature man of twenty-seven.

The first few years of their marriage were fairly pleasant, she supposed, although she was little more than a squaw to him as they camped alone all over the territory. After a while, the novelty of his bride wore off, and his true nature began to emerge. As he aged, he became more and more intolerant of her slightest mistake, and her collection of scars began to multiply with his frequent beatings. She stood his abuse for thirty years, before deciding it was time she ended it. One night he came home drunk without the supplies he was supposed to have traded for his pelts. It was not the first time he had done so, causing them to have to do without basic staples, like coffee, flour, and sugar. She complained and received a broken nose for her trouble. The actual cause of Long Sam Swift's death was an iron skillet applied to the side of his head with every ounce of strength her sturdy body could muster, and not the arrow of a Pawnee warrior. She had rehearsed the story of his death by a war party so many times in her mind that she had almost come to the point where she believed it was true. The years that followed his death were her happiest, and she found that she was very good company for herself. Times became more difficult as the years passed, however. The firing pin in his rifle broke and she didn't know how to fix it, so she threw it off the cliff at the end of the rock ledge below her cabin, the same place she had rolled his body over the edge to drop to the bottom of the canyon. Five years after Long Sam's death, his horse died, leaving her on foot and with a shotgun, good only for small game. But that was enough. There was enough small game to keep her supplied with meat, most of it caught with snares she taught herself to fashion. And then Cam and Mary and the two children wandered into her world, and she suddenly missed being with people. Contrary to what she had repeatedly told herself, she did not want to die an old woman alone. And she realized that, more than anything else, she wanted to go with Mary and the children. She would be a good aunt to Grace and Emma. Being around them made her feel young again. *What if Mary finds out I killed my husband?* she thought, then relaxed her mind. *How in hell is she going to find out, if I don't tell her?* "We'll make a go of it," she said.

"What?" Mary asked, entering the room just then.

"Nothin'," Ardella said, and gave her a big smile. "I was just thinkin' how I can't wait to get workin' on your boardin'house with you."

Mary answered her smile with one in return. "Yes, we'll make a go of it."

"That's what I just said," Ardella remarked. "Are the girls in bed?"

"Yep. They're just waiting for their aunt Ardella to come tuck 'em in."

"Well, I best not keep 'em waitin'."

• • •

"Damn!" Cam grimaced as he replaced the shot glass on the bar. "It's been so long since I took a drink of likker I forgot how much it burns." He and his two friends stood at the small counter at the front end of the dining room. The bar was not a proper one, but served the purpose with a counter of wide planks resting on two beer barrels. Cam waved Larry away when he held the bottle over his glass for another shot. "No, thanks. One drink of that stuff is enough to suit me for a while."

"You know," Bob commented, "I heard Mary tellin' about how she was gonna build her a boardin'house, and what's her friend's name—Carmella?—is gonna help her run it. But I didn't hear her say nothin' 'bout you."

"Ardella," Cam corrected.

"Yeah, Ardella," Bob said, "but I didn't hear nothin' 'bout you."

"Yeah, Cam," Larry chimed in, "you're still ridin' with her. What are you gonna do? You gonna keep the lady happy every night after she's worked all day?"

"Yeah," Bob echoed. "Has ol' Mary put you out to stud?"

"You know," Cam told the two grinning faces, "the two of you ain't got one bit brighter since the last time I saw you." He shook his head in mock disgust.

"Well, what are you aimin' to do?" Bob asked. "I ain't never heard you say. When you folks left us, you was just gonna guide her up to see her brother-in-law."

"I don't know," Cam answered, "drift, I reckon. I made a bargain with her that I'd see that she got where she wanted to go. So I reckon that's Fort Collins. After that, I ain't got no plans. Hell, you heard what happened to her brother-in-law. Do you think I shoulda just said, 'So long, good luck' and left her and those two little girls there?"

"No, I reckon not," Bob replied. "I was just japin' you a little bit. I'da done the same as you. So would Larry. I didn't mean nothin' by it." It was obvious that he had touched a raw nerve in Cam's mind.

Cam recovered at once, realizing that he might have shown a hint of irritation. "I'm sorry. I guess I'm gettin' a little touchy." Hearing himself answer Bob's questions made him realize that he really didn't have any plans after Mary and the kids were safe. He hadn't even thought about the day when he'd be through with them. When he really thought about it, the prospect made him feel kind of melancholy. He kinda liked being Emma's *uncle Cam,* but what the hell would he do in Fort Collins? He had no trade of any kind. All he knew was cattle and horses, and he wasn't ready to go back to that just yet. He had money from the weapons and saddle he had sold, an extra horse that was worth a little, plus he knew Mary would insist upon paying him handsomely for his services, no matter how much he protested that his price was forty dollars. "I reckon it's time I turned in for the night," he finally said. "What time will you be pullin' outta here in the mornin'?"

"Not till after breakfast," Larry said. "We've got a short day tomorrow."

Cam nodded. "Well, I'll see you in the mornin'," he said, and left to go bed down with the horses. He was almost positive that Mary was going to take the stage to Cheyenne, but he would have to wait until he saw her at breakfast to decide if he was going to be on it with her.

He walked out the front door of the inn and had started toward the stables before he remembered he had told Ardella that he would stop by her room so she could change the dressing on his wound. Hesitating, he almost decided to skip it, for already the wound was healing to his satisfaction and he was stronger every day. A slight smile crossed his lips then as he pictured the scolding he would suffer from Ardella in the morning. *What the hell?* he thought. *It won't hurt to put a clean bandage on it.* He did an about-face and walked around to the back door.

The two rooms that had been added to the original building were connected to it by a short hallway and an outside door in the middle. Cam took the two steps to the door, went to Ardella's room, and rapped on the door, quietly, so as not to wake Mary and the girls if they were sleeping. Ardella opened the door at once. "Come on in, Cam. I was startin' to think I was gonna have to go drag you outta the barn to take a look at that wound. Come on over here and set down on the bed. I got a pitcher of clean water and some fresh bandages. Mrs. Kelly gave me an old sheet to use for bandages." When he had parked himself on the edge of the bed, she continued. "Take that shirt off so I can get at it."

She proceeded to untie the old bandage and went to work with a washcloth to clean away some of the dried blood. "Won't be long before it won't need no bandage," she said. "You heal quick, just like Long Sam. The thing that helps it to heal fast like that is that poultice I slapped on there when I found you."

"I reckon," Cam said, although he was not convinced it should deserve much of the credit.

She finished cleaning the area around the wound and wrapped a fresh bandage across his chest and shoulder. "There you go. You can put your shirt back on now." He was in the midst of pulling it on when the door suddenly opened and Mary walked in. "Oh!" she exclaimed. "I didn't know . . ." Obviously embarrassed, she didn't finish her statement. "I should have knocked."

Ardella threw back her head and laughed at the shocked expression on Mary's face. "Well, that's all right. We was through, anyway, weren't we, Cam?"

"I reckon," Cam replied, with no clue as to what Ardella found so hilarious, "soon as I get my shirt on. Then I reckon I'll leave you ladies to get to bed." Walking past Mary, he said, "I'll see you in the mornin' at breakfast. Have you pretty much decided to ride the stage on in to Cheyenne?" Mary nodded. "We can decide in the mornin' what you wanna do with the horses."

After the door closed, Ardella suggested to Mary that she might want Cam to take the horses to Cheyenne. "You'd most likely get a better price for 'em there. They might take 'em off your hands here, but I doubt they'd give you much money for 'em." She studied Mary's face closely, for she had read her first reaction when she walked into the room and found Cam getting his shirt on. To Ardella, there was no mistaking Mary's concern. "Maybe you'd rather get rid of the horses here, so Cam can ride the stage with us."

"No," Mary replied at once, then paused while she thought the matter over. Frightened by her reaction to the scene she at first thought she was walking in on, she feared she had developed an interest in her young guide beyond that of a paid employee. She promptly lectured herself that her reaction had been ridiculous to even imagine. Ardella was merely changing Cam's bandage. The thought of anything beyond that was what Ardella found to be so amusing. But the discovery of deeper feelings for her soft-spoken protector troubled her a great deal, especially since she could not imagine a successful outcome for such a union. After a few more moments of thought on the matter, she told Ardella what she had decided. "I'm thinking of giving Cam those horses, as part of the payment I owe him. If we find we need horses when we get to Fort Collins, we'll get them there. I don't think we need Cam's protection anymore. From here, into Cheyenne at least, we aren't supposed to risk much danger of road agents. And if we do, I feel confident with Bob and Larry to see us through."

"Plus, you got me and my rifle," Ardella interjected, "unless you're fixin' to turn me loose here, too."

"No, no," Mary quickly responded. "I'm counting on you to stay with me. I need your help and your strength." She patted the plaintive woman on the shoulder. "Besides, I couldn't deprive my two girls of their aunt Ardella."

"Well, I'll do my best to look out for you," Ardella assured her, "but if a time comes when you think I ain't pullin' my share of the load, all you have to do is tell me and I'll leave."

"Don't even think such a thing. You're stuck with me."

Chapter 13

Cam was at breakfast half an hour before the women showed up with the girls, and happened to be there at the same time as Bob and Larry. He took the opportunity to advise the two of the "luggage" they would be transporting, although he chose not to tell them of the real value of it. "The lady got a little bit of gold from her husband's interest in the mine, and that's what she's countin' on to set herself up in business, so I'd sure hate to see her lose it."

"We ain't got no strongbox on this coach," Larry said, "it bein' one of the small ones. But I don't think we'll run into any trouble between here and Cheyenne. We ain't for a long time now."

"You ain't ridin' with 'em, then?" Bob asked.

"Reckon not," Cam replied. "I'll be comin' on behind you with the horses."

"Well, me and Larry will take care of 'em," Bob assured him.

"If you do run into trouble, don't forget you can count on Ardella. She has a rifle and knows how to use it, so you might wanna let her carry it with her in the coach."

"Good to know," Bob said. "I'll sure keep her in mind." He looked right and left to make sure there was no one else to hear. "She looks tough enough to whip a grizzly."

Cam chuckled. "I don't think she'd back down from one, and that's a fact."

"Well, we'd best get movin', Larry," Bob said, pushing back from the table. "Sure good seein' you again, Cam."

"I'll load Mary's things when you get hitched up," Cam told them as they were leaving. He started to get up, but Mary, Ardella, and the girls came in the back door. Emma ran ahead to greet Cam, so he had to stay a few moments to hear what was on her mind after a night's sleep. "I just finished my breakfast," he told Mary and Ardella. "I'm thinkin' I can load your things on the stage as soon as they're ready to go." He wondered at the odd little smile Ardella favored him with as he spoke, but dismissed it as just one of the rambunctious woman's many eccentricities. Mary, on the other hand, had a definite look of concern on her face.

"Cam," Mary said, still standing while the others sat down at the table, "I need to talk to you a minute, back in my room."

Curious, he replied, "Sure. Is somethin' wrong?"

"No," she said, "nothing's wrong. I just want to talk to you in private." She looked around her at the half dozen passengers filing in around the long table, then turned and walked back to the door. He followed her out the door and down the short hallway to her room.

"I see you pulled all your gold sacks out in the middle of the floor," he commented upon entering the room. "Where'd you have it, under the bed?"

"Yes, we did," she confessed with a slight smile. Then the smile disappeared immediately as her face took on a serious facade. "Cam, I think it's time to release you from your obligation to watch over me and my girls. I think we'll be fine from here on, and it's not fair to delay you any further from where you were going when we first met."

He wasn't sure what she was telling him at first, but then it began to sink in. "You mean you're firin' me?" he asked.

She reacted at once. "No, don't say that. I'm not firing you. It's just that I think we'll be safe from here on in, and I don't want to bind you to any sense of obligation you might feel you have. You should be free to go on with your life, the life I interrupted with my troubles. In your efforts to keep me and my children safe, you've been shot twice. I'll never forget that, and I'll always be grateful to you for coming to my aid when I so desperately needed someone I could trust. I think Emma may have been right when she called you an angel."

He was more confused than hurt. He knew there was no reason to fire him before he saw them safely to Fort Collins, but it felt as though he was being fired. "Hell, Mary, you're the one callin' the shots. You don't have to worry about lettin' me go. I just thought I'd feel better knowin' you were safely in Fort Collins. But you're probably right, there ain't much chance you'll run into any trouble between here and Cheyenne, anyway. I'll help you load up your possibles on the stage. Bob and Larry oughta be able to tell you where you can deposit that gold. You've got some horses to do somethin' with. I'll still take them down there for you."

"I'm giving you the horses," she said. "I don't need them, and I think you certainly deserve them." Before he could comment on that, she continued. "And I'm giving you the payment I promised."

"Mary, you don't owe me anythin' but the forty dollars we agreed on, and you really ought'n owe me that, since you're givin' me a lot more'n that in those horses and saddles."

"I owe you my life, and the lives of my babies. How can I ever repay that?"

He smiled and said, "You don't owe me anythin'. We're square. Now, you'd best get back in there and get some breakfast before they throw it to the hogs." He walked over and held the door for her. She shook her head sadly, knowing she was leaving someone who meant so much to her. Before she walked out the door, she paused, went up on her tiptoes, and kissed him on the cheek. Then she hurried up the hall, not trusting herself to look back at him.

When Bob Allen walked into the dining room and announced that the stage was going to leave in thirty minutes, everyone at the table hurried to their rooms to get their belongings. While the passengers had been eating their breakfast, Cam went down to the stable to get what odds and ends had been left there with the packs. He put them on one of the horses and led it over to the back door of the inn. As a favor to Cam, Larry drove the coach around to the back to make the loading easier. Cam unloaded the luggage off the packhorse, then helped the women load the items from their rooms. Also helping in the loading, Bob soon realized that there was quite a bit more weight than he had assumed. He cast a suspicious eye in Cam's direction and commented, "I'd say the lady came away with more than a little bit of gold from that mine. No wonder those outlaws were chasing after you. Maybe we shoulda been drivin' one of the Concord coaches and six horses, instead of this one and four horses." A good portion of Mary's fortune was packed in the front boot, under the driver's box. The rest was packed in the rear boot, causing some of the passengers' luggage to have to ride on top, along with two colorful suitcases with bullet holes.

"I'd say she's got enough to build a right nice boardin'house," Cam replied. "It's her whole future, now that her husband's gone, so take care of her, Bob."

"I will," Bob said.

When everything was loaded, Cam checked the canvas cover to make sure it was secure. Unknown to him, it was all there except for one bag of gold dust. He failed to notice Mary when she walked over to the packhorse he had tied to the stair rail at the back stoop, and slipped the missing sack inside an empty bag on one of the packs.

When all was ready, Cam stood by while the passengers boarded the coach. Ardella gave him a hug, then climbed up on top where she could breathe, she said, rifle in hand. Emma and Grace each gave Cam a hug, and Emma had to be pried loose from his leg by her mother. "Why aren't you going with us?" Emma wanted to know.

"I got other things I gotta do right now," Cam told her. "I'll come see you when I get a chance."

"Promise?"

"I promise. I'll come see you," he said, with no idea when that might be, if ever. He knew of no other reason to go to Fort Collins.

The last to get on board was Mary Bishop. She smiled at Cam and whispered, "Thank you for everything."

He nodded in reply and touched a finger to his

hat brim as he stepped back away from the coach and looked up to meet Bob's gaze and one quick nod confirming his promise to take care of her. He stood there in the yard and watched the stage depart until he could no longer hear Larry's shouted commands to his horses and the coach rolled out of sight. It was an odd sensation he was aware of, and he realized that he had never missed anyone since his mother died. But this feeling he now experienced was an empty feeling, as he imagined it would be if one lost a family. *Uncle Cam,* he thought, and smiled when he thought of Emma and Grace—and Mary and Ardella. They *had* been his family for the short timc thcy were together. *I'm getting downright sentimental,* he told himself, sighed, and returned to the back stoop to get the packhorse. "I'm free to go where I damn well please again," he told the sorrel. He would have to think about that and decide if he wanted to go back to the Black Hills, or head for Montana maybe. "First, I gotta see about the horses." He led the sorrel back to the stable to decide what to do.

He cut his six horses out of the corral and tied them to the rail while he evaluated them to decide which one he would ride and which one to keep as a packhorse. The other four he planned to sell, along with the three extra saddles. There was not much time spent in selecting his saddle horse; he would keep the dun he had been riding. As for his packhorse, he settled on the other sorrel, thinking it the stronger of the two, so he went about trans-ferring the pack rig from the one he had used that morning. It occurred to him as he removed the straps that Mary had forgotten to pay him the forty dollars they had agreed upon. He had to chuckle at the thought, for she had been so adamant that she was going to pay him. It didn't matter to him that she had forgotten. He would have helped her for nothing, anyway. And besides, he was well paid in horseflesh. Thinking there was nothing but a couple of empty cloth sacks left on the packhorse, he pulled the rig off and almost dropped it. "What the hell?" he muttered, then saw where the weight came from. "Well, I'll be . . . She forgot one." He immediately thought to throw his saddle on the dun and chase the stage down, but he hesitated. He had unloaded the dust from the packhorse, and he was sure he had loaded every sack on the stage. Shaking his head with a sigh and a chuckle, he realized that she had not forgotten after all.

The next bit of business was the sale of his horses, so he went into the stable looking for Lou, the man charged with running it. He found him in the tack room, working on a harness. Right from the start, Lou didn't show much interest in buying any horses, but he walked outside with Cam to take a closer look. "I'm gonna be honest with you, mister," Lou told him. "Mr. Kelly ain't gonna be interested in buying any more horses. He raises his own, and he's got a lot more than he needs to run this ranch. You can talk to him about it, and he might give you a little somethin' to take 'em off your hands, but it wouldn't be much." When Cam grimaced in response, Lou suggested an alternative. "You'd be a sight better off if you was to take those horses down to Cheyenne. They're always lookin' for good horses, and they'll give you a decent price for 'em."

Cam scratched his chin while he thought about it. Cheyenne wasn't in the direction he was figuring on going. There had to be someplace else where he could sell them—Custer City, maybe, or Deadwood. He hesitated. Cheyenne was a lot closer.

Seeing him struggling with the decision, Lou said, "Fellow to see in Cheyenne is Jim Pylant. He's got a ranch right outside of town—sells a lot of horses to the army. He's most likely your best bet."

"What the hell?" Cam decided. "I ain't in a hurry to go anywhere, and that ain't but fifty miles or so. Jim Pylant, huh? I might as well get the most I can for the horses." A factor that figured in with his decision making was the fact that he was now in possession of the most wealth he had ever had in his entire life. He wasn't sure of the value of the sack of dust that Mary had slipped into his saddlebag, but it had to be considerable. He could just give the horses away if he so chose, but that would go strictly against his nature. He had been forced to scratch out a meager living ever since he was big enough to ride a horse, and he wasn't going to change his respect for money at this point. Gold dust was good to have, but it ran out, just like everything else. "Well, thank you for the advice," he said to Lou. "I reckon I'm goin' to Cheyenne."

With thoughts of missing his adopted family already in the back of his mind, he set out along the stage road to Cheyenne, leading a string of horses behind him. It was still early on a clear, bright day, and it felt good to be riding without having to constantly peer over his shoulder lest someone should overtake him to do harm to him or those he cared for. There was no need for hurry. It was going to take him two days, because of the extra horses he led, so he figured he might as well make it two leisurely days. Crossing Horse Creek well before noon, he let the horses drink, then pushed on, following the stage road. There was still daylight left when he struck Lodgepole Creek and the horses were showing signs of tiring, so he followed the creek a little way upstream to make his camp.

Cotton Roach slow-walked his horses into the yard at Chugwater Station, his eyes constantly darting back and forth warily for any sign of the people he trailed. It was already dark and his horses were in need of rest, since they had been ridden hard all day. He wasn't sure how far behind he was, but he was going to have to stop for the night, so he decided he might as well stay in the inn. He could use a good meal, paid for with some money he had found at Foley's, and he might get an idea how far behind Red Bandanna he was, if they had happened to stop here as well.

He nudged his weary horses toward the stable, where he saw a man at a corner of the corral, pumping water into a watering trough. Lou looked up as the white-haired stranger rode up to him. "Howdy," he said. "You look like you've been ridin' hard. You thinkin' about puttin' 'em up for the night?"

"Maybe," Roach replied. "How late do they serve supper over there at the hotel?"

"Oh, it ain't too late. They'll fix you a plate even if they've started to clean up."

"I reckon I'll leave my horses here, then," Roach said, and dismounted. Lou looked quickly away when Roach glanced up and caught him staring at his bound-up hand. Something about the sinister scowl on the stranger's face told him it was best not to ask questions about it. While Roach removed his saddlebags, he said, "I'm lookin' for some folks, a man travelin' with a woman and two young'uns, leading some horses—mighta had somebody else with 'em—thought they mighta stopped here."

Lou didn't answer right away. Judging by the stranger's appearance, that shock of white hair that reached his shoulders and eyes like marble chips, he wasn't sure he should. Seeing his reluctance, Roach said, "He stole them horses and I've been trailin' him for a couple of days."

Lou was surprised. "Are you a lawman?"

"That's right," Roach said.

"Well, I'll be . . . That feller was here, all right, couple of days ago. I never woulda took him for a horse thief, though—seemed like a nice feller, and those folks he was with—"

"Wearin' a red bandanna tied around his neck?" Roach asked.

"Yeah, I think he was," Lou said, pausing to remember. "If that ain't somethin'. Goes to show you can't judge a man by his looks."

"Which way'd they head outta here?"

"The women and two little girls got on the stage to Cheyenne," Lou said. "The feller you're lookin' for rode outta here on the stage road, and he was leadin' your horses."

"The women took the stage, eh?" That was something he had not anticipated. He was thinking about the gold they were carrying, and wondered if it went on the stage or with Red Bandanna. If it went on the stage, that meant it was already out of his reach. It was enough to frustrate him, especially when he was so certain that he and Cheney had them cornered on that mountain where Cheney broke his neck. But he still had the one driving force to keep him on his quest to find the man who had ruined his hand. He was determined to have his revenge, and that might be more important to him than sacks of gold. “I’ll go get me some supper and a room,” he told Lou. “I’ll be leavin’ early in the mornin’.” He had no way of knowing how far ahead of him Cam might be, but his horses were in no shape to start out after him tonight, so he resigned himself to the possibility of a longer hunt. There was a chance he might pick up Cam’s trail, but he would be lucky to do so, since there were many tracks on the stage road. It seemed pretty obvious to him that Cam was headed for Cheyenne, just as Mabel Foley had said, and it figured that he would follow the road, especially so if he was no longer carrying a fortune in gold.

“Right,” Lou replied. “I’ll be here before sunup, always am.” He watched the man depart, saddle-bags over one shoulder, rifle in hand, as he walked toward the inn. “No, sir,” Lou mumbled, “you sure can’t judge a man by his looks. That’s one lawman I wouldn’t want comin’ after me.”

It was still early in the morning when Cam left Lodgepole Creek for the short ride into Cheyenne. When he arrived, he was amazed to see how much the town had grown since the last time he had seen it. The first thing he came to on the main street was a stable, so he pulled up in front of it and dismounted. "Good day to ya," a short, gray-whiskered man with a bald head greeted him as he came walking out of the stable. "You lookin' to stable them horses?"

"Howdy," Cam returned. "No, I'm lookin' for a fellow who has a ranch near town, name of Jim Pylant. You wouldn't happen to know where that is, would you?"

"Well, sure I do," the stable owner answered. "Everybody knows where Jim Pylant's spread is."

When he went no further, Cam prompted him. "Everybody but me," he said.

"Right, except you," the owner agreed, and laughed. "Excuse me, young feller. I reckon it's too early in the day to get my brain workin'. I figured you might be in town for the cattlemen's meetin'. That's where Jim Pylant is."

"Where's that?" Cam asked.

"Over at the Cheyenne Star." He turned and pointed to a saloon about halfway down the main street. "Jim left his horse here."

Cam thought that over for a few moments, trying to decide what to do. "A cattlemen's meetin', you say?"

"Yeah, it ain't a big to-do, just three or four of the bigger outfits havin' a meetin' to talk about boundaries and whatnot, so as not to step on each other's toes, I reckon. They're meetin' in the back room at the Star. Just a chance to see which one of

’em can hold the most whiskey, if you ask me.” He paused for a moment while he watched Cam deciding. “If you’re just lookin’ for his ranch so you can deliver those horses, I can tell you how to get there.”

“Well, I’m hopin’ to sell four of these horses, and I heard he buys horses,” Cam said. “Course, I’m lookin’ to sell those saddles, too, since I won’t have no use for ’em if I ain’t got horses to go under ’em, or fannies to sit on ’em.”

The bald little man laughed again. “Well, that makes sense. I couldn’t help wondering when I saw you leadin’ horses in with empty saddles—couldn’t help wonderin’ what happened to whoever was settin’ in the saddles.”

Cam smiled in response. “I reckon it does look kinda strange at that, but it ain’t what it looks like. The folks who were ridin’ in those three saddles took the stage in from Chugwater night before last, two ladies and two little girls.”

“I saw ’em,” the man exclaimed, “saw ’em when the stage rolled into town, with that one ol’ gal ridin’ on top of the coach with a rifle!” He paused at once and said, “Don’t mean no disrespect.” When Cam merely smiled, he went on. “My name’s Porter Thompson. Folks call me Smiley.”

“Cam Sutton,” he returned. “So they made it all right?”

“Yep,” Smiley replied, “and I know why you’re askin’. That one lady put a whole load of gold dust in the bank this mornin'. Mr. Proctor over at the bank said Bob Allen and Larry Bacon—they drive the stagecoach—sat up guardin' it all night at the stage office till the bank opened."

Cam smiled at the picture that created in his mind. "Well, it didn't take long for word to get out about what the lady was carryin', did it?"

"Hell, half the folks in town knew about it last night," Smiley said.

"How safe is her gold in that bank?" Cam asked, immediately concerned that, after all they had come through to get it to Cheyenne, it was now known by everyone in town to be sitting in a bank, waiting to be robbed.

"Safe enough," Smiley assured him. "Mr. Proctor's already hired a couple more guards, and the sheriff's gonna keep an eye on the bank, too, till they change it to paper money and ship the gold out on the train."

"How 'bout if I turn my horses out in the corral till I find out if I'm gonna stay in town or not?" Cam asked. Smiley nodded. "I'll go down to the saloon and see if I can get a chance to talk to Mr. Pylant."

"That'll be fine. You know, I buy horses from time to time. How much are you lookin' to get for them four?"

"Well, I don't know," Cam said. He paused to stroke his chin while he thought. "They're all good, sound horses, but I ain't lookin' to ask a lot for 'em—about fifty dollars apiece, I reckon."

"Whoa!" Smiley blurted as if shocked. "Two hundred dollars for the four of 'em? That's a little steep, ain't it? I mean, they ain't nothin' but plain ol' cow ponies."

"Maybe Pylant might look 'em over a little closer," Cam told him. "That bay is as strong a horse as a fellow could want, and that black one is a Morgan as far as I can tell. What would you give?"

"I don't know," Smiley said, then proceeded to look the horses over with a close eye. Although he tried, he could really find no obvious flaw in any of them. After another look at the bay's teeth, and an inspection of the gray's hooves, he finally stood back as if to look at them as a group. "I swear, that gray's got a wild look in his eye, kinda spookylike."

"He's the gentlest of the bunch, but he's strong as an ox," Cam commented, and he thought of the dappled gray gelding the first time he had seen him, with the black Spanish-style saddle and the scornful killer astride him. "What'll you give?" he asked again.

"I don't know," Smiley repeated, "a hundred dollars."

"Apiece?" Cam responded.

"Shit no!" Smiley blurted. "For all of 'em."

"Hundred and fifty, and I'll throw in the three saddles."

"Why, them saddles are pretty wore out," Smiley protested. "They ain't worth much."

"I expect I'd best go see if I can talk to Mr. Pylant. I've been told he pays a fair price for good horses," Cam said, and put a foot in the stirrup, preparing to mount.

"All right," Smiley said, "a hundred and fifty."

Cam took his foot back out of the stirrup, and extended his hand. They shook on it, and Smiley said, "I'll have to get you the money outta the bank. I don't keep that much money here in the stable. Whaddaya say I run over there before the bank closes and I'll meet you in the saloon afterwards and we'll have a drink?"

"Sounds fair to me," Cam said. "I'll help you take the saddles off the horses you just bought, and I might as well leave my two here for the night, too, since it looks like I'll be stayin' over." He pulled his saddle off the dun and relieved the packhorse of its small load, then stowed it all in the stall Smiley said would be his. "I'll go on over to the hotel and get myself a room. Then I'll meet you at the Cheyenne Star." He drew his rifle from the saddle sling, picked up his saddlebags, and started out across the street.

"I'll be there directly with your money," Smiley assured him.

Cam felt like treating himself for a change. His little adopted family had arrived in Cheyenne safely, Mary's gold was secured, and she was probably on her way to Fort Collins. The men who had chased them were no longer constantly on his mind. He had evidently lost them, thanks to Ardella's knowledge of the mountains she had lived in for so many years. So he asked for a room on the second floor that faced the street, paying in advance. "That looked like a bath-house on the back of the building," Cam commented to the desk clerk.

"Yes, sir," the clerk replied. "Would you like to get a hot bath?"

Cam hesitated for a moment before answering, "Yes, sir, I believe I would." He had never had a bath in a tub with hot water, and he figured it was about time he tried it. Having never before been so flush with money, he decided he'd spend a little of it. Turning his attention back to the clerk, who was awaiting his decision on when he wanted his bath, he said, "First, I need to buy me a new shirt and a couple of other things. Then I'll order up one of those baths."

"Yes, sir," the clerk said. "All I'll need is enough time to heat up some water, so you just let me know. You should be able to find a shirt across the street at Freeman's." He pointed toward a dry goods store next to a barbershop.

"Much obliged," Cam said, picking up his room key from the counter. The barbershop put another idea in his head that he might consider, but first he had to meet Smiley in the saloon. As he ascended the stairs to the second floor, he realized that he felt like the first day upon reaching a cow town at the end of a long cattle drive—with the exception of having a hell of a lot more money in his pockets. He even forgot for a few moments that he missed Mary and the girls.

When he got to his room, he went inside and turned the key in the lock to see how securely the door closed. Satisfied that it was a sturdy enough barrier to discourage curious petty thieves, he looked around the room in search of a hiding place for the sack of gold dust in one pocket of his saddlebags. "Ain't that fancy?" he muttered when he spotted the washstand with a pitcher and basin. He walked over and looked in the pitcher, and found that it had been filled with water. He was truly living like a rich gent, if only for a night. There was no obvious place to hide his gold, however, and he immediately reminded himself that if it was obvious, it wasn't a good place anyway. Then he saw another item that spoke of affluence, a chamber pot. *So you don't even have to walk out to the outhouse behind the bath-house,* he thought. *That'll be the best place to hide the gold.* He peered into it to make sure it had been cleaned since the last use. Then, holding the sack over the pot, he hesitated to consider if he should just give it to the clerk. They probably had a safe. He gave it another moment's thought, then dropped it in the pot. *Anybody figuring to rob the place knows there's money in the safe. Most likely wouldn't bother with my room after one look at me.* Satisfied that the odds were in his favor that his gold would be safe while he was gone, he locked his door and went downstairs on his way to the Cheyenne Star.

Smiley was not there when he walked into the saloon. He hesitated to look over the few men sitting around a couple of tables playing cards before going to the bar and ordering a glass of beer. He took his beer to a table and sat down where he could watch the door for Smiley. He sipped the beer slowly, but was almost finished, and beginning to wonder if Smiley was going to show up, when the bald little man pushed through the swinging doors. "You been waitin' long?" he asked. "It took me longer'n I figured at the bank."

"Just long enough to finish a glass of beer," Cam said. "You got the money?"

"Right here," Smiley answered, and produced a neat stack of bills. While Cam quickly put the money away, Smiley called out to the bartender, "Fred, lemme have a shot of whiskey and a glass of beer." Then back at Cam, he asked, "You want another?" When Cam said he did, Smiley ordered that from Fred, too, and then he produced a folded-up paper from his pocket. "I need you to sign this," he said.

"Sign it?" Cam asked. "What is it?"

"It's a bill of sale," Smiley told him. "When that U.S. marshal comes to town lookin' for them horses you stole, I'll show him that I paid for 'em, fair and square." He grinned to show Cam he was joking.

Cam signed the bill of sale, and then sat awhile with Smiley, who seemed anxious to tell him all the things that were happening in Cheyenne that were going to make it a better town. "Sure, it's got a reputation as a wild, wide-open town, but there's a lot of good solid folks moving in around Cheyenne, folks like Jim Pylant that you was askin' about. It's gonna be a decent town for women and children, people like that lady you were askin' about."

"Mary Bishop?" Cam replied. "She's headin' back home to Fort Collins, might already be on her way, if she was able to arrange transport."

"She's stayin' right here in Cheyenne, accordin' to what Mr. Proctor told me when I was in the bank."

Cam couldn't believe he heard right. "Mary Bishop, the woman with two little girls?" he asked incredulously. "Why would he say that?"

"I think Mr. Proctor got hold of her when he saw all that gold she had," Smiley said. "He's a smooth talker, Garland Proctor is. He said she decided to invest her money here in Cheyenne, 'cause she sees a lot more opportunity here than that other town she was thinkin' about."

"Fort Collins," Cam supplied.

"Yeah, I reckon. Mr. Proctor said she was thinkin' on buildin' a nice roomin' house with a dining room."

Cam was stunned. He had to give himself a few moments to grasp all that had happened in such a short amount of time. It was the last thing he would have expected to happen. All she had talked about was getting back to Fort Collins where she at least knew a few people. After he thought about it for a few minutes, he shrugged and decided it really didn't matter where she decided to light. He just hoped she would be happy here, and the girls would like it. Ardella, he wasn't worried about. She was one soul who could adapt to living in hell itself. Further conversation on the subject was interrupted when the door to the back room opened and several of the ranchers attending the meeting walked out.

"Well, I reckon the meetin's over," Smiley commented. "That's the feller you were askin' about, Jim Pylant."

Cam looked up to see a tall, lean man, with a neatly trimmed brown mustache and wavy brown hair. He paused just outside the back room door to carefully settle his flat-crowned hat upon his head so that the brim was just above his eyebrows. Then, spotting Smiley sitting at the table, he walked over to speak to him. "Well," Smiley greeted him, "I didn't hear no firearms goin' off. Did all you ranch owners agree not to shoot each other?"

"Nobody got shot," Pylant replied. "I don't know if we accomplished anything or not."

"I got some new horses I just bought," Smiley said. "One of 'em looks like a Morgan, the kind them army officers like to ride. You oughta take a look at 'em before you leave town."

Cam cocked a suspicious eye at Smiley. He had a feeling that he had just been skunked by the stable owner. He started to get mad but then decided it was kind of amusing. *Hell, I got what I wanted for them,* he thought. *Maybe the joke's on Pylant, if he ends up buying them. He could have gotten them a hell of a lot cheaper if he'd bought them from me.*

"Who's your friend, Smiley?" Pylant asked, smiling at Cam.

"This here is . . ." He glanced down at the name Cam had signed on the bill of sale. ". . . Cam Sutton. He just brought in the horses the new lady in town was totin' her gold dust on."

"Oh, Mrs. Bishop," Pylant said. "I met her and Mrs. Swift in the hotel dining room last night. They'd just gotten off the stage." He offered his hand to Cam. "You must be the fellow who guided them through some pretty hazardous times."

"I brought 'em as far as Chugwater," Cam replied modestly. "She decided to take the stage on in."

"I think Garland Proctor and I talked her into staying right here in Cheyenne," Pylant said. "She's a fine woman. I think she'll do well here. I've volunteered my services to help her get her boardinghouse built at a fair cost."

"I reckon she was lucky to run into you," Cam said, still a bit overwhelmed by how much had been accomplished in such a whirlwind fashion.

"I'm supposed to have a meeting with her in the morning at the bank," Pylant said. "I told her I'd stay in town a couple of days to help her line up a couple of good carpenters. Does she know you're in town?"

"No," Cam replied. "Fact of the matter is, I wasn't plannin' on comin' to Cheyenne, but I changed my mind 'cause I figured I had a better chance to sell some horses here." He glanced over at Smiley and said, "But I decided to give 'em away instead."

"Somebody should have warned you about dealing with Smiley," Pylant said, and punctuated his comment with a chuckle. "Like I said, I'll see Mrs. Bishop in the morning. I'll tell her you're in town."

"Thanks just the same, but there's no need to bother," Cam insisted. "Sounds like she's fixin' to be plenty busy, and we wound up our business back at Chugwater Station, anyway."

"All right, then," Pylant said, signaling a

conclusion to the conversation. “Glad to make your acquaintance, Cam. Smiley, I’ll stop by the stable sometime before supper and take a look at those horses you stole from Cam.” He left them with a broad smile on his handsome face.

“That’s the man that’ll probably be runnin’ this town before long,” Smiley commented as they watched Jim Pylant moving toward the door, with a wave for the bartender as he went out. “He’s done more than anybody else to draw decent folks to Cheyenne, just like he done with that Bishop lady. Hell, if she’s got money to invest in a town, it might as well be our town.”

Cam still had his eyes on the swinging doors after Pylant had disappeared. “Is Pylant a family man?” he asked.

“Yes and no,” Smiley answered. “His mama and daddy live with him out at his ranch, but he ain’t married, if that’s what you mean.”

Cam didn’t comment, but for some reason he couldn’t explain, that information disturbed him. His rational mind immediately asked the question *Why do I care, one way or the other?* Still, he couldn’t help forming a picture of the handsome and smooth-talking rancher dazzling Mary, and it bothered him. He was beginning to regret coming to Cheyenne, instead of heading back north. “What?” he said when he realized that Smiley had asked him something.

"I said, do you want another glass of beer?" Smiley repeated.

"No, reckon not. I gotta go over to the store and buy me a shirt and some things." He pushed his chair back from the table and got to his feet. "I reckon I'm buyin' the drinks, since I'm the one that sold the horses."

"Well, now, I hoped you'd say that," Smiley laughed. "I 'preciate it. It was a pleasure doin' business with you."

"I'm just payin' for the drinks you've got on the table," Cam said. "Anythin' after that, you're on your own."

Smiley laughed again. "Fair enough. Like I said, pleasure doin' business with you. Tell you what, I won't charge you nothin' for boardin' your horses. How's that?"

"That'll help a little. Thanks." He stopped by the bar and paid the tab, then went out the door.

"Yes, sir," Ed Jervey greeted the tall young man when he walked into the store. "What can I help you with?"

"I need a new shirt," Cam said. "This one's a mite loose, and it's picked up some stains that won't come out."

"It does look like you musta lost a lot of weight," Jervey said.

"I ain't lost any weight," Cam explained, "it's just that the shirt's too damn big." He was still wearing the shirt that Ardella had given him. *Long Sam Swift must have been as big as Ardella boasted,* he thought.

"Well, I can fit you with a nice hundred percent cotton shirt, or a wool one," Jervey said. When Cam said he preferred cotton, Jervey brought out several from his shelves. "This one here is the latest thing out. It's got a pocket on it."

Cam looked at it but couldn't see a need for a pocket. "I reckon I'll take that blue one without the pocket," he said. "I got pockets in my vest. That's what I wear a vest for."

"Right you are," Ed Jervey remarked. "Just thought I'd show it to you, because it's different. I doubt it'll catch on. How 'bout britches? You need a pair? I've got some nice wool britches, but I've also got some denim pants most of you cowboys like, from Levi Strauss."

Cam ended up buying two shirts and a pair of Levi britches after trying them on. He liked them so well that he kept them on and told Jervey to throw his old pants away. Jervey pointed out that the old ones had a bullet hole in one leg, anyway. He outfitted himself in new underwear and socks, and on a last impulse, he took a good look at his red bandanna as he was about to tie it on. "This thing's about ready to go, too. How 'bout a blue one to go with my new shirt?" Feeling like a new man, after spending close to fifteen dollars, he went back to the hotel to leave his spare shirt and order up his hot bath. After checking the pot under the bed to make sure his gold dust had not been disturbed, he walked down to the bath-house.

He took a long time to soak in the tub. For a man who had never had a bath in anything but a river or creek, the tub bath seemed luxurious, and whenever the water began to chill, he rang the bell sitting beside him on a table, and a young boy brought in another bucket of hot water. It was decidedly different from the last bath he had taken, mostly by accident, when he had stumbled upon Mary's gold sacks in the creek. Finally, when the tub threatened to overflow, he reached for the towel. *If I sit in here much longer, I'm liable to shrivel up to nothing,* he thought. "That oughta hold me for a while," he commented to the boy who had brought the hot water. Then, feeling his new prosperity, he reached in his pocket and pulled out fifty cents for the boy.

Back in his room again, he took another look at his new clothes in the mirror. There was one more thing that he had never done before, a shave and a haircut from a real barber. It was a waste of money, he told himself. *But dammit, I'm gonna remember this day, July 13, 1878, as the one day I treated myself like a highfalutin gentleman.* So he went to the barbershop.

Chapter 14

He was seated in the hotel dining room shortly after it opened for supper, almost finished with a plate of some kind of stew, which contained chunks of meat that he could not readily identify. But the taste was all right, so he cleaned his plate and pushed back a little from the table to give his stomach room to work on the meat while he had another cup of coffee.

He heard her walk into the room before he heard the voice. "My Lord in heaven," Ardella exclaimed. "Is that you?"

Turning around, he was surprised to see her. "Ardella, looks like you made it all right," he said, grinning at her reaction to his cleaned-up appearance.

"Cam," she gushed, "what are you doin' here? We thought you was headin' north."

"I thought I was, too," he replied, "but I couldn't sell the horses back in Chugwater." He went on to tell her how he wound up there in the hotel. "I didn't expect you and Mary to be here." He didn't tell her that he had learned earlier that they were still in Cheyenne, or that the main reason he was eating so early was to avoid an awkward meeting like this one.

"I didn't expect to be here myself, but the

banker and this other man grabbed hold of Mary as soon as they saw how rich she is. Got to tellin' her how much bigger Cheyenne is than Fort Collins, and how much the town is growin'. Before she knew it, she was agreein' with 'em, and here we are, gonna build a fine new boardin'house right here." She paused then and took a step back to admire him. "I swear, you fixed yourself up somethin' fancy, and you smell to high heaven, like a big ol' flower blossom."

"I can't help that," Cam said, thoroughly embarrassed. "I didn't get a chance to stop that barber before he sloshed about a bucket of that stink on me."

She chuckled delightedly, enjoying his embarrassment. "Now you're startin' to turn red, just like a rose." She pulled a chair out and sat down. While she waited for her supper to arrive, she told him all that had happened since they said good-bye to him at Chugwater. "Mary and the girls weren't ready to come to supper yet, so I came on by myself. You know me, I'm hungry all the time. I'm glad I did—I mighta missed you."

He was thinking about excusing himself and leaving to avoid seeing Mary and the girls, and he wasn't sure why he felt that way. He didn't have a choice, anyway, because when Ardella's plate arrived, the waitress asked him if he'd like more coffee, and Ardella answered for him.

“Yeah, he does, thank you. He’s gotta stay and talk to me for a while.” She interrupted her rambling talk for a moment when she saw someone enter the dining room.

He turned to see what had caught her attention, and immediately saw why. There, pausing in the doorway, scanning the entire room, was a sinister-looking man with long dirty white hair, his eyes like two blue-hot coals as they peered out from under ominous dark eyebrows. He had the look of a predator as he swept the dining room with his gaze, coming to rest on Cam and Ardella, moving on, then coming back to them as if uncertain, before walking back to the door, where he paused once again to look over the room. Of particular interest to Cam was the way the man wore his handgun, and the fact that he wore it into the dining room. His holster was on his right side, with the gun handle forward, which would indicate he was left-handed. Then Cam spotted the reason. His right hand was bound with what appeared to be rawhide cords, and the hand looked to be misshapen.

“I reckon it’s a good thing that man don’t seem to see whoever he’s lookin’ for,” Ardella commented when he abruptly left the room. “ ’Cause he looked like he was ready to shoot ever’body in the place.”

Cam had to agree with Ardella. The man had an evil look about him, and it was apparent that he was looking for somebody—and whoever that somebody was might be in for a rough night.

"Cam!" he heard the child scream, and turned to see Emma running toward him with Grace close behind. Both girls piled onto his lap, almost strangling him with their hugs. Beaming openly, Mary walked across the room to greet him as well. "I knew you wouldn't break your promise," Emma said gleefully. "I told Grace you'd come to see us."

Obviously glad to see him, Mary said, "Well, if this isn't a surprise. We thought you'd be riding up in the Black Hills by now." She admitted to herself that she envied the girls' ability to just run up and hug him.

"Well, like I told Ardella, I was gonna head up that way, but I wanted to sell the horses you left me with, and Cheyenne was the best place to take 'em, so I rode on down here." He reached up and gently loosened Emma's stranglehold on his neck. "I hear you're fixin' to settle down right here in Cheyenne," he said to Mary.

"Yes, it seems like a better idea than going back to Fort Collins," she said, then went on to tell him about her meetings with Garland Proctor and Jim Pylant. "They're so willing to help me get started," she concluded, "that I just didn't believe I'd get that much help in Fort Collins."

"I know you'll be fine," Cam said, "especially since you've got Ardella to help you."

"Tell him how good he smells," Ardella said, with a great big grin.

"I noticed you've gotten all cleaned up," Mary commented, "new clothes, too. Is there some special occasion?"

Feeling the flush in his face beginning to spread, he fought to control his embarrassment. "Nope, just the occasion of needin' a shirt that ain't two sizes too big, and a pair of pants to replace those wore-out britches I was wearin'. That's all."

"Long Sam was a big man," Ardella interjected proudly.

"Well, I've got to be goin'," Cam said. "I'll let you folks get on with your supper."

"Where are you going?" Mary asked. "Can't you stay and visit with us while we eat?"

"I told Smiley down at the stable that I'd be right down there to finish up with those horses he's buyin'," he lied. "I shoulda already been there. He'll think I'm backin' out."

Clearly disappointed, Mary said, "Maybe later. I hope you got a good price for the horses."

"Not as good as I should have," he replied as he got up from his chair. He reached down and mussed Emma's hair. "You behave yourself, Skeeter, and do like your mama tells ya. Grace, you keep her straight." He turned to leave.

"Will we see you again?" Mary asked.

"I don't know," he said, "maybe. You're gonna be pretty busy, sounds to me, so I don't wanna get in the way." He walked briskly to the door then, so as to end the conversation before he was foolish enough to confess that he wanted to see her again.

A most interested observer of the awkward exchange between the two, Ardella shook her head slowly. It was plain to see that the two had strong feelings for each other, but neither one wanted to admit it, for reasons all their own. *It's a damn shame,* she thought, *but it ain't for me to say anything about it.*

"Do you think we'll see him again?" Mary asked Ardella when Cam had gone.

"I don't know," Ardella replied. "Do you wanna see him again?"

"Well, of course," Mary answered. "Cam is a good friend, and the girls would really like for him to visit often."

"I expect you'd best let him know, 'cause I don't think he knows. He's thinkin' he got fired, so he ain't likely to hang around. A man like Cam won't stay long any place he feels like he ain't needed."

Her answer only served to confuse Mary more, because she could not bring herself to tell him. "He should know that he's welcome," she finally said, ending the discussion.

Outside the dining room, Cam almost ran into Jim Pylant, who was on his way inside. "Sorry," Pylant said, "I didn't see you coming."

"It was my fault," Cam insisted. "I reckon my mind was on somethin' else." He stepped aside to let him pass.

"Cam Sutton, wasn't it? Did you find your friends, Mrs. Bishop and the others?" Cam allowed that he had just left them. "She's a fine lady," Pylant went on. "I was hoping I would see her at supper, but I'm running a little bit late."

"Well, she's still in the dining room," Cam said, and headed for the lobby door, suddenly needing some air, the picture in his mind of the highly polished man, standing beside him in his coarse new clothes. He didn't like the thought of the comparison in Mary's eyes. He suddenly had an urge for a drink of whiskey, something he didn't crave very often. *And then,* he decided, *I'm gonna get my stuff out of that fancy hotel room and get the hell out of this town.* He finally and completely admitted to himself that he was jealous, an emotion he had never experienced before, and he didn't like the feel of it. So he figured the best remedy for the affliction was to remove himself from the source. As soon as he settled on that, he said to hell with the drink of whiskey, turned around, and went back into the hotel. A drink would only delay his departure.

It didn't take him but a few minutes to pick up his saddlebags and rifle, retrieve his bag of dust from the chamber pot, and turn his key over to the desk clerk. "Ain't you even gonna stay the night?" the clerk asked. "Is there something wrong with the room?"

"Nope," Cam said. "I just gotta be goin'. How much do I owe you?"

The clerk scratched his head, still surprised. "You paid in advance. Did you get in the bed, take the quilt off?" Cam replied that he had not touched the bed, and he hadn't used the chamber pot. "Well, you owe fifty cents for the bath and I guess that's all."

"Fair enough," Cam said. "I 'preciate it." He collected his refund and left.

Smiley Thompson was as surprised as the hotel clerk had been when Cam came to get his two horses. He stood talking to him while he put his saddle on the dun. "I thought you was thinkin' 'bout hangin' around town for a couple of days. You ain't spent all that money I just paid you for them horses, have you?"

"I just changed my mind about stayin'," Cam said as he tightened up on the cinch. "I think I'll head back north."

"Where'bouts you headed up north?"

"Just north. I'll know when I get there."

Smiley shrugged, figuring Cam was not unlike many other drifters who blew through Cheyenne with the east wind. "Well, if you get back this way any time soon, I'll still make good on that promise of free board for your horses."

"This fellow, Pylant," Cam couldn't resist asking, "he runs a pretty big outfit, does he?"

"His is the biggest spread in the county," Smiley said. "You thinkin' 'bout lookin' for a job?"

"Shit no," Cam answered in no uncertain terms. "I expect I'll go back to punchin' cattle somewhere. I don't know much about anythin' else, but it ain't gonna be around here." He went into the corral to put a bridle on his packhorse and lead it outside. "Looks like you picked up another new horse," he said, looking at a paint that wasn't there earlier.

"Feller just left that horse today," Smiley said. "Strange-lookin' feller, looks like a damn wild animal."

"I think I saw him in the hotel dining room a little while ago," Cam said. "Long, white-lookin' hair?"

"That's the one," Smiley said. "He looks like a lot of that wild bunch that used to come ridin' through here a few years back."

"Well, I reckon I'll get started while I've got a little daylight left, maybe make it to Lodgepole Creek tonight," Cam said when he finished packing the sorrel. He stepped up into the saddle and turned the dun's head toward the stage road he had ridden in on.

Mary had ample cause to feel optimistic after her meeting in the hotel dining room with Jim Pylant.

He had assured her that he knew a responsible man who would build her boardinghouse exactly as she wanted it, and offered his assistance in any other matters that might discourage a lady when it came to establishing a business. Jim was a most gracious and proper gentleman, unusual for a man who raised cattle for a living. He seemed also to take pride in his appearance, deservedly so, for he was certainly a handsome man. These were the thoughts that occupied her mind as she left the hotel and hurried down the street to pick up some things she had forgotten to buy at the store. She feared that it might be too late, but maybe the store hadn't closed. It was still early in the evening. So occupied was she that she was unaware of the man walking quickly up behind her until she was suddenly snatched sideways into the alley between the bank and the dry goods store. One powerful arm pinned her arms to her sides while a rawhide-bound hand clapped roughly over her mouth, stifling her screams, and she was lifted off her feet and carried to the rear of the bank where a paint horse was tied.

"Remember me?" Cotton Roach growled as he pressed her hard against the wall. Her eyes, wide with horror, told him that she did, even in the fading light of the alley. "You've been leadin' me on one helluva chase, but I knew I'd finally catch up with you—you and that son of a bitch ridin' with you." He pressed a little harder against her to make sure she understood. "Now, I'm just wantin' to have a little talk with you. I ain't gonna hurt you if you behave. Understand?" Unable to move, she tried to acknowledge with a flick of her eyelids. "I'm gonna take my hand off your mouth," he went on, "so you can tell me what I wanna know. If you make one squeak for help, I'll shut you up for good. You understand that?" Again, she signaled with her eyelids.

Very slowly, he removed the offensive hand from her mouth, while locking his penetrating gaze upon her eyes. "Mr. Smith," she gasped, terrified to see the strange-looking man who had ridden on the stage with her and her children.

"Yeah, Mr. Smith," Roach replied contemptuously. "Where is that son of a bitch that's been leadin' you all over the territory, the one that wears that damn red bandanna? He's caused me a helluva lot of trouble, killed my partner, and more than that he owes me for this." He whipped his injured hand up before her face, causing her to flinch, thinking she was about to be struck.

Finding her voice again, she answered him. "I don't know where he is. He was here, but he left. He didn't tell anyone he was leaving." Terrified moments before, she watched the reaction in those dead blue eyes and realized he was uncertain about his next move. Emboldened by his indecision, she said, "You'd better get away from here as fast as you can. When the sheriff finds out you're here, he'll arrest you for robbery and murder."

He slapped her hard across her mouth, causing it to bleed. "I told you to behave yourself!" he warned. "You ain't tellin' the sheriff nothin', unless you wanna end up dead. Now, here's what you're gonna do. I figure the trouble you cost me oughta be worth about thirty-five thousand dollars, so you're gonna go to the bank and get it. Then I want that bastard with the red bandanna to bring it to me. You got that straight? Now, you listen real careful, 'cause I'm gonna tell you where he's gotta bring it. There's a line of hills about a mile outta town on the road to Laramie. One of them hills has a rock tower stickin' up outta the pine trees about a hundred feet high. That's where he'll bring the money."

Mary listened carefully, astonished that the man expected her to comply when he surely should know that as soon as he freed her, she would go to the law instead. Amazed by the man's stupidity, she couldn't help asking, "Why do you think I'll do what you say once I'm free?"

His lips parted slowly in a smug smile. "Maybe because I've got a little girl tied up in a neat little bundle. I think I heard you call her Emma when she couldn't quit runnin' her mouth on the stage-coach."

"Emma!" Mary gasped, stunned to the point of almost fainting. "No! That can't be! I just left her!"

His contemptuous grin spread once more across his rough features. "That's a fact—left her and her sister playin' on the hotel porch. Only, she ain't there no more."

"Oh my God, please!" Mary pleaded. "Please don't hurt my babies! I'll get you the money."

"Well, I ain't got but one of 'em. The other'n went in the hotel 'bout the time I rode up, but that littlest one oughta be worth thirty-five thousand." Thoroughly enjoying her distress, he said, "I'll take real good care of her, unless I see a posse comin' after me. If that happens, I'll just gut her like a fish, but I'll hang her up somewhere where they can find her real easy." He grinned when he saw her grimace at the thought. "And remember, I want that bastard with you to bring me the money, and nobody else, or the kid gets slaughtered."

Her heart was pounding so violently in her ears that she feared she would miss his exact instructions. "He's gone," she implored. "I don't know where he went, but he's already left town."

"What?" he demanded angrily. "You're lyin'."

"No, I swear to you, he's gone and didn't tell anyone where he was going, or why."

He hesitated then, hit by another wave of frustration, while he had to think of how that changed things. He believed she was telling the truth, and his first impulse was to try to find which way he went, for the longer the man who had shot his hand remained alive, the deeper the passion for revenge cut into his soul. But he also felt he was entitled to the woman's gold. "All right," he finally decided. "You, and nobody else, can bring the money and I'll give you the little girl. You got till noon tomorrow, and then I'm leavin', and I ain't gonna be botherin' with no little girl. So if you want her alive, you'd best be there before noon tomorrow with my money." He grabbed her by the throat and pulled her face up to almost touch his. "I can see about five miles in every direction from that rock, and if I see one extra person with you, you can say good-bye to sweet little Emma. You got that?"

"Yes," she answered, drained of strength, her knees threatening to collapse. He released her, and she had to catch herself to keep from falling. He took two steps back, planted his feet, and struck her beside her face with his fist. She slumped to the ground, dazed, while he stepped up in the saddle unhurriedly and rode off behind the buildings.

"Mary!" Ardella cried out when she saw her staggering out of the alley, holding on to the side of the building for support. "Oh my Lord," she gasped, and ran to help her. "What happened?" Before Mary could answer, Ardella blurted, "Emma! She's gone. Grace said some man grabbed her and ran off with her."

“I know,” Mary choked out. “He took her, that man on the stagecoach, that Mr. Smith. I’ve got to go in the bank, got to get money to buy her back.” She tried to push by her.

“Wait,” Ardella pleaded, “Mary, the bank’s closed. Tell me what happened.”

“Noon, tomorrow, he’ll kill her if I don’t give him the money,” Mary sobbed. She finally let Ardella put an arm around her to support her, and bit by bit, she related the incident that had just taken place.

Equally concerned, but infinitely calmer in the face of crisis, Ardella took a moment to think the situation over. “Dammit, we need Cam.”

“Cam’s gone,” Mary cried. “The desk clerk said he checked out. I’ll have to carry the money.”

“You’ve got till noon to get that money,” Ardella said. “We need Cam.”

“I’ve got to get my baby away from that man,” Mary sobbed.

“He ain’t likely to do her no harm, not if he wants that money. You go on back to the hotel and stay with Grace. She needs you right now. I’m gonna go to the stable and see if I can find out where Cam went.”

“Yes, ma’am,” Smiley Thompson said. “He sure did, took outta here a couple of hours ago.”

“Did he say where he was goin’?”

“No, just said he was headin’ north.” He paused

a moment to recall. "He did say he thought he might strike Lodgepole Creek tonight, and he took outta here on the stage road."

That at least gave Ardella a chance to find him, but she might have to ride all night. Well aware that she had to be back before noon the next day, she decided it was worth a try anyway. "I'm gonna need to rent a horse from you, that one," she said, pointing to a sorrel standing near the back of the corral. "That's the one I was ridin' before we got on the stage."

When Smiley brought out a couple of saddles from the tack room, he said, "I don't remember which saddle was on which horse."

She pointed to one of them. "That one," she said. "The stirrups are already set for my short legs." In a matter of minutes, she was in the saddle and she paused another minute to decide whether to go to the hotel to tell Mary what she was going to do. "No, hell," she muttered, and wheeled the sorrel toward the road to Laramie.

Darkness was rapidly overtaking her as she pressed her horse to keep up a steady pace, while not pushing it to go too fast. There were rough places in the stage road that could break a horse's leg in the dark. She hoped that Cam had not been in a hurry when he left town. She had ridden perhaps three or four miles when it became so dark that she reluctantly slowed her horse down to a walk, cursing the fact that there was no moon that night. Her attention was glued to the road before her horse's feet, so much so that she was surprised by the sorrel's greeting nicker. Looking up then, she was startled by the dark shadow of a man on a horse right in front of her. Alarmed, she pulled back hard on the reins, realizing too late that she was without a weapon of any kind.

"Ardella?"

"Praise the Lord!" she exclaimed, in great relief. "Cam, is that you?"

"Yeah. Where are you goin'?"

"Lookin' for you!" she responded.

"What for? Is somethin' wrong?"

"There's a helluva lot of somethin' wrong," she replied, and related all that had happened in the last few hours.

In the darkness, she could not see the anguish in his face when she told him of Emma's abduction and the demand for ransom. While he digested all that she told him, many other pieces of the puzzle fell into place. Mary identified the kidnapper as one of the gang that held up the stage—the paint gelding he had seen in Smiley's stable. When they were at Ardella's cabin, he had spotted one of the men who came after them riding a paint. The man with the bound right hand in the dining room had to be the same man he thought he wounded at the stage holdup. "Where's Mary now?" he asked.

"She's back at the hotel with Grace, and she's

about to come to pieces. She'll feel better knowin' you're back. We thought you were gone for good. Why'd you come back?"

"It don't matter now," he said. "We've got to get back to town. I've got work to do."

Mary ran to him as soon as he walked in the door, and embraced him. "Somehow I knew you'd come," she said tearfully. "Cam, he's got my baby."

"I know," he told her calmly, with no show of the distress he felt inside at the thought of his "Skeeter" in the brutal hands of a killer. "I'm gonna do everythin' I can to get her back, so I want you to tell me everythin' he told you to do."

"He said he wants you to bring the money," she told him. "Cam, I think he wants to kill you! He said you crippled his hand. I didn't know what to do, but I told him you were gone. I guess I'll get the money and take it to him, and he'll let Emma go."

"I'll go, but I ain't gonna wait till mornin'," Cam said. "If you don't hear somethin' from me by the time the bank opens in the mornin', go ahead and do like he said. Take him the money."

At once alarmed, Mary questioned him. "What are you going to do?"

"I'm goin' to get Emma," he said calmly. Turning to leave then, he told Ardella, "Look after her and Grace."

"I will," Ardella assured him, "but I can go with you to give you a little help."

"No, you stay with them. I'll have a better chance alone."

Chapter 15

When he left the hotel, he went straight to the stable. Finding the corral empty and the doors locked, he went to the small house behind the stable where Smiley lived, but he found no one at home. Knowing where to look next, he went to the saloon and found the little man seated at a table with two other men. "Hey, I thought you was gone," Smiley called out when Cam walked in the door.

"I was," Cam said. "I'm back now. I need to leave my horses at your place."

"All right. Sit down and have a drink with us. We'll go over to the stable directly."

"Thanks just the same, but I'm in a hurry," Cam insisted. "If you just let me in, I'll take care of 'em and lock up when I'm done." The grim look in his eye conveyed an urgency that Smiley couldn't miss.

"All right," he said. "I was about ready to go home, anyway." He got up from the table, paused to tip his glass back to make sure he had gotten every drop, then followed Cam out the door after a quick good night to his two drinking companions.

As soon as Smiley unlocked the door, Cam led his horses in, pulled his saddle off, unloaded his packhorse, and turned them over to Smiley, who said he would feed and water them. "Much obliged," Cam said, and pulled his rifle out of the saddle sling.

Smiley watched him as he checked to make sure his rifle and handgun were fully loaded, started to ask him why he was so tight-lipped tonight, but decided against it. He walked out to the front door and watched Cam walk briskly up the street, in the opposite direction from the hotel. He had a feeling. *That fellow's up to something I don't want to know about.*

According to what Mary had told him, the big rock that Smith, or whatever his name was, had picked for the exchange was only about a mile out of town. With what he had in mind, he figured it better to be on foot. He didn't want to worry about hiding a horse or having it nicker or whinny and give him away. So in the dark of the moonless night, he strode purposefully along the road to Laramie. In what was probably a mile or a little more, he came to the designated meeting place. It was easily recognized. The end slope in a chain of hills, covered for the most part with a thick pine belt, stood apart from the others because of a massive tower of rock that reached up from the surrounding pines. He paused to look at the hill before leaving the road.

He did not expect to find Roach and Emma there. He credited the man with more sense than to camp there where he would run the risk of having someone sneak up on him during the night. No, he was sure that Roach was hiding out with Emma somewhere some distance from this place, and there was little chance it could be found if Cam searched all night for it. After a general scan of the area, he left the road and followed a path that led up to the base of the rock. He could only guess the purpose for the path, for there was nothing there but a small clearing around the rock. He turned to look back at the road, then moved to several spots, deciding on the best one to watch for someone on the road. *This is where he'll probably stand and watch,* he thought. Using this as his target, he then moved off into the trees to find the best spot to set his ambush. Moving up the slope a little, he tested a couple of places, seeking one that would give him good visibility of the target while providing him with some pro-tection. After he made a selection, there was nothing more to do but settle in and wait for morning.

First light found him asleep, half covered by pine boughs he had cut from the trees to conceal himself. He awoke with a start, alarmed that he had fallen asleep, but he heard nothing beyond the whisper of a morning breeze as it caressed the pines. How soon would Roach show up? He could only guess, but he had to be ready for him to appear at any moment. So he moved up to position himself at the base of one of the larger trees and sat down to wait, pulling the pine boughs up around him.

The time dragged by with no sign of anyone on the road below him. Positioned as he was, he could only see the road from Cheyenne. But to see the road on the other side of the hill, he would have had to move to a spot where his target area at the base of the rock would no longer be clearly seen. So he decided it best to sit tight and wait for Roach to show up with Emma and hope he had hidden himself well enough. Still, there were no sounds other than the wind and some rude arguing among a flock of crows. The sun was well up in the sky now. He had no watch, but he figured it surely close to the time the bank should be opening. He would have thought that Roach would be there by now. Again, the cawing of the crows high over the hill above him shattered the morning quiet. And suddenly it struck him! Without having to think, he dived out of his pine bough cover, but not quick enough to avoid the rifle slug that slammed into his shoulder. He rolled over on his belly on the downhill side of the tree trunk in time to evade the shot that quickly followed the first and ripped off a piece of pine bark.

With no idea how badly he had been hurt, Cam had no choice but to ignore the wound. It was in his left shoulder, and at this point was more numb than painful, and his shoulder still worked, so no bones or joints were injured. He berated himself for not allowing for the fact that Roach might have been holed up in the hills behind the stone tower and, like him, was on foot. He should have been alert the first time the crows scolded the intruder to their forest. His problem now was the fact that he didn't know exactly where the shots had come from, only that Roach was somewhere on the hill above him. Hugging the ground, he moved to the other side of the tree and tried to scan the trees above, hoping to spot a muzzle flash if another shot was fired. Even if he spotted one, he was afraid to return fire, because he couldn't chance hitting Emma, if the outlaw was holding her close to him. He was still trying to decide what to do when Roach called out to him, "Hey, rifleman! You bring my money?"

"Where's the little girl?" Cam yelled back.

"Too bad you moved," Roach shouted, ignoring the question. "I had a bead on the middle of your back. You hurt pretty bad?"

"Yeah," Cam returned. "Why don't you come on down and take a look?"

"Maybe I will."

The response came from a slightly different direction, so Cam knew he was moving. His best bet was to keep him talking, and he thought he knew how to do that. "Hey, how's that hand of yours? That was a helluva shot that crippled your hand, wasn't it?"

"You son of a bitch," Roach replied in anger. "It was a lucky shot, and it's gonna be an unlucky shot for you, 'cause I'm gonna kill you for it."

"Is that a fact?" Cam responded. "How you gonna do that without comin' down here to get me?"

"Maybe I'll just slit this little brat's throat and see what you can do about that—see if you've got the guts to come up here to stop me."

That was one thing Cam did not want to hear. "Anythin' happens to the kid, you don't get the money," he called back, while inching farther away from the tree toward another tree, still trying to locate Roach's position. It occurred to him that if Roach had Emma with him now, she might have made some noise, a cry, or a plea for help. He decided to try to find out. "Emma," he yelled, "if you're up there, let me know. Make a noise, anything." There was no sound in reply. "Where's the girl?" Cam challenged.

"Right where I want her," Roach returned, "and right where she'll stay till I get what I want from you."

That last threat came from a spot farther down

in the trees. *He's moving down the hill to try to flank the spot I'm in,* Cam thought. "Why don't you come on down here and see if you're man enough to get what you want, you yellow dog?" Cam called out, then quickly slid over farther in the underbrush and crawled up the hill. Moving as quietly as he could manage, he tried to position himself to be above and to the side of the tree he had first taken cover behind. There was no more taunting from the kidnapper, which told Cam that he was moving in for the kill, so he rose to his feet and moved quickly toward a game trail directly above the clearing around the base of the rock tower. Just as he crossed the path, Roach appeared on it a dozen yards below him. Both men were taken by surprise. Both reacted instantly, turning to fire with no time to aim. Both men went down, Cam as a result of the bullet that tore the sole on his boot, Roach with a bullet in his hip. When Cam hit the ground, he immediately rolled over and over to find cover from the barrage of shots from Roach, as the critically wounded outlaw cranked cartridge after cartridge into the chamber. Unable to clearly see his target as Cam continued to roll down the hill, Roach desperately fired away at the bushes between the trees until the click of the hammer against an empty chamber signaled an empty magazine.

It was no more than a moment, but the silence was deafening as Cam got to his feet and stepped out from behind a tree to face Roach, his rifle aimed at the outlaw, who stood painfully favoring a smashed hip. His face twisted with hatred and pain, he cranked the lever on his empty rifle again, then threw it away from him. He tried to straighten up to stand squarely facing his despised adversary, his left hand poised to reach across his body to draw the .44 holstered on his right side.

"You wouldn't make it halfway there," Cam told him. "You're done. Where's the little girl?"

"Who are you?" Roach asked, trying to stall. "What's your name?"

"Cam Sutton. What's yours?"

"Cotton Roach."

"It suits you," Cam said, well aware of Roach's attempt to stall long enough to surprise him. "Pleased to meet you. Now, where's the little girl?"

"Oh, her?" Roach responded with a smirk. "She's dead." He saw the shaken look on Cam's face that indicated a moment's loss of concentration, the moment Roach was hoping for. Like a flash of lightning, he reached for the handle of the .44 strapped to his side. In that moment, he was reminded of a well-known law—the fastest draw will always come in second to the squeezing of the trigger on a rifle already cocked and aimed.

Roach crumpled to the ground, gut-shot, still trying to pull his handgun from its holster. As he walked cautiously toward him, Cam quickly chambered another round and silenced the struggling gunman. He stood over the body for a long moment, looking at the man who had hunted him. Then, his thoughts returning to Emma, he determined to find her, wherever this demon had left her. Gazing up at the tree-covered hill above him, he feared that her innocent little body could have been discarded anywhere along the ridges that extended for a mile or more. He looked down at the bullet hole in his new shirt to note that the wound seemed to have stopped bleeding for the moment. *Take care of it later,* he thought, and turned to begin following the game trail on up the hill, assuming that it was the way Roach had come down. *He must have a horse back up there somewhere,* he thought. *I'll ride it along these ridges until I find Emma.*

The trail led him to the top of the first hill and across a hogback to the next. As he approached what appeared to be a small meadow down the side of the hogback, he spotted the paint horse he had seen at Smiley's stable, standing saddled and tied to a tree. He left the trail and went down through the trees to the clearing. Not twenty feet from the horse, he saw her. Bound and gagged, she was tied to another tree, and as Cam hurried to her, she looked up at him with eyes completely devoid of fear. As soon as he removed the gag from her mouth, her first words were calmly said.

"I knew you'd come and get me. I told that bad man that you would come to get me and that he was going to be in trouble then."

He almost choked on his emotion. "That's right, Skeeter, I was gonna come to get you, no matter what."

Standing in front of the bank, Mary, Ardella, and Grace anxiously waited for it to open. They had been there for almost an hour, and Mary's pleas with a bank employee to let her withdraw the cash she needed were unsuccessful. She was told that it was too large a sum to be released by anyone but Mr. Proctor, so she would have to wait until he arrived. "Surely it must be nine o'clock by now," she worried.

"It can't be long," Ardella tried to assure her. Her main concern was the fact that there had been no word from Cam since the night before.

"Mama, look!" Grace exclaimed, pointing toward the end of the street.

The two adults turned as one to look. What their disbelieving eyes saw was Cam riding down the middle of the street on a paint horse with Emma sitting in the saddle in front of him. Ardella was handy to catch Mary by the elbow and support her when Mary's knees threatened to fail her. It was only for a few moments, however, for then she recovered enough from the past sleepless night to run to meet her daughter.

Cam reined up when he saw Mary running to meet them with Grace and Ardella not far behind. It struck him that this was his family, the only family he could remember, and now the family he did not want to lose. He lifted Emma from the saddle and lowered her into Mary's arms, then sat a moment to enjoy the mother-and-daughter reunion. In the midst of the hugs and kisses she was showered with, Emma managed to whisper something in her mother's ear. Mary smiled, then looked up at the tall young man in the saddle, and said, "You were right, darling, he is an angel."

"Well," Cam declared, "I reckon that pretty much takes care of things, and the family's all back together again, so I guess I'll go put my new horse in the stable for the night and see about this hole I just got in my new shirt."

"It doesn't seem to be bothering you that much," Mary said. "Why don't you come back to the hotel with us? Ardella and I can take a look at that wound. If Ardella can't fix it, then we'll go to the doctor."

"Yeah," Ardella said. "Let ol' Dr. Ardella take a look at it." She realized that neither Cam nor Mary heard her remark. "You never did say why you came back last night," she said to Cam.

He shifted his gaze from Mary's for only a moment to reply. "No, I reckon I never did," was all he said.

Impatient, Emma tugged at her mother's arm

until Mary bent down to hear her daughter's whispered question. In reply, Mary said, "Why don't you ask him?"

Emma turned at once to look up into Cam's face. "Can you come live with us?" she asked.

He was taken by surprise, but he answered at once. "I reckon that's up to your mother." He looked at Mary then, his eyes searching.

Mary smiled. "I think we can work something out."

Grace, standing beside Ardella, thought she heard a sob caught in her adopted aunt's throat. She looked up to discover the tough old lady smiling broadly with tears streaming down her cheeks.

Center Point Large Print
600 Brooks Road / PO Box 1
Thorndike, ME 04986-0001 USA

(207) 568-3717

US & Canada:
1 800 929-9108
www.centerpointlargeprint.com